First Date

First Date

Krista McGee

THOMAS NELSON
Since 1798

NASHVILLE   DALLAS   MEXICO CITY   RIO DE JANEIRO

Published in Nashville, Tennessee, by Thomas Nelson. Thomas Nelson is a registered trademark of Thomas Nelson, Inc.

Published in association with literary agent Lauren Yoho of D.C. Jacobson & Associates, an Author Management Company, www.DCJacobson.com.

Thomas Nelson, Inc., titles may be purchased in bulk for educational, business, fund-raising, or sales promotional use. For information, please e-mail SpecialMarkets@ThomasNelson.com.

Publisher's Note: This novel is a work of fiction. Names, characters, places, and incidents are either products of the author's imagination or used fictitiously. All characters are fictional, and any similarity to people living or dead is purely coincidental.

Scripture quotations are taken from the NEW AMERICAN STANDARD BIBLE®. © The Lockman Foundation 1960, 1962, 1963, 1968, 1971, 1972, 1973, 1975, 1977. Used by permission.

Library of Congress Cataloging-in-Publication Data

McGee, Krista, 1974–
  First date / Krista McGee.
    p. cm.
  ISBN 978-1-4016-8488-4 (soft cover)
  1. Orphans—Fiction. 2. Reality television programs—Fiction. I. Title.
PS3613.C457F57 2012
813'.6—dc22   2011030772

Printed in the United States of America
11 12 13 14 15 16 QG 6 5 4 3 2 1

To my husband, David.
Your passion for Christ and
dedication to family inspire
me daily. I love you.

Chapter 1

You're going to be on television, Addy," Mr. Lawrence said, as if it were a good thing. As if all seventeen-year-old girls dreamed of being told that and Addy should jump up from her seat, squeal, and thank him for the opportunity.

"The show is supposed to be a cross between *America's Next Star*, *Survivor*, and *The Bachelor*, with a little Miss America thrown in."

Addy tried to calm herself. On the walk from her AP US History class to the office, she had imagined dozens of possible scenarios as to why the principal would want to see her in the middle of the day. *Suddenly my fear that I've bombed the SATs doesn't seem quite so awful.*

"It's called *The Book of Love*." Mr. Lawrence looked at Addy with eyebrows raised.

The wrinkles on his forehead were very much like the lined paper Addy left on her desk when she was called out of her class to come here. The paper she should be working on right now.

"The president's son is going to choose a date for his senior prom on live television."

Addy wasn't a big fan of teen magazines, but she would have to be blind not to know about Jonathon Jackson. His movie-star looks and leader-of-the-free-world father made him the poster of choice for many teenage girls across the country.

"But I thought he was dating that girl from the Disney Channel," Addy said.

"Janie Smart?" Mr. Lawrence leaned forward, his eyes dancing. "Where have you been? They broke up last month. It was huge news." He clicked his mouse a few times, then turned his computer screen to face Addy.

She read that Jonathon had asked Janie to come to a state dinner with his parents and she refused. Apparently, Janie had already made plans to promote her new TV movie in LA. Jonathon was supposedly very upset—as was the journalist whose article Addy was reading.

"Who turns down a chance to meet heads of state so she can schmooze with Mickey Mouse?" He shook his head.

So Jonathon ended the relationship. Teenage girls across the country must have rejoiced at the news. "He broke up with his girlfriend and decided to choose his next date on reality TV?" Addy rolled her eyes. "That makes no sense."

"Actually, it makes a lot of sense. Jonathon Jackson will make a fortune from this." Mr. Lawrence looked at Addy, his expression full of hope. "Our school stands to make a fortune as well."

"Our school?"

"You will represent our school in the competition," he announced with a clap. "If you win, even if you make it to the Top Thirty, our school will receive so much publicity, our numbers will double, maybe even triple, next year."

Addy knew her small Christian school was struggling to bring in new students. With the economy crumbling, many couldn't afford to pay its rising tuition costs. She had heard rumors that if something didn't change soon, the school would close next year. While she certainly didn't want to be forced to transfer schools her senior year, she was not about to sacrifice her self-respect in order to keep it open.

"I'm honored you think I could do this, Mr. Lawrence," she began, hoping she wouldn't hyperventilate midsentence, "but I'm *really* not interested."

Addy was the last girl who wanted to be in a reality TV show. *I don't even try out for school plays. Not since that time in third grade when I was forced to play a molar in* Tooth or Dare.

"It's already done." He leaned back and reached into his desk drawer for a large white envelope. The envelope had a mock presidential seal on the front, the eagle replaced with a chubby, winking cupid holding "The Book of Love." Addy's name was drawn on a piece of parchment paper in one of the cupid's hands. Jonathon's name was on the other.

Her face got warm. "People on reality TV are there for a reason." She stood and looked toward the door. "They want attention. *I* don't want attention. I want to get good grades and get into an Ivy League school. Period."

"Listen, Addy, you can be exactly who you are, and if you generate a large enough fan base, you can write your own ticket." He motioned for her to sit down. "Look at what has happened to some of these reality TV stars." He began clicking again, but Addy turned the computer screen back toward her principal.

"But I don't want to be a reality TV star." She slumped back into the leather chair. "I don't want to be any kind of star at all. Why don't you ask Alice Harrington or Tiffany Weaver or one of those girls? They'd *kill* for an opportunity like this."

"That's exactly why I *didn't* choose them. One hundred schools were contacted. They were chosen at random from every secondary school in the country. We are privileged to be one of them. We can each send one girl. I imagine most of the principals will be picking their drama stars and head cheerleaders. I think we can have an edge in the competition by sending *you*."

"Is that supposed to be a compliment?" Addy bristled, once again standing to leave.

"Sorry. That didn't come out right. Please, sit back down." Mr. Lawrence waited as Addy dropped back into her seat. "I don't believe our school was chosen by chance. God was in that 'random' drawing." He walked around his desk and sat beside Addy. "Mrs. Lawrence and I talked about this for a while last night. We've watched you grow up, and we know the kind of young woman you are. You will represent our school well, but you will also represent Christ well. That's why I believe our school was chosen—to give Jesus some good press for a change."

Addy's heart raced. From the time she was young, people expected her to be a spiritual giant because her parents had been missionaries. She knew she could never live up to those expectations, so she learned to stay quiet and live in the shadows. So far, that tactic had worked for her.

"Look what you and Lexi have accomplished this year with the girls' Bible study." He blinked back tears. "Twenty girls staying after school on Mondays to study God's Word. And you initiated that."

Addy shook her head. She and God had had many arguments before she finally talked to Lexi about starting that Bible study. Her friend was thrilled at the idea, but Addy was nervous about being in charge. What if she messed up? What if no one came? But in the end, she knew it was what God wanted her to do, so she obeyed.

But this TV show. This is a lot more difficult than leading a Bible study for girls at my school. She didn't mind talking about her faith with other Christians, but sharing her faith with those who didn't believe terrified her.

"I can't," she said, her voice barely audible.

"Pray about it, Addy. Please. I have, and I am convinced God wants you in this."

"But, Mr. Lawrence—"

"God will let you know if this is right for you."

That was exactly what she was afraid of. "When do I have to make a decision?"

"Your flight leaves at nine o'clock tomorrow morning."

Chapter 2

T he Book of Lo-o-ove," Lexi, Addy's best friend since third grade, said, looking at the glossy folder with the chubby cupid on the front.

The pair had been given permission to leave school early. Mr. Lawrence wanted Addy to have time to peruse the information packet from the show. Lexi was allowed to go along as moral support. Settling into a booth at their favorite coffee shop, the girls sipped frappuccinos.

The bell above the door announced another customer had entered.

"It's Spencer, Addy." Lexi drew out his name, like a second grader beginning the song, *"Spencer and Addy, sittin' in a tree . . ."*

Addy put the menu in front of her face. "Lexi, what have I told you about whispering?"

"That was loud?" Lexi looked at Addy with a frown.

Addy peeked over her menu. "Oh no. He's coming over here. I'm going to kill you."

Lexi waved at him. "Hey, Spencer. Want to join us?"

Addy put down her menu and looked up. Spencer Adams was the cutest boy at school. Because of his Cuban heritage, Spencer had creamy olive skin and dark brown hair, with eyes to match. And suddenly those eyes were looking right at Addy.

"Thanks, but I have to get right back to school." He motioned toward the door. "I'm an office aide, and the coffeemaker in the teacher's lounge isn't working." Spencer pulled out a piece of paper containing several orders.

Lexi opened her mouth to say something else, but Spencer was already walking away.

"That went well." Lexi watched Spencer walk to the counter and talk with the pretty barista. "He spoke to you. That only took five years. Maybe by the time you're thirty, you can have an actual conversation."

Addy fanned herself with the menu. "I doubt he even knows my name."

"Because you don't talk to him. You've been crushing on him since we were, what, twelve?"

Addy looked at her friend. "I find him attractive. That's all. I like brown-eyed boys."

"Jonathon Jackson has brown eyes." Lexi grinned.

"Please. If Spencer Adams won't give me the time of day, then the president's son definitely won't."

"You never know." Lexi picked up the packet. "Your names could be written in *The Book of Love*."

"Very funny."

"What kind of name is that, anyway? *The Book of Love*?"

"It's from an old 1950s song, Lex."

"Who listens to music from the 1950s?"

"Uncle Mike." Addy shot Lexi a "duh" stare.

"That's oldies music?" Lexi snorted. "I thought he had committed some crime and listening to that music was his punishment."

Addy laughed. "You better not say that to him."

"Why not? I'm just about as big as he is now. I can take him." Lexi flexed her biceps and grinned.

Addy looked at her friend and had to agree. At just under six feet tall and just over two hundred pounds, Lexi Summers was a force to be reckoned with.

"Oh, I see." Addy pointed to the middle of the first page of information. "Chad Beacon recorded an updated version of the song. It's going to come out the same week the show premieres."

"Chad Beacon? Who's that?"

"Lex, seriously. Where were you last spring? Chad Beacon is our age and won *America's Next Star*. Don't you remember how half the girls in school kept talking about him? They put posters up in the bathroom stalls and everything. It was crazy."

"Last spring." Lexi tapped her fingers on her chin. "What was happening last spring? Oh, I remember. Last spring I was the first sophomore ever to hit one thousand points in basketball."

"Anyway, back to the reason we're here, please." Addy straightened the papers on the table. "You have to help me find a good reason to tell Mr. Lawrence I won't do this."

"Interesting, because Mr. Lawrence told me I was here to help you find a reason *to* do this." Lexi sipped her drink. "Quite a conundrum we're in, isn't it?"

"You can't honestly be thinking this is a good idea."

"Why not, Addy?"

"You've known me almost my whole life. Why would you think this is something I'd want to do?"

"You didn't ask me if I thought this was something you'd want to do." Lexi sucked the last of her frappuccino. "You asked me if I thought this was a good idea."

"And why is it a good idea?"

"Hello." Lexi put her elbows on the table and leaned toward Addy. "Number one, Jonathon Jackson is super hot. I mean, come on. Have you seen him?"

"A perfect reason for me *not* to go." Addy leaned back. "He's got all kinds of girls throwing themselves at him all the time. Which means, number one, he wouldn't ever be interested in me. And number two, he's probably incredibly conceited."

"Fine, let's say you have no chance with the boy."

Addy rubbed her temples.

"Reason number two: You're on TV. Addy Davidson, a television superstar. Every girl at school will want to be you. Every boy will want to date you. Spencer Adams will be the first in line." Lexi lowered her voice in an attempt to sound like Spencer. "'Oh, Addy. I've been blind all these years. Why have I been dating the cheerleaders and the pretty coffee girls when you've been right here, right under my nose all this time? I love you, Addy.'" Lexi made loud kissing noises and several customers turned to look. Spencer, grabbing the last of his order, among them.

Addy sank farther into her seat. "Shh."

Spencer walked past the girls without even a nod. The bell rang as he left the shop and Addy sighed. "Look, I don't even want to date. Not right now."

"Because nobody's asked you out."

Addy stuck her tongue out at her friend. "We've talked about this before. God first, boys later."

"I know." Lexi sighed. "But we can appreciate all the fine merchandise without having to buy anything."

Addy laughed. "I don't want to window shop. I want to get through high school with a good GPA."

"And get into an Ivy League college," Lexi finished. "I know. But, Addy, seriously. You have been chosen to be on TV. And it's only for, what, a month? A month out of your life to enjoy fame and pampering and . . . what else?" Lexi looked through the papers in the information packet. She pointed to the second page. "Ooh, challenges and contests. That sounds fun."

"Are you even listening to me?" Addy tried to pull the papers from Lexi's hand, but her friend turned to the side and kept reading. "I don't want to be on a show where I'm trying to win a date with a boy. It's embarrassing."

Lexi pointed to the third sheet. "Look, it says you won't even get an actual date with Jonathon until the very end. Once you've proven your worth."

"I don't want to prove my worth." Addy grabbed the papers and stuffed them back into the envelope.

"Stop being so stubborn. Go on the show. This is a once-in-a-lifetime chance."

"I know you mean well, Lexi. But I can't do this. It's not for me." She looked at her phone. "I'm going home. At least I know Uncle Mike will be on my side. He'll help me tell Mr. Lawrence no."

❧

"You told Mr. Lawrence I would do this?"

Her uncle had been waiting for Addy when she got home, her suitcase out and clean laundry folded on her bed.

"Calm down, Addy-girl." He pulled travel-sized shampoos and conditioners out of a Walmart bag. "This is nothing to be afraid of. It's an amazing opportunity. Talk about being a light in the darkness. Your parents would be so proud."

"*Don't* bring them into this, Uncle Mike. This is not the same."

He opened his mouth to respond, but Addy held up her hand to stop him. "And even if it were, I don't want it. Mom and Dad *died* being a light in the darkness. Is that really the goal you want me to strive for?"

It was a low blow. They both knew it.

Mike put down the bag and squeezed her shoulder. "I know this isn't something you'd choose, but God can use you—"

"Why would God want to use *me*?" Addy pulled away from her uncle and hugged herself, fighting panic. "I'm not like my parents. I'm just . . . me."

"Addy-girl, sit down." He waited as she reluctantly

dropped to her bed. "Have I ever told you that your mom was scared when they left for the jungle? She told your grandpa and me at the airport she was worried she'd let people down. She sounded a lot like you do now. She was sure others could do a better job than she could. You know what your grandpa said to her?"

She shook her head.

"He told her those thoughts were from the enemy, not from God. God had called her to that village, so she could trust that he would help her accomplish his tasks for her there."

"But they were killed, Uncle Mike." Tears rolled down Addy's cheek and she fought to keep herself from completely breaking down.

He sat next to Addy and held her. "God had a reason for taking your parents home. He brings good even out of evil."

Addy doubted she would ever think of her parents' murder as a good thing, but she had decided long ago that trusting God was a wiser choice than hating him.

"You know the first thing that came into my mind when Mr. Lawrence told me about this?" Uncle Mike asked.

"This is crazy—my niece doesn't need to embarrass herself by going on a dating show?"

"No." He put his arm around Addy. "I thought of Daniel and the lions' den."

Addy looked at him. "What?"

"Daniel got thrown into the lions' den for his faith. But what happened because of that?"

"God saved him," Addy said.

"And?"

"And?" Addy asked.

"And then the king knew Daniel's God was the true God and it changed the entire country."

"I might buy that reality TV is the lions' den." Addy pulled away from her uncle. "But I'm no Daniel."

"I bet Daniel didn't think he was Daniel either." He kissed the top of Addy's head, then left her alone, knowing she needed time to think.

She walked to her bathroom and splashed cold water on her face. Looking in the mirror she saw an absolutely ordinary teenage girl. Her brown hair was just brown—no highlights or streaks. Just a boring medium brown. It was thick enough to be a hassle, but not a hassle Addy wanted to bother with, so most mornings she just put it up in a high ponytail and that was it. Her eyes were brown. Not the deep brown her mother had, but like her hair, a medium, boring brown. Her height was average. Her weight, a little below average.

She knew her uncle was trying to encourage her, but Addy was sure that, even at her worst, Addy's mother was ten times better than Addy could ever be. Better at life, better at Christianity, better at stepping out and doing things that scared her.

I'm not my mother. I'm definitely not Daniel. I can't do this. Please, God. Choose someone else.

Chapter 3

"This is the craziest thing I have ever done." Addy looked from her uncle to Lexi to the Lawrences, who had come with her to the airport early that morning. After a night spent praying and fighting, she had finally surrendered to what she knew God was asking her to do.

"Who wrote the book of love?" Lexi sang in her horribly off-key voice and Addy held up her hand.

"No more, please. You sang that the whole way here."

"I think I should record it and make it your ringtone." Lexi laughed.

Uncle Mike wrapped Addy in a huge hug. "I love you, Addy-girl," he whispered in her ear. "I'll be praying for you every day."

Mr. Lawrence handed Addy a manila envelope, filled with her homework assignments for the next week. "I'll be sending you one of these every week. Your grades won't suffer in the time you spend away. I promise. Mrs. Lawrence and I are so proud of you."

Addy grabbed her carry-on bag and walked away, looking back one last time before boarding the plane that would take her to the lions' den.

ॐ

Three hours later, Addy and ninety-nine other girls were stuffed into four charter buses. They had been picked up at the airport in Nashville and directed to one of the sleek, black buses waiting to take them to The Mansion—the massive home in mid-Tennessee where the "chosen" would meet Jonathon Jackson for the first time.

The longer Addy stayed on the bus, the more uncomfortable she became. She had no business with these girls. They were beautiful, prepared, and determined. Addy felt like the ugly duckling—only she would have been happy to be kicked out of the family and sent to live on an island all by herself. Forget turning into a swan at the end. Invisibility would have been preferable.

Her seatmate, a stunning African American girl, started painting her nails beside Addy. The fumes were suffocating. Addy moved to open the window beside her to get some fresh air.

"No!"

"What are you doing?"

"I spent five hours at the salon. Shut that window right now."

Five pairs of hands clawed at the barely open window. Addy moved out of their way as the girls around her clicked the window shut and glared at her. Her seatmate returned to her nails.

Addy closed her eyes. Some of the other contestants had tried to engage Addy in conversation, but she just pretended to be asleep. She didn't want to talk to them. She had nothing to say. All they seemed to want to do was squeal and croon about the show, its star, and their plans to be his prom date.

An hour later, the buses were parked in front of The Mansion. Waiting. Cameras had been positioned on all sides, bright lights facing the bus doors. Addy remained in the back—hoping for an electrical malfunction—while the rest of the girls powdered, sprayed, stuffed, and adjusted.

"Number seventy-four," shouted a man in a Yankees baseball cap.

Since we are cattle, thought Addy, *none of us has a name. Just numbers.* And when the numbers were called, the girls would each take one last glance in her compact mirror, paste on a Miss America smile, and step out of the bus, ready for her close-up. Most of the time, the exit wasn't quite right— too many shadows, a noise from the crew, a microphone misplaced. So number seventy-four would get back on the bus and reexit, same plastic smile in place.

Addy was number ninety-seven. By the time her number was called, it was two in the morning. Not once had she reapplied makeup, brushed her hair, or even glanced in a mirror. She knew from the information packet that only thirty girls would be chosen from the initial one hundred. Addy was determined to be in the majority. Mr. Lawrence could give her detention for the rest of the year. She didn't care. Served him right for choosing her over Tiffany. Addy had warned him she would be a bad choice.

"Number ninety-seven," shouted Yankees Hat, the edge in his voice reflecting the late hour and the overload of aerosol-laced estrogen he had been inhaling.

Groaning, Addy shuffled to the front of the bus.

"*You're* number ninety-seven?" Yankees Hat said.

"Can we please just get this over with? I want to be voted off as quickly as possible."

"Fine by me."

Addy squinted as the bright lights assaulted her eyes.

"Back on the bus, ninety-seven. No squinting."

"I've been in a dark bus for thirteen hours." Addy rubbed her temples. "What do you expect?"

"*Again*, ninety-seven."

Addy walked on the bus and reached into her purse for her sunglasses.

"No sunglasses," grouched Yankees Hat. "Jonathon needs to see your face. This is your first impression, you know."

Addy knew. The "coaches" who had traveled with them on the buses and the executive producer had all made sure the girls knew that Jonathon Jackson would be standing at the door to The Mansion, waiting to greet each of them personally.

"You will exit the bus, walk slowly to the porch, shake

17

Jonathon's hand, tell him something about yourself, then walk into The Mansion," they had been instructed. Over and over again.

Most of the girls had spent the entire bus ride agonizing over what to tell the hunky president's son. "I love baseball too," "I'm president of my junior class, so I know what it's like to have so much pressure on you," and "I can't wait to get to know you"—deep breath, chest out, wink—"better" were some of Addy's favorites.

She forced herself to keep her eyes open as she exited the bus. Again. She smiled warily at camera two as instructed, then walked over to a mark on the porch, just a foot away from the president's son.

"Hello. I'm Jonathon," he said as deep brown eyes met hers.

For a moment, Addy forgot why she was so frustrated. Jonathon Jackson was the best-looking guy she had ever seen up close. He had sandy brown hair that lay perfectly over his forehead, a straight nose, straight white teeth, a hint of a tan, and even a little stubble on his face. And he smelled so good. Not that cheap, musky cologne boys like Spencer Adams bathed in, but a subtle, very masculine scent. Addy couldn't stop herself from closing her eyes and inhaling.

"*Cut,*" yelled her biggest fan. "Ninety-seven, you have to speak! And *keep your eyes open*. Go back to the bus and do it again."

She suddenly remembered the source of her frustration.

Forgetting the warmth of Jonathon's eyes and his amazing smell and focusing instead on her burning desire to be as far away from lights and Yankee baseball caps as possible,

Addy marched back to the bus, then walked over to the president's son and shook his hand.

"Hello, Jonathon. My name is Addy Davidson. I have *no* desire to be part of this 'competition,' and I suggest my name be the very first you take off the list."

Shaking with adrenaline, she turned on her heel and stalked through the door to The Mansion, but not before noting a hint of a smile in the First Son's eyes.

Chapter 4

"Well, if it isn't the little showstopper," Hank Banner, the show's host, as well as one of the producers, said.

He was the stereotypical Hollywood insider. Addy guessed he was in his thirties, but with the sprayed-on tan, whitened teeth, highlighted hair, and three-hundred-dollar ripped jeans, she couldn't be completely sure.

"I thought I knew all of the contenders, but I guess I was wrong. Well played." Hank held his fist out.

Addy put her hands up apologetically. "No, you don't understand. I didn't mean to say that. I was just so tired . . ."

"Hey, no need to make up stories with me. We're on the same team here. I want the show to do well; you want publicity." Hank allowed his outstretched hands to complete the sentence.

"I don't want publicity." She shook her head. "I really didn't want to come on the show. But I shouldn't have said what I did."

His smile faded. "You didn't want to come on the show?"

"Not really." Addy shrugged.

"You didn't want to come on national television and have a chance to be discovered? You didn't want a chance to win a date with the most recognized teenager in the world? You didn't want to have thousands of dollars in clothes and trips and gifts lavished on you?"

"It's a huge honor, I know."

"No, I don't think you do know." Hank raised his voice, his entire demeanor changing. "Do you know how many girls fought to get on here? How many phone calls from parents I got, begging me to give their precious daughters this chance?"

"N-no."

He looked across the lawn at a beautiful Hawaiian girl and waved. "That's Lila Akina. Her parents own a pineapple plantation. They are substantial supporters of this show, committed to its success. They have proven their sincerity, and their daughter is thrilled to be here. She will do well."

Suddenly smiling again, Hank looked down at Addy and folded his arms. "Look, here's how it's going to go: play by my rules, and I can guarantee you a spot in the finals. You've got underdog potential." He leaned forward, just inches from her face. "Don't play by my rules, and you're out. Got it?"

No, I don't get it. Addy stumbled backward in an effort to regain her personal space. And dignity.

"You've got ten minutes to get to the rose garden," Hank said, turning to leave. "I suggest you spend the walk over thinking about what I just said."

"I think you're insane," Addy wanted to say. Was he really trying to get her to bribe him? Was he thinking Uncle Mike would bribe him? That's a laugh.

Oh, God, maybe I misunderstood you. You can't want me here on this show. If this is the lions' den, then I've spent my night here. Send me home.

Ten minutes later, Addy was looking at the same man, but he wasn't the same man. Hank had suddenly transformed into a cool older brother, talking to the girls as if they were all his favorite people.

"You have to sell yourselves to America, girls." Hank smiled. "Get those beautiful faces on TV as much as you can. That's the way it works. People see you, they recognize you, and then the sky's the limit. This could be your big break." He walked between the rows of girls, smiling and winking. He was looking toward the paparazzi's cameras too, probably hoping to get his own spot in one of the magazines they represented.

"And don't forget, Jonathon will be watching the footage every week as well. As a matter of fact, he's watching it right now. He's getting to know you so he can decide who will be his Top Thirty."

Squeals of delight pierced Addy's ears as the girls reacted to this news. They were all talking at once, wondering what Jonathon was thinking, who would be in the Top Thirty, how much they wished everyone could make it because they were all best friends—did the camera catch that? No? Maybe they'd better say it once more.

"Don't forget, little ladies, this show is live. Every episode, every week. America will be watching right along with you."

A girl next to Addy screamed and clapped her hands. Several others followed.

"It's more exciting this way," Hank said, his eyes darting to the cameras. "Nothing phony or rehearsed. Reality TV at its best. We might even start a trend." Hank laughed and glanced again at the cameras. "At least, that's the plan."

Addy had to get away. As soon as Hank finished his pep talk and dismissed the girls, she walked toward the woods that bordered The Mansion.

She just needed to get past the crowd and to the gate. The bodyguards were there making sure no unauthorized person entered the grounds, but dozens of men and women with cameras and press passes lined the fence in front, pushing forward and shouting at the girls.

"Hey. Over here."

"What's your name?"

"What's happening in there? Hey, girl."

Groaning, Addy kept her head down, hoping the paparazzi would see she wanted to be left alone. The cameras and microphones just got closer. Obviously these people were not familiar with nonverbal communication.

"Leave me alone," Addy shouted as she kept walking.

Several minutes later, she looked up, finally far enough away from the cameras that she could enjoy the scenery.

It was beautiful. Being a Floridian, Addy was used to see-ing palm trees and lakes and pastel-colored houses. March looked much the same as January. Here she was greeted by a dense forest, green with spring leaves, rolling hills, and majestic trees. Addy found a dry spot at the edge of the for-est and sat, enjoying the peace and quiet.

Glancing back at The Mansion, Addy sighed. Under any other circumstance, she would have loved being here. The house, they were told, was over 150 years old, built just before the Civil War. The owners were abolitionists who bought the property in order to help runaway slaves. Theirs was one of the stops on the famous Underground Railroad. Hank had only gotten permission to use the house because of the show's star. Who refused the president's son?

Addy couldn't help thinking of the home in *Gone with the Wind*, one of her favorite old movies. Uncle Mike and she watched it every Christmas.

"Your mama and I would watch that movie whenever it came on TV," he'd say. "No DVD players when we were growing up, Addy-girl."

Whenever Mike talked about his childhood, his eyes would close and Addy could tell he was reliving those memories.

"Because the movie was so long, Mom would set up a picnic for us in the living room. We'd always have a pitcher of grape Kool-Aid and a batch of Mom's chocolate chip cookies." He would laugh. "She was a great mom, Addy. The best. But that woman could never make anything with-out burning it. We'd need the whole pitcher of Kool-Aid to wash down those cookies."

In memory of both women, Mike re-created the pic-nic, laying down a blanket and making cookies—usually burned—as Addy and he watched a movie they both could quote almost verbatim. Inevitably, Mike would tear up and tell stories about his sister. Addy knew the stories as well as she knew the film, but she never tired of either.

Addy often wondered what her life would have been like had she grown up with her mom. She loved Mike, but she missed the presence of a mother, helping her through the times in life only a woman could really understand.

Her mother would have liked The Mansion very much. It looked a lot like Tara from *Gone with the Wind*: two stories of red brick, with four massive columns rising all the way to the top of the roofline. There was a porch at the entrance and a balcony on the second floor. Homey white rockers with intricately designed quilts thrown over them sat on the front porch, matching white end tables in between. Vases filled with wildflowers were on each table.

"This house is a national landmark," Hank had said when asked why the girls couldn't sleep there.

He had looked around to make sure there weren't any cameras in sight before continuing. "We can't risk you breaking anything in there. But the trailers we've got for you are top of the line. These are the same kinds of trailers the big stars stay in when they're filming. But you'll take turns hanging out in The Mansion. The show needs casual shots for the premiere. America needs to believe you live there. Just be careful when you're sitting on that furniture, got it?"

Addy couldn't wait for the whole thing to be over. The premiere was just a few more days away. The night after that, Jonathon would choose his Top Thirty. Addy was certain she would be the first to receive the "good-bye daisy" from him. She'd run back to the trailer and pack while the other sixty-nine girls vied for their "I'm so sad he didn't pick me. We were made for each other" shot.

Addy turned around when she heard the canter of a horse behind her.

Jonathon Jackson pulled the reins on a powerful gray-and-white horse. "Oh, hi."

Those eyes again. "Hi," Addy said, the awkward silence broken only by the horse's heavy breathing.

"Are you enjoying yourself?"

He was obviously trying to be polite. Addy was surprised at how pleased she felt at his attention. Then again, she was no different from the other girls. A silly teenager swooning over a cute boy.

"This is a beautiful place." What an imbecile. She was alone with the *president's son* and all she could think of was "This is a beautiful place"? She grimaced at the thought.

"Am I bothering you?" Jonathon asked.

She looked up and the vulnerability on his face shocked her. Was *he* actually feeling awkward around *her*? Or maybe afraid? She was, after all, the jerk who told him off.

Jonathon cleared his throat, jolting Addy from her thoughts.

"No. I'm sorry. Sometimes I just start thinking and forget to talk . . . That sounded stupid." Addy closed her eyes and groaned, wishing she were anywhere but here.

He laughed, dismounted, and sat beside her on the grass. "You're different," he said with a smile.

An amazing smile, Addy noted. *Perfect.*

"What's your name again?"

"Addy Davidson." Holding out her hand to Jonathon, she added, "It's nice to meet you."

"Really?" He gave her a teasing grin. "I never would've guessed from our first meeting." He took her hand and shook it.

Addy's ears heated. She quickly dropped his hand and looked down. "Okay, so I'm not thrilled to be here."

Jonathon glanced around and whispered, "Can I be totally honest with you?"

Addy was again struck by the look in Jonathon's eyes. *More than vulnerable. Almost childlike.* Her heart softened for a moment. *Maybe he isn't so bad.*

Or maybe this was a trick. Maybe Jonathon was just like Hank—putting on a show when people were around so he'd look good for the cameras. Of course that's what he was doing. How could Jonathon be any different from Hank? He was the one starring in the show, after all. She'd already been embarrassed by Hank. And by her own stupidity in what she said to Jonathon at their first meeting.

No more. I've done enough damage. I'm keeping my mouth shut until I'm on that plane home.

"Addy?" He looked at her, his eyebrows raised.

"Actually, Jonathon, I need to go. I'm sorry. I'm sure one of the other girls would be happy to talk with you, though. Would you like me to send one of them out?"

"No thanks. I just thought—" He cut himself off, looking completely bewildered.

"I'll see you later." With that, Addy walked away as

fast as she could. She didn't slow down until she heard the pounding of the horse's hooves fading in the distance.

The roar of the paparazzi soon replaced that sound and Addy was again assaulted for information, pictures, and guesses about what was next. She pushed her way through the crowd of lights and cameras, groaning.

How many hours until she'd be free from this picturesque prison?

$\mathcal{K}$ara

BOOK OF LOVE: So, Kara, tell us a little about how you made it here to *The Book of Love*.

KARA: I had my father bribe the principal . . . (she laughs). Really, it all happened so fast. The hardest part was packing. I mean, really, one suitcase? One? And everything has to be in those tiny little bottles. Do you see all this hair? Three ounces is barely enough for one shampoo. What is the world coming to when a teenage girl is only allowed one suitcase and a few tiny bottles of hair products? It's terrible. What was your question again? How did I make it here? I'll bet Mrs. Kawolski is watching this, wondering the same thing. I don't know. Maybe my dad *did* bribe her. I sure hope she gets something outta this.

BOL: I can certainly see that famous New York spunk in you, Kara. Was it hard leaving home and coming down here to Nashville for the show?

KARA: Leaving home was hard. I've never been away from my folks for more than a week—and that was just for summer camp. Pop kept trying to convince me to let him come along—be my bodyguard. But

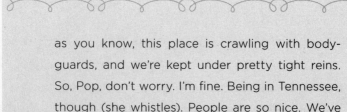

as you know, this place is crawling with body-guards, and we're kept under pretty tight reins. So, Pop, don't worry. I'm fine. Being in Tennessee, though (she whistles). People are so nice. We've got caterers here and cleaning people, hair and makeup folks, and they're all so friendly. And those accents. I am determined to learn how to talk like them before I leave. Hi, y'all. How're you doin' toda-ay?

BOL: (Laughs) Keep working on that southern drawl, Kara. Now, what do you like to do in your spare time?

KARA: Spare time? What's that? (She laughs) I keep pretty busy. School, of course, is my main priority right now. If I can just get through chemistry and trig without my brain melting, I'll be happy. After school, I am either in dance, voice, or acting lessons, at rehearsals, or hanging out at the mall with my friends. When I'm not doing those things, I'm home with the folks watching reality TV shows. I love reality TV (she winks).

BOL: I have a feeling reality TV is going to love you. Now, Kara, for the last question: Describe "The Perfect Boy."

KARA: Isn't that an oxymoron? Just kidding. The perfect boy? For me, I'd want someone just like my pop. He's awesome. He knows how to make me laugh when I'm getting upset. He listens and offers just enough advice, but not so much that I feel like I'm being told what to do. He is fun and silly and he's always there for me.

BOL: Sounds like your dad is a great guy.

KARA: He is . . . Did he pay you to say that?

BOL: No, did he pay *you*?

KARA: (Laughing) That was a good one. Thanks for the interview.

BOL: Hey, that's my line. Thank you, Kara. I'd wish you good luck, but I don't think you're going to need it.

Chapter 5

Okay, ladies, you watch the show as America watches it. We're putting it up on the big screen outside so you'll all get to see it." Hank had really poured it on earlier that afternoon, and the girls had shrieked their excitement.

"The show will start right at eight o'clock tonight. You are sitting in your assigned seats, so make sure you go right there before the show. The cameramen have the seating assignments, so they can get shots of you during the show."

The girl next to Addy, a petite blonde with a southern accent, leaned over to her. "We're all the way in the back. How are the cameras going to be able to see us over all those tall girls in the front? It's not fair."

Addy shrugged. She had been thinking the same thing. *But I don't think this girl would appreciate that I think it's a good thing.*

"All right, girls." Hank looked at his phone. "You just have a few hours to eat, get dressed, and be ready for makeup. You'd better get going."

Most of the girls could hardly wait.

Addy's mood, however, had only soured in the days since she met Jonathon in the woods. She hated the way she was acting.

This isn't me. It's some Frankenstein version of me: someone who is rude to boys and hates authorities and plots ways to escape uncomfortable situations.

Her uncle's face came to mind uninvited. If he saw her right now, he would be so disappointed. He had taught her to always do what's right, no matter the circumstances, to be kind to others no matter how they treated her. He had taught her to be like Jesus. But being selfish was just *so* much easier.

Uncle Mike would say she needed to apologize to Jonathon for being unkind. Addy *hated* apologizing. She did it because the guilt would eat at her until she did. But she still hated it.

In her trailer, Addy lay on her bed, trying to read. Realizing she had read the same page at least four times, she put down the book and closed her eyes.

"Don't you want to get changed?" Kara, Addy's trailer mate, asked.

Addy grimaced. She had managed to avoid conversation most of that week. With a hundred girls crawling around the grounds, the trailers were stuffed to capacity. Addy's trailer had four girls in it—and most of the time, the other three girls were off having fun together. Hank had arranged game nights, bowling tournaments, and movies on the big screen for them. Kara and her other trailer mates had been enjoying all the show had to offer, and Addy was more than happy to stay behind in the quiet trailer and read.

Though the girls were required to spend the mornings doing schoolwork, Addy found that three hours wasn't enough. So she spent her afternoons finishing assignments and getting ahead on others. She enjoyed the independent study. No waiting around for her classmates to finish assignments or ask questions that had already been answered in the teachers' lectures. The other girls thought her a little odd for enjoying her schoolwork so much. Most of them did just enough to say they were done, then spent the rest of their study time texting friends back home or updating their Facebook or Twitter statuses.

Kara had invited her to all the events the others attended. But Addy declined. Having to hear all the giggling and squealing at mealtimes and meetings was enough. Addy felt some guilt over that.

If God really wants me here, then I really should try to be a better example. Of course, if he doesn't want me here, then I might as well just lie low and wait to get kicked off with the other sixty-nine girls.

"Addy," Kara asked again. "Hello. Are you changing before the premiere? There are some awesome clothes in the costume trailer. And they're free. I got this." She twirled around in a ruffled white skirt, teal tank top, and cropped jacket. "I'm sure we could find something for you too."

"No, I don't want to create any more laundry to bring home." *Please, just leave me alone.*

No such luck. Kara walked over to Addy's bed and sat at her feet. "You really don't want to be here?"

"No." Addy sat up and stretched. "No offense, but I am not interested in parading myself around to get the attention of a *boy.*"

Kara didn't say anything but remained sitting on Addy's bed.

I'm a jerk, Addy thought. *Why am I acting like this?* "I'm sorry, Kara. I shouldn't have said that. I just want to go home."

"Don't worry about it. I'm from New York. I'm used to people saying what they do and don't want."

Addy laughed. Maybe Kara wasn't so bad. She was certainly pretty. Kara had deep auburn hair that hung halfway down her back, huge green eyes, and the body of a dancer. She looked the part of a beauty queen wannabe, which was the primary reason Addy had avoided her. She assumed all the girls here were brainless beauties looking for attention. But anyone who could handle Addy at her rudest couldn't be *that* bad.

"So you really think we're all here just because we want to go to prom with the handsome Mr. Jackson?" Kara raised an eyebrow.

"Well . . . yes." Addy shrugged. "Aren't you?"

"I'm not going to lie—he is a whole lot cuter than the boys in my high school. But I've got much bigger plans than going to prom."

"Really? What are they?"

"I'm going to be a world-famous actress."

Addy gave a slow nod.

"What?"

"Nothing."

"Listen, missy. I know nothing, and that wasn't a nothing nothing. That was a something nothing. So spill it." Kara leaned in. "You don't think much of actresses, huh?"

"How can you get that from one word?" Addy sat up and hugged her knees to her chest.

"Why are you avoiding my question?"

"We're all entitled to our own dreams. Yours is to be an actress. That's great. I wish you luck."

"Could you be more condescending?" Kara crossed her legs. "If I do nothing else the entire time I am on this show—which will be the entire show, including prom with the young Mr. Jackson—I will get you to talk, Miss Davidson. So you can talk now, or I can keep talking until you talk. What's it gonna be?"

Addy shook her head and bit her lip to keep from smiling. "Forget acting. You should be a lawyer."

"Whatever. Stop changing the subject, smarty-pants. You don't think highly of actors because . . . ?"

Addy took a deep breath and looked at Kara. "What's the point? I mean, really, *if* you make it—and that's a huge 'if'—you're hounded by the press and every aspect of your life is scrutinized. And how many actors are normal? No drug problems, no messed-up marriages, no botched plastic surgeries? Other than the money, what's so great about it?"

"What's so great is that it's what I want to do more than anything else in the whole world." Kara waved her long, graceful arms all around the already-crowded trailer to make her point. "I want to move people. Actresses can be part of something bigger than themselves. We can make people think. We can make statements. We can change the world."

Addy laughed. She liked this girl.

"What are you laughing about, Addy?"

"Sorry." Addy coughed. "You're just so . . . dramatic."

"Thank you." Kara took a bow.

Suddenly, a voice at the door barked that the viewing would begin in forty-five minutes. They needed to be out on the lawn "pronto."

"C'mon, roomie," Kara said. "It's time for our close-up."

Ready or not, here I come.

Chapter 6

"Addy, you've got to see this." Kara was shaking Addy awake, pulling on her arm so hard Addy had to sit up or fall out of bed.

"What in the world are you doing? I'm tired." Addy wrenched her arm free and picked up the alarm clock on her nightstand. "It's six thirty in the morning."

"Doesn't matter." Kara laid her computer on Addy's lap. "Look."

"Chad Beacon?" Addy stared at the computer screen. The *America's Next Star* winner had his mouth wide open in a shot from last night's show. He had sung "The Book of Love" at the premiere.

"Oh, sorry." Kara grabbed the computer and stared.

"He's beautiful, isn't he? I mean, look at him. I hate to say it, but he's even cuter than Jonathon. That blond hair. All those muscles. And he must be, what, six foot three at least?"

Addy groaned. "Yes, he's cute. You really needed to wake me up at six thirty to tell me that?"

"No. I'm talking to you about the show. I just got sidetracked."

Addy rubbed her eyes. "Your point?"

"People started blogging as soon as the show ended. *The Book of Love* was the hottest show on television last night. Over fifteen million people watched. Fifteen million. Do you have any idea how huge that is? Of course you don't. Let me just tell you, it's *major*. No show has those kinds of numbers on the first night. Most shows are happy to have half that. A third is great. And get this, they loved it. *Loved* it. All the major websites have our pictures front and center. I have fifteen hundred friend requests on Facebook."

Addy yawned. Why couldn't she have been given a roommate who was mute? And comatose. But without all the machines making beeping noises.

"Addy. Did you hear me? Snap out of it. We're famous!"

"I heard you. People in Kentucky heard you. And, again, *I don't want to be famous*. I want to be asleep."

"Too bad," Kara chirped, grabbing her laptop and setting it on Addy's bed. "Because *you*, my reluctant celebrity, are *the* sound bite from last night's show."

"What?"

Kara tapped her computer and Addy heard herself talking to Jonathon through the tinny speakers. *"Hello, Jonathon. My name is Addy Davidson. I have no desire to be part of this* 'competition,' and I suggest my name be the very first you take off the list."

She lay back down and threw the blanket over her head. "No, no, no, no, no . . ."

Laughing, Kara ripped off the blanket. "Addy, this is everywhere. People love you. Or hate you. But who cares! They know your name. Look, I just Googled *Addy Davidson* and there are 85,641 hits. Listen to this: 'Addy Davidson might just be the smartest eleventh grader in the country. While the other girls were prepared with flowery words and blinding smiles, Addy hit below the belt. Jonathon Jackson might have been shocked, but America is in love.'"

Oh, God. Please let me still be sleeping. Let this just be the world's worst nightmare.

"Addy. Say something."

"I think I've said enough. This is crazy. Why me? I don't want this. I want to go home and fill out college applications and read books."

Addy shut Kara's computer, walked to their tiny bathroom, and slammed the door behind her. She turned to the mirror and examined herself. Her hair was all over the place—completed by a huge bump around the center of her head where her hair had been in a ponytail the day before. Her eyes were puffy and her face had lines from her pillowcase imprinted on it. Not the prettiest sight to see.

And now that face and hair were being broadcast all over the Internet. People were logging on to see her and comment about her and criticize her.

Addy closed her eyes and took a deep breath. Why was this happening to her? Why couldn't *Kara* be the "sound bite"? She would have loved it.

The rest of the morning went by in a torturous blur. Hank called to demand that Addy make an appearance so the press could get a shot of her. She walked into The Mansion with a bodyguard to protect her from the hundreds of cameras, newspeople, and screaming teenage girls who either thought she was their hero or cursed her for being such a jerk to "Jahhhhnathuhn."

After lunch—an orchestrated event at The Mansion with twenty-five girls who tried desperately to make the cameras look at them—Hank called Addy in for a private meeting.

Without cameras around, Addy knew Hank would not be in "cool older brother" mode.

Pacing in the spacious sitting room, Hank raked his hand through his pseudo-sun-bleached hair and sighed. "I was afraid of this."

"Afraid of what?"

"This. You." Hank motioned toward her like she was a deadly virus. "Who's helping you, Addy?"

"What?"

"You heard me." Hank crossed his arms and glared at her. "Someone told you to say that to Jonathon. Who is it?"

"N-no one. It was a mistake. I'm sorry."

"Sorry that you're the front-runner or sorry you're all over the Internet? Funny, for someone who swears she doesn't want attention, you sure are getting a lot."

"I didn't want any of this to happen. Honestly."

Hank growled, "I spent half the night talking with parents. Parents who have been playing by my rules and are now feeling cheated because you come along and do your thing and their kids are barely even noticed."

Addy stiffened. "Hank, what do you want me to say? I'm sorry. I didn't plan this, and I certainly wasn't coached to do this. I'm sorry you're angry, but it isn't my fault."

"It most certainly is your fault," Hank yelled, then calmed himself before continuing. "Let me make one thing crystal clear: this is *my* show. I've worked long and hard to get here. I am the host and I am a producer—and I call the shots. Me. Not you. Do you understand that?"

Addy refused to say another word. Hank stared at her and she stared right back.

"Look, I have no choice but to keep you on another week." Hank raked a hand through his hair again and grunted. "But that's all you get. I'm still willing to work with you. I know potential when I see it, and you've got it. But only if you understand that you work for me, and not the other way around. I don't want you to sneeze without checking with me first. Got it?"

Before Addy could even consider a reply, Hank stormed off.

Walking into The Mansion's living room, Addy thought things couldn't get worse. She wanted nothing more than to go back to her trailer and call Uncle Mike. He would know what to do. He would at least be a friendly voice. Instead she heard Hank's voice addressing the contestants.

"Girls, I want all of you to gather in the living room for some casual shots. Just sit and talk, act as naturally as you can. Be careful on the couches, though. Only two or three on each, the rest can just stand behind them. Don't sit on the floor. You are young *ladies*," he added. "And hurry up. We need to get the other groups in for *their* camera time."

Cameramen swarmed in from all directions, blocking the exits. Lights and boom mics crowded the ceiling. The girls, each applying more layers of ultrashiny lip gloss, vied for a spot in front of the huge gilded mirror above the marble-topped table in the foyer. They were all chatting about how beautiful everyone looked, how much they liked Dawn's eyes and Lila's hair and Hannah's shoes. Eyes darted to the cameras after each compliment.

"Dan, no mics on this. We'll be playing music under these shots. Cameras only."

The girls suddenly switched tactics. Smiling toward the cameras, they moved en masse to Addy. "So, Addy," began one of the girls, a southerner with long blond hair and a big mouth, "how long did it take you to come up with that line the other day?"

"Yeah," piped in another contestant, a beautiful Latina, her hazel eyes flashing, "we didn't know we'd have to start playing the game so early. You think you're pretty smart, huh? Well, you've messed with the wrong girls. Just wait until those cameras are off. We'll—"

Addy was shocked at the contrast between how they looked and what they were saying. Suddenly Kara pushed her way through the crowd, smiling and yelling at the same time.

"Leave my roommate alone or I will make your beautiful faces look like a scene from a horror movie."

Addy couldn't help laughing as she watched Kara—always smiling her thousand-watt smile—turn the angry mob into a group of frightened little girls.

Maybe actresses aren't so bad after all.

Chapter 7

And the worst part is that I'm in the Top
Thirty, Uncle Mike." Addy had finally
gotten some free time, so she returned
to her favorite spot in the woods and called her uncle as
soon as she cleared the paparazzi.

He laughed his deep, husky laugh. She could picture
him smiling through his salt-and-pepper mustache, his
hazel eyes dancing.

"Addy, my girl. This is a good thing. Really. Remember
what James tells us: the testing of your faith develops
perseverance."

"Uncle Mike," Addy whined. "I don't want perseverance. I want out."

"How are you handling things? Getting angry, frustrated, biting people's heads off?"

"What, are you hiding in the trailer?"

He laughed again. Even at her most upset, Addy was reassured by that sound.

"I just know you, girl. You're just like your mama. She would get like that when she was trying to handle difficult situations all by herself. And do you know what our daddy would tell her when she got like that?"

"What?"

"He'd sit her down, put his arm around her, and say, 'There's one God, baby, and you're not him.'"

She smiled.

"Are you asking for his help, Addy?"

She sighed. "No."

"Are you reading his Word?"

Addy winced. "No."

"Then you're not handling things well. How can you expect to get through this if you're not talking to God about it?"

"What does he care about this stupid TV show?"

"Absolutely nothing. But he cares a great deal about you. He also cares about those other girls. And Jonathon. Even Hank."

"Aw, Uncle Mike, you *almost* had me."

Another laugh. "Don't get so caught up in what's happening around you that you forget what's going on above. God has a plan for everything. He's not looking down and saying, 'Oh man, what in the world has that Addy Davidson gotten herself into now?' He put you there. For a reason.

You don't have to go around preaching. Just be a light. Be Jesus to those people. And remember, it's the meanest ones who need him the most."

"I love you, Uncle Mike."

"I love you too, Addy-girl. Hang in there. I'm here whenever you need to talk."

She hung up the phone and looked up into the cloudless sky. Uncle Mike was right. She *had* been getting too caught up in what was going on around her. She had been completely self-absorbed, too self-absorbed to even consider what God might want to accomplish through this whole mess.

She closed her eyes. *Lord, please forgive me for my behavior, my attitude, and my anger at the situation.* She asked God to help her remember that she was happiest when she was obeying God, as Uncle Mike always said. She had certainly experienced the reverse of that the last few days.

She entered her trailer and found two of her three roommates packing. They were throwing their belongings in their suitcases like boxers throwing punches.

Allison looked up. "What, have you come to gloat too?"

Addy looked over at Kara, who had also made it to the Top Thirty, and saw that roommate lift her arms in surrender.

"I'm not gloating," Kara said, an edge to her voice. "I'm in my trailer."

"Watching me and Lindsey pack to go home."

"And now Addy is here too," Lindsey said. "You don't say a word to us all week, and now you want to be here?"

Kara stood from her bed. "Just because you're miserable doesn't mean we have to be miserable."

Lindsey faced her. "Just wait, Kara. Your turn is coming. I think Hank has already picked his favorites. So you'll eventually be off too. Just like us."

"We're not gloating, Lindsey. Really." Addy placed her hand on Lindsey's shoulder. "You know, I'm pretty good at packing. Would you like a hand?"

Lindsey looked at Addy, and Addy could tell her roommate was wondering if she was being sarcastic or sincere. So Addy sat on the floor and began folding Lindsey's shirts and helping her place them in her suitcase. "My best friend's mom owns an upscale clothing store in Tampa. One time she showed me how they fold shirts for the displays." She demonstrated. "See?"

Lindsey sat beside Addy and sighed. "Thanks. I'm sorry. I just really wanted to stay on, you know? Everybody back home expected me to make it. I'm so embarrassed."

Addy handed her a pair of jeans and smiled. "You know what, we'll all be off eventually. Even the winner. You just get a head start. You get to sleep in your own bed and go back to school with your friends."

"But I go back a loser."

"Did anyone else from your school get on this show?"

"No."

"Anyone from your city?"

Lindsey laughed. "No."

"So you got an experience no one else around you has ever had. You're going to go home a celebrity."

Kara shut the door behind Lindsey and Allison as they left. "That was nice, roomie."

"What was?"

"That, with those girls. They were all nasty and you calmed them down." Kara placed her suitcase on the bunk that had been Allison's. "I was ready to get into it with them."

"They're disappointed." Addy shrugged.

"Not the word I would have used to describe them." Kara laughed. "Anyway, enough about that. We're in the Top Thirty and we get this whole trailer to ourselves now. Woo-hoo. I say we decorate it. I'm thinking sparkly beads hanging from the doors and maybe a disco ball."

"Yes, that's exactly what this trailer needs. Sparkle." Addy rolled her eyes.

"I'll make a star out of you yet, Miss Addy."

Lila

BOL: So, Lila, why should you be chosen to be Jonathon Jackson's prom date?

LILA: Well, I am the only island girl here. All these other girls are from the mainland. Not that there's anything wrong with that, you know. I like mainlanders. But we island girls are special. More relaxed. And I think Jonathon needs some relaxation in his life. He must be so stressed, being the son of the president and all. It must be so hard. I can help him enjoy life and ride the waves. I'm a lot of fun, so he'd never be bored. I can bring him home to meet my family, put him to work in the fields. We would have a special luau in his honor. I'll bet he's never experienced anything like an authentic Hawaiian luau. My parents are some of the best cooks on the island.

BOL: Tell us a little more about your family, Lila.

LILA: They are the greatest. My parents own a pineapple plantation on the island of Maui. The plantation has been in the family for four generations—I'm thinking of majoring in business so I can take over when my parents retire. But I have twin brothers—eleven years old—and they are so smart.

If I choose to pursue a career in the arts, I'm sure they could run the business.

BOL: The arts, huh? Is that what you'd like to do?

LILA: I just don't know. So many people back home expect me to continue to study dance and music. And I love both so much. I'd love to combine them both somehow and use those skills to help under-privileged children. You know, kids who would never be able to afford lessons on their own. So many people have helped mold me into the person I am today. I just want to give back, you know?

BOL: That's great, Lila. Not many girls your age, with your talent and beauty, think of others. Good luck with all your plans. We look forward to seeing more of you on *The Book of Love.*

Chapter 8

The crew had been given a day off, so Addy was enjoying what she hoped would be a relaxing, camera-free day. She had just opened her Bible when Hank's voice came over the intercom.

"All right, girls." He sounded put out to have to be talking to them. "Just because the crew has the day off doesn't mean you do. Get dressed and get out here. You've got fifteen minutes."

Dozens of comments flew into Addy's brain—none of them kind. She looked down at her Bible, then looked up. "I know, I know. Love your enemies."

"Who are you talking to?"

"Sorry, Kara." She had thought her roommate was asleep.

Kara sat up and stretched her long arms. *She even stretches gracefully,* Addy mused.

"So what do you think about this Top Thirty?" Kara said.

"What do you mean?"

"Do you really think Jonathon chose us? Or were we chosen *for* him?"

Addy hadn't mentioned her conversations with Hank to Kara. It seemed pointless. But Addy knew there was much more going on behind the scenes than just a teenage boy choosing his prom date.

"Addy, hello. Did you hear me?"

"Yes. Sorry, Kara. I was thinking."

"And . . . ?"

"I don't know."

"Want to know what I think?"

"That's rhetorical, right?" Addy smiled.

"Ah, my friend, you're learning." Kara laughed and pulled her long legs up to her chest. "None of us are from the same state. All ethnicities are represented. All sizes. All hair colors." She flipped her auburn mane. "Coincidence? I don't think so. It's way too politically correct for a seventeen-year-old boy. It's all about audience. If the producers want all of America to watch *The Book of Love,* then all of America has to be represented."

"So we're just pawns in the hands of the producers, then?"

"Exactly," Kara said, a triumphant look filling her face.

"And this is the life you have chosen for yourself?" Addy grinned.

Kara stood, clutching her heart. "Oh, you got me. But," she began in a pseudo-Shakespearean accent, "I, my de-ah, am a true act-trees. Thy silly words may prick, but they do not pierce." She walked around the trailer, long arms filling the space. "Nay, I say, nay. I wilt not succumb to thine attacks on my profession. I act, therefore I am." With that, Kara made a deep bow, sending Addy into a standing ovation. Both girls were laughing when they heard a knock on the door.

"Let's go, girls."

"Seriously, though, Addy. This is like a game. There are rules, strategies. All we have to do is figure out what those are, and we'll make it all the way to the Top Five."

"Hold on there, Juliet," Addy said as she changed into shorts and a T-shirt. "I have no interest in staying that long, remember?"

"Addy, you can't leave me here."

"And what makes you so sure *you're* staying?"

Kara replied with a swat from a pillow to Addy's head.

The girls were still laughing as they walked around The Mansion to the spacious backyard. Hank was sitting on a director's chair, sipping a huge iced coffee from a green straw.

Addy looked around and realized Kara was exactly right. There were brunettes, blondes, redheads, African Americans, Latinas, Asians, an American Indian, a Pacific Islander, three who looked like plus-sized models, and two who looked like negative-sized models. From their voices, she could tell they were a mixture of southern girls, New Englanders, at least three from the Midwest, and a sprinkling of others from around the country. They all had one thing in common, though. They were stunningly beautiful.

Addy suddenly felt like a weed in a rose garden.

"Addy, what's wrong? Are you sick?" Kara asked.

"No." She tried to smile. "I'm just feeling out of place."

"Why?"

"Remember that song from *Sesame Street*—'One of these things is not like the others'?"

"Yeah, so?"

"I'm the thing that's not like the others."

"What are you talking about?"

"Kara, look around. All of you are beautiful. Then there's me."

"Addy Davidson." Kara placed her hands on her hips. "You're prettier than any of these girls. I'd give anything for that body. Not to mention your hair . . ."

"You don't have to say that. I really don't care what I look like—"

Addy was interrupted by Hank yelling for the girls to come closer. He must have been full from his iced coffee—it was too much for him to *go* to the girls. And his eyes looked more tired than normal.

"All right, ladies. Let's hurry and do this. I was out in LA yesterday. Just flew back last night. I am tired and cranky, and I want to walk through this as quickly as possible so I can go back to my hotel and sleep. Okay?"

Addy was amazed at how self-important Hank could make himself sound in just thirty seconds.

"One of you will be Jonathon Jackson's prom date," he

announced as the girls jumped and yelled. Hank motioned for them to be silent with a wave of his beverage. "But as you know, this isn't your average reality TV dating show. Being pretty and charming isn't enough. Jonathon's date must be a well-rounded young woman. Beautiful, yes, but also smart, athletic, talented. He is the president's son, after all. So you will be tested in several areas. We will have different competitions every week for the next five weeks. The night after each competition has been aired, Jonathon will choose five girls to leave."

A collective groan came from the crowd. "Until the final week, when we are left with the Top Five. Believe me, you want to make it that far. That's the week you get to go on a date with Jonathon Jackson. So work hard and listen to everything we have to say. This is a great opportunity for you girls. Take advantage of it. Also, from now on, each morning will begin with boot camp with Lacy." He grinned. A beautiful and incredibly fit woman appeared at his side. "This doesn't replace your schoolwork. It comes before it. You will be out here at 6:00 a.m. ready to work out. That will be your first activity tomorrow morning."

More groans.

Hank silenced the girls with a glare as Lacy jogged away. He reached into a leather satchel and pulled out a three-ring binder with the show's logo on the front. He took his time flipping through to find the right page. Addy looked around and noted that all twenty-nine girls were quiet, too scared of Hank's wrath to make another sound.

"The focus for *this* week will be the arts. Each of you will have a sixty-minute meeting with either a voice, piano, dance, or acting instructor. You choose whichever of those to which you are most inclined. The instructor will help you get started on a presentation, and you will give that presentation Thursday evening—on camera, in a theater downtown. Any questions?" Several girls raised their hands, and Hank took out his cell phone and pointed to one of the assistant directors standing nearby. Obviously, he was too busy to talk to any of the girls personally.

Addy bent over, head in her hands, fingers kneading her temples.

As if I don't already feel ridiculously out of place—now I'm supposed to perform? What is he thinking? What kind of idiotic beauty pageant is this? And why am I stuck in it when I could be home, lying in my comfy bed, reading a book? In silence.

"Addy." Kara broke into Addy's mental tantrum, grabbing her arm and pulling her toward The Mansion. "Come on, let's go. We've got work to do. Music books, CDs, monologues . . . any of this getting through? We're performing onstage at the end of the week. Let's pick our pieces so we can work on them today and be ready for our lessons tomorrow."

Addy glared at Kara, then stalked off, shaking her head and muttering to herself.

Kara was right behind her, though. She grabbed Addy by the shoulders, forcing her to stop. "Addy, you know what I've noticed about you?"

Addy groaned. "No. What, Dr. Kara?"

"I've noticed"—Kara arched one eyebrow in a "watch it, sister" slant—"that you get angry when you're uncomfortable. You don't want to admit you're scared or nervous, so you get angry to cover it up."

Addy turned and walked away, too upset to even speak. *After a few days' acquaintance, Kara thinks she can analyze me? Please.* Addy power-walked her way toward the trailers.

She rounded the corner of the massive front porch just as Jonathon came from the other side. Addy narrowly missed running right into him. She gazed up just in time to throw an irritated glance his way.

"Hey," Jonathon called after her. Addy was surprised to see he appeared even more irritated than she did.

"You know, most girls are excited to be here." Jonathon shook his head and sighed. "I mean, I don't expect you to fall all over me. But do you really think acting like that will get you attention?"

"What?" Addy sucked in her breath. "I don't want attention."

"That's not what Hank says."

"And what does Hank say?" Addy put up her hand to stop him. "Never mind. I don't want to know. I just want to go home."

"There's something we have in common."

"Thanks." Addy's voice was laced with sarcasm, and she bit her tongue to keep from saying anything else she'd regret.

"No, that's not what I meant . . ." Jonathon appeared conflicted. He rubbed his temples and looked at Addy, his eyes softening. Melted chocolate.

Addy was confused, almost ready to apologize. But she was interrupted by Lila, the Hawaiian bombshell with a grass skirt for a brain.

"There you are, Jonathon." Lila tossed her long black

locks like she was in a shampoo commercial. "Hank told me you wanted to see me. That's so cute. Come on, I'll take you into The Mansion. I was just about to practice for Thursday night." Lila grabbed Jonathon's arm and led him toward the door.

Jonathon looked puzzled, but he went along. As they walked away, Lila glanced over her shoulder and gave Addy a "he's all mine" smile. Addy fought the urge to stick out her tongue in response.

Addy walked away, her heart and mind racing. She was angry. She was embarrassed. She felt like an idiot. Her uncle would be disappointed with her behavior. *She* was disappointed with her behavior. Jonathon was upset with her. Even Kara was put out. Addy was supposed to be the light here, but instead she was causing more problems than anyone else. She broke into a jog and arrived back at the trailer sweaty and out of breath.

Sitting on her bed, Addy thought about what Kara had said. Did she really use anger as a cover? She thought back to her response to going on the show, her treatment of Jonathon—every time she saw him—especially her most recent outbursts.

Kara was right.

With reluctance Addy made her way back to The Mansion.

Okay, God. I hear you.

Chapter 9

S till nothing?" Kara inquired.

Addy, surrounded by books that might as well have been written in Latin, was trying to find some sort of talent to display at the performance.

"Nothing. Unless sitting onstage and reading silently counts."

"Sorry, chick. Not gonna happen."

Addy had met with an acting coach for her required hour the day before. Less than fifteen minutes into their session, the coach recommended that Addy "consider another arena in which to display her talent."

As Addy opened up yet another book of monologues, Lila poked her head into the room.

"Oh, hi, girls. Can't find anything?" She smiled. "It must be hard. Especially for you, Addy. I saw you with the acting coach yesterday. Tsk, tsk, tsk. Not pretty. But I guess you're used to that—not being pretty."

Lila picked up a book, flipped through it, then tossed it in the pile. "Don't worry. I'm having trouble finding something too. Voice lessons for six years, dance lessons for seven. And I'm in the theater track at my performing arts school. Five minutes just isn't enough." She laughed. "Oh well. I'm sure I'll come up with something."

Trash talk. Beautiful Hawaiian trash talk. Addy's initial impression that there was nothing under that long black hair was wrong. Lila was brutal. But brutal with a smile. A deadly volcano disguised as a grass-covered mountain. She was trying to intimidate Addy.

And it was working.

Thankfully Kara was there to rescue her.

"I don't know, Lila. You only have a couple more days. If you wait too long, you might get up on that stage and freeze. All those lights, millions of people watching . . . it's scary. *Really* scary." Kara's face was deadly serious. Addy felt like she should be playing screeching horror film music in the background.

Lila's eyes grew wide, then hardened. "Oh, I'm not scared, ladies. Not at all. In fact, I was just trying to make *you* feel better. I've had my piece ready for a while. It's something I perfected at home. Won first place at my school's talent show."

"A performing arts school has a *talent* show? I go to a performing arts school—*musical* theater track—and our teachers wouldn't dream of putting together a talent show. It's so *juvenile*." Kara spat out the last word like it was poison.

"Wh-what?" Lila was flustered. Beaten at her own game. "I don't . . . I mean, we have . . . well, whatever." She regained her composure. "My piece is fantastic. You won't want to miss it. I'm sure it'll be the highlight of the night." With that, she swept out of the room, wanting, no doubt, to get in the last word.

Kara winked at Addy.

"I didn't know you went to a performing arts school."

Kara grinned. "I don't. And Lila probably doesn't either."

"Oh." Addy laughed. "Trash talk."

Kara burst out in loud laughter. "Exactly."

The girls continued to work for the next two hours, listening to CDs, thumbing through piles of scripts, until Eric, one of the assistant directors, came into the room.

"Hi, girls." Eric was one of the few nice ones on the show. He actually treated the contestants like humans instead of cattle. "We need to take some video of you talking about yourselves, for your package before the performance."

"Package?" Addy inquired.

"TV lingo for video clip."

"Oh."

"So who's first?" Eric looked from Kara to Addy.

Kara jumped up. "I'll go. Can I freshen up a little first?"

"Sure. Why don't both of you meet me at the gazebo in ten?"

The taping of the first part of the "package" went as smoothly as Addy guessed it could go. Because Eric was so kind, Addy felt relaxed. She just answered the questions as they came. How old are you? What are your hobbies? How were you chosen to be on *The Book of Love*? The answers came easily. Until the end.

"Tell us about your parents," Eric said, glancing at his notes.

"My parents?"

"Yes, you know—mom and dad—you have some, right?" He laughed. Until he saw Addy's strained face and watery eyes.

She did not discuss her parents with anyone but Uncle Mike and God. The subject was difficult. She didn't want to share their story with anyone else. Especially not with fifteen million strangers.

"You know what?" Eric closed his binder. "I think we have enough. Dan, go ahead and wrap that." He smiled apologetically at Addy and squeezed her shoulder. "I'm sorry if I brought up a painful subject. I won't mention it again, okay?"

She must have looked more upset than she thought or he wouldn't have felt so bad. Her mouth had gone dry, and she asked to be excused to go to the catering table for a drink.

Addy was sipping a Diet Coke when Kara sat beside her.

"Let's go for a walk, roomie."

"I'd rather not," Addy replied, eyes on the ice bobbing in her drink. She could tell by Kara's tone that she wanted to talk. Addy hoped her tone revealed her desire to remain silent.

"Addy. You need to talk."

"No, I don't."

"See, you're angry. Because you're uncomfortable. And because you know I'm right."

"I thought you wanted to be an actress, not a psychiatrist." Addy nudged Kara's shoulder with her own.

"We all have to have something to fall back on."

"I really don't want to talk about it." Addy looked back down at her drink.

Kara pulled Addy up by her arm, spilling Diet Coke on the perfectly manicured lawn. "I know. But you need to. Come on, let's go."

God, help me, Addy prayed.

Tell her, was the reply.

Chapter 10

I was six and a half when my world came crashing down," Addy began. "We lived in a little jungle village in Colombia. My dad was the village doctor; my mom was the nurse. They had lived there for several years and they loved it. My dad had been a doctor for a while in the States, but he didn't like it. Didn't feel totally fulfilled."

Addy couldn't bring herself to admit that her parents were missionaries. She prayed that God would understand. "My mom felt the same way, so they sold everything they had and moved to Colombia. I was born there. My first memories are running around with the village kids, playing in the rain forest, watching monkeys jump from tree to tree and trying to follow them."

"Wow," Kara exclaimed.

Addy forgot how unique her childhood was. Because it was *hers*, it just seemed normal. "Anyway, our village was pretty remote, so we didn't often hear much from the 'outside world.' But when I was six, some people moved into the village next to ours."

Addy's mind raced back to that day, to the familiar memory that never left her.

"What language are they speaking, Daddy?" Addy gazed past her father, beyond the low-lying branches of the tree. Several men were speaking quietly. They were looking around and pointing toward her village.

"Shh, honey. Be very still." Daddy stroked Addy's hair, listening carefully to what the men were saying.

Addy waited for what felt like hours. She sat down, staring up at the colorful birds making their way from tree to tree. She wanted one of them to come down to her so she could play with it, but Daddy wouldn't want her to use her bird-calling voice then, so she remained silent.

When the men left, Daddy picked up Addy and threw her on his shoulders. Normally she loved this. They would take walks and Daddy would tell her the names of all the trees and the plants. Addy would touch the different leaves, some slick, others almost furry, and try to recall their names.

This time, though, Daddy didn't walk. He ran. Addy gripped his neck as he picked his way through the dense forest to her village. Mommy was outside, talking with her friends. They were cooking over a fire. Addy hoped they would make something sweet tonight.

"Laura, gather the elders. Now."

Mommy's eyes widened, and she ran toward the other huts, calling out the names of the men in the village. Everyone came outside, and soon almost the entire village was in their small hut.

"I overheard some men in the next village. They were speaking Spanish. I could understand some of it." Daddy looked at the people and closed his eyes. "They are going to use the village to process drugs. Cocaine."

Addy wasn't sure what cocaine was, but she knew about drugs. Some of the villagers had taken drugs. They did bad things. Mommy and Daddy helped some of them stop. "Dr. Joshua, this is not our business," one of the elders said. "Leave it be. We cannot stop them if they want to do this."

"We must stop it," Daddy said. "You've seen what these drugs do to people. Imagine them getting into the hands of thousands more. We can't allow it. I will go into Mitú and tell the authorities. Who will come with me?"

At first no one spoke. Addy raised her hand. "I will, Daddy. Then I can see Sarah and Miss Stacy too." Some of their American friends lived in Mitú. Addy loved to visit them the few times a year her family went into the larger city.

"No, sweetheart," Mommy said. "Not this time. But, please, one of you at least. Have we taught you nothing? Will you really allow these men to come and do this?"

"Mrs. Laura," another elder spoke. "It is not our business. It is bad luck to put ourselves into another man's affairs."

"Luck? There is no luck. There is right and wrong. This activity is wrong. God would not want us to ignore it."

"We will not go with you, Dr. Joshua," the oldest man in the tribe said, and the others nodded in agreement.

Addy's mother wiped a tear and Addy hugged her, not fully understanding all that was happening.

Two days later, Daddy returned from Mitú.

The day after that, the police arrived. The men from the other village, the ones Daddy had overheard talking about the drugs, were right behind the police. They started screaming for everyone to come outside. The police stood beside them.

Inside their hut Mommy sobbed. "The police are corrupt. They will kill everyone!" She picked Addy up and handed her to their maid. "Please escape with Addy."

"No, I couldn't. You go. You are her mother." The maid set Addy down.

Addy began to cry and cling to her mother's legs. "Mommy, hold me. I'm scared."

"I can't go." Mommy lifted Addy and held her tightly to her chest. "They know who I am, what I look like. If I tried to escape with Addy, they'd come after me and kill us both. Please take her so she can live."

Between sobs, Mommy told the maid where Miss Stacy lived in Mitú. "Don't you dare stop running until you get there."

Mommy kissed Addy on both cheeks, tears streaming down her face. "I love you, sweetheart. Daddy loves you too. So much." Mommy held Addy again. She took a ragged breath and continued. "But God loves you more. He will always be with you. And no matter what happens, he is good. He has great plans for you. Never forget that."

Then Mommy handed Addy to the maid and walked out of the hut. Addy saw, through a gap in the wood planks of the wall, her mother thrown beside her father on the hard ground in front of their hut.

The maid snuck out the side opening of the hut, hiding behind a large barrel until she was sure no one was watching, then she ran into the jungle.

Addy heard more shouting. Then gunshots. Then silence.

She closed her eyes, the memory overwhelming.

Addy couldn't speak any longer. She was that scared little girl clinging to her maid's leathered shoulder again, silenced by a hand that shook with sobs of her own.

Kara's arm wrapped around Addy in a protective hug. She was crying too.

"They were good people, Addy," she murmured.

Emotionally drained, Addy could only nod in agreement.

Chapter 11

ddy slept from that afternoon until the next morning. But no one was exempt from "Boot Camp with Lacy," not even an orphan exhausted from telling her horrifying life story to a sympathetic roommate. So she reluctantly woke up at 5:50, threw on shorts and tennis shoes, and joined the other girls for the workout.

The exercise really wasn't all that difficult. Having been raised by an avid outdoorsman, she found running laps was not a big deal, nor were the aerobics that followed. Some of the other girls struggled to keep up, though. Addy looked back to see them stooped over, with hands on their knees. Jessica, however, was right beside Lacy, barely even out of breath.

She's insane. The exercise might not be a problem. But listening to Lacy's incredibly annoying voice is brutal. No way I'd be right up there beside her.

Addy tried to tune out Lacy as she thought about what had happened the day before. She had never told anyone that story. She didn't need to tell Uncle Mike. He had lived it. He was in Colombia within twenty-four hours of getting the phone call from the mission board. "She's in the bedroom," Miss Stacy told Uncle Mike. "She's been in there since they arrived. I've tried to get her to eat, but—"

Uncle Mike burst into the room and lifted Addy into his arms. He held her so tightly, she could barely breathe. He was shaking. Addy felt hot tears on her cheek and realized he was crying. Rocking her back and forth, he repeated, "I'm so sorry. I'm so sorry."

Addy felt numb. She couldn't cry. She couldn't remember walking through the jungle. She kept hearing the gunshots in her mind. She knew her parents weren't coming, that the men from the other village had shot them. But she couldn't feel anything. She just wanted to sleep.

But Uncle Mike kept crying and rocking. He refused to leave her side. He forced her to drink some juice and, later, to eat beans and rice. He didn't ask her to talk. Not that day, not a few days later when they got onto the airplane.

Addy looked out the airplane window as everything she knew began to fade away, and then she cried. She unbuckled her seat belt and ran for the exit.

"I want to go home. I want Mommy and Daddy." Addy didn't care that the people on the plane were all looking at her. All she knew was that the plane was rolling away from everything she knew, and she wouldn't allow it. "Take me home. Take me home."

Mike grabbed Addy in his arms and cradled her like he would a tiny baby. He carried her back to her seat. Addy kicked and cried.

"No!" The tears were coming so fast she couldn't even see. "Let me go. Take me home. I want my mommy!"

Flight attendants rushed over and demanded that Mike and Addy buckle up. The plane was taking off. Mike refused to let go of Addy. He sat in his seat, Addy still in his arms. She finally grew tired of fighting. The next thing she knew she was waking up, still in Mike's lap, her face dry and sticky from her tears.

Uncle Mike had helped her as she adjusted to life in the United States, so different from life in her village in Colombia. He took her to a counselor so she could work through all she had experienced. He took her to a tutor so she could improve her English. Mike gave up his longtime career in the army to work as a policeman in Tampa so he could be near Addy more. A confirmed bachelor in his forties, Mike became father and mother in one tragic day.

Emotions she had thought were long-gone resurfaced: abandonment, anger, fear. But Kara's words kept coming back to her. *They were good people, Addy.*

They were. As Addy ran, she saw her parents' death through the eyes of a stranger. They were good people doing good things. They died a horrible but noble death. They died for what they believed in. For the people they loved. They died doing what God asked them to do. She was too scared to admit that to Kara. Not yet. But she needed to.

I need to stop thinking so much about myself. I'm acting like a whiny little toddler not getting her way. Why do I do that? All the time? Why can't I just automatically do what's right and think what's right?

Addy pictured her uncle's face and knew what he would say. She was here because God put her here, because he had a plan. For now, this was her village; these people were her tribe. Would she be like her parents, doing what was right no matter what, honoring God regardless of the consequences? She didn't know why God would choose *her* of all people, nor did she know what she could do for him. But one thing she did know: God had her here, in this place, for such a time as this.

Chapter 12

Oh, sweetie. You know I love you. I'm your biggest fan and all that. You know that, right?" Kara stalled, pacing from Addy's bed to her own. Addy already knew what she was going to say.

"It stinks. *I* stink." Addy laughed. "I know. But you know what? I don't care. This is the talent portion of the competition, and this is my talent."

"But a kazoo?" Kara asked, her dark eyes wide. *"Really?"*

"You heard me sing; you saw me try to act. Dancing is most *definitely* out of the question. What other options do I have left? It *is* original. None of the other girls will be out there with a kazoo."

"Yes, and I do appreciate the new, more positive outlook.

But, Addy, you're going to get ripped apart when you do this. Hank might come up on the stage and strangle you himself."

Kara imitated Hank's swagger and tried to impersonate his "angry brother" voice: *"Addy Davidson.* Is this a joke to you? A *joke?* Do you know how lucky you are to have gotten this far? How much money has been spent housing you and feeding you and making sure you are well cared for? You ungrateful, stupid *beep-beep beep-beep beep-beep.*" Kara winked. "Since this is a 'squeaky clean' show, I censored all the curse words."

"Thanks," Addy said, laughing.

"Seriously. Is this how you want to go out?" Kara sat on her bed.

"I'm not going to try to be something I'm not. This is who I am."

"You are a kazoo player?" Kara crossed her arms.

"You know what I mean. I know what I can and cannot do. And one thing I cannot do is seriously compete with people as talented as you and the others here. It's ridiculous to even try."

Addy leaned forward, a huge grin splitting her face. "It's a nice one, by the way, the kazoo. Not the dollar-store plastic kind. Metal. Shiny. See?" Addy held out her kazoo so Kara could admire it. "No, no. Don't touch. I just tuned it."

Kara rolled her eyes and sighed. "At least tell me you're going to dress up."

"I will. I have my appointment with the wardrobe people at one thirty, thank you very much."

"Good for you. So what are you thinking? Shiny to match your kazoo, or white to show it off?"

"Like I'd tell *you*." Addy laughed. "You, Kara McKormick, are the competition. I couldn't trust you with something as important as that. My dress is *my* secret." Addy managed to stick out her tongue right as Kara hurled a pillow at her face.

The rest of the week went by quickly. Boot camp in the morning followed by breakfast, schoolwork, photo shoots, and rehearsals. In between all that was "camera time" and one-on-one talks with Jonathon, though Addy hadn't had her turn with the latter just yet. In some ways, she was dreading it. She had felt a load lift from her shoulders once she told Kara about her past. But that didn't change the fact that she owed Jonathon an apology.

Oh, God, haven't I learned enough lessons? Couldn't I just send Jonathon a note? On my way to the airport?

But she would have to face Jonathon. And an audience. Ironically, both ended up happening on the same day. She was the last girl to sit down with Jonathon. She was sure Hank orchestrated that. Probably hoping they wouldn't have enough time and she'd be bumped. Unfortunately for Hank, the morning went by smoothly and Addy sat in the staged meeting room inside The Mansion promptly at 10:00 a.m.

"Wait one minute." Eric fixed the angle on a huge light so Addy was totally, not just partially, blinded. "Okay. Just go ahead and talk. Pretend we're not here."

Addy moaned. "I definitely have a greater respect for actors now. I don't know how it's possible to 'act naturally' when surrounded by a room full of people."

Jonathon laughed, nodding. Their conversation was a little awkward, though not unpleasant. She was not about to apologize to him in front of the whole crew, but she was determined not to add to her list of offenses.

When their allotted time was over, Addy asked if she could speak with Jonathon privately. Because it was the last interview of the day, he said he had a few free minutes. So as the crew packed up their supplies, Jonathon led Addy to the kitchen and leaned against the counter.

"What would you like to talk about, Addy?"

She hadn't noticed before how pleasing his voice was. When they were being taped, she was focused on answering the questions without saying "um" too many times. But now, without all the distractions, she really heard him. His voice was deeper than most boys', and so proper.

"I need to apologize to you for my behavior."

He stood up straight. "No, don't. Actually . . ."

"Jonathon, I *need* to do this." Addy tried not to lose focus as she looked into his eyes. "I've been rude to you and you've done nothing to deserve it. I'm sure it's no secret that I didn't want to be on this show. But I shouldn't have taken out my frustration on you. I shouldn't have taken it out on anyone. I was acting like a child, and I am sorry for that."

He shook his head and smiled. She felt her toes tingle. "Thank you, Addy. I accept your apology." He folded his arms. "Can I ask you a question?"

"Sure." Addy looked into Jonathon's eyes and felt her heart race.

"Why did you come, if you didn't want to be on the show?"

"Because . . ." Addy took a deep breath. *Because God wants me to be here? No way. I am not saying that. I can't.*

Jonathon's eyes softened. "That's okay. You don't have to tell me."

"No, it's just . . . I'm not used to attention. I don't really want it. But my principal wanted me to come. I told him to pick someone else. I knew I would make a fool of myself here."

He touched her arm and she felt an electric shock. "I think he made a great choice. You're real. I like that. And you're not making a fool out of yourself."

Addy's face felt like it was on fire. "Let's see if you still think that after tonight."

Anna Grace

BOL: Good morning, Anna.

ANNA GRACE: Actually, it's Anna Grace.

BOL: Oh, excuse me, Anna Grace.

ANNA GRACE: I'm sorry, I don't mean to be rude, but I was named after my grandma and she passed away just last month (dabbing her eyes with a tissue). That name is special.

BOL: I'm sorry to hear about your grandmother. Would you like to postpone the interview?

ANNA GRACE: (Straightening up) Oh no. No. It's just that I get sad when I think about her. But I know Grammy is up in heaven, looking down on me and smiling. I know she's proud of me for being in this competition. And if there are TVs in heaven, she's got everyone gathered 'round one, watching me right now.

BOL: Okay. Well . . . tell us how you were chosen to be part of the show.

ANNA GRACE: I was sitting in my homeroom class taking roll. I'm the class representative, so it's my job to take roll and help the teachers however I can. As I was taking roll, the assistant principal, Mr. O'Neal,

buzzed in and asked that I come to the office. I was a little nervous but I went. And as I was walking, I noticed several other girls going that way too—our class secretary, the head cheerleader, the president of the drama club. We were all talking on our way over, and we just couldn't imagine what Mr. O'Neal could want from us. But then he sat us all down and told us about the show. Our little ol' Alabama high school was chosen to participate in a reality TV show. We couldn't believe it. Well, we were all so excited. I couldn't believe I was even being considered. It was truly an honor. Well, Mr. O'Neal said he'd be talking to our parents and our teachers, trying to find out which one of us would be the best choice for the show. He told us it was a new kind of show, so it wasn't just about being pretty or charming. The girl he chose would also have to be talented, smart, an all-around great girl. That's what he said y'all were looking for. Well, I would never say I was all those things. But I guess the others thought I was because they chose me. And here I am.

BOL: Yes, here you are. That was quite an answer . . . Why don't we just skip to the last question: Describe "The Perfect Boy."

ANNA GRACE: The perfect boy? Well, he's about six feet tall, has light brown hair, brown eyes, his father is a prominent politician, and he is currently looking for a prom date.

BOL: That was certainly specific. And do you think you are *his* perfect girl?

ANNA GRACE: Well now, I don't know about that. But I certainly hope I'll get the chance to let him find out.

BOL: And there you have it, folks, Miss Anna Grace Austen. Thank you very much.

Chapter 13

"Anna Grace, you'll be fine," Addy said. "I heard you practicing earlier, and you are amazing. You sound like a professional."

"Well, I have been taking voice since I was four," Anna Grace said, fanning herself. "I don't know why I'm so nervous."

Addy hugged her, surprising even herself at this display of emotion. "Don't be nervous. If you sing even half as well as you did at practice, the audience will be blown away."

Anna Grace smiled. "Thanks, Addy."

"You're next, Anna Grace." Eric motioned for the young woman to stand in the wings.

She left and Eric walked over. "And how are you, Addy?"

"More nervous than I've ever been in my entire life."

"Understandable. The latest numbers I've heard are twenty million viewers—"

"Not helping," Addy said, hands over her ears.

"Picture everyone in their underwear?"

"Even worse."

"Break a leg?"

Addy chuckled. "With my luck, I just may."

Their banter was interrupted by the first angelic notes of Anna Grace's song, and Addy glanced down at the kazoo in her hand. *What in the world am I doing?* Maybe she could fake an asthma attack. Or a heart attack. That would buy her more time. Maybe even send her home. *Home . . . No cameras, no packages, no talent shows. God, I would give anything for this to be just one very long dream. I'm ready to wake up. Anytime now . . .*

"All right, Addy. There'll be a three-and-a-half-minute commercial break. Get in place and then Dan will give you the thumbs-up sign. Your music will start right after that. Got it?"

"If I say no, can I get out of it?"

Eric pushed Addy onstage, where she walked to the blue *X.* Downstage center was what Eric called it. She wasn't allowed to move from that *X.*

Addy wasn't sure she'd be able to move anything ever again. Thousands of faces looked at her, cameras were hugging the stage. Behind those cameras, millions of people were sitting at home watching her. She had never been so terrified in her life.

"The next contestant tonight is Miss Addy Davidson,"

Hank said from his post at stage left. The audience erupted in applause and the stage lit up around her.

God, help! Addy took a deep breath and lifted the kazoo to her lips. She closed her eyes and tried to pretend she was in the trailer with Kara, just practicing, as she had the last few nights.

Kara had helped Addy find background music suitable to accompany her kazoo. The two decided a patriotic piece would be best, and Kara insisted on "The Star-Spangled Banner" and taught Addy how to hum "runs"—a series of notes like the pop stars sing—to be included at the end. On "Oh say, does that star-spangled banner yet wave," Addy hummed her heart out, putting her whole body into the effort, just like Kara had shown her.

The audience began laughing and clapping.

They actually like it. Thank you, Coach Kara.

By the time Addy hit the last line, "O'er the land of the free and the home of the brave," the audience in the Nashville theater was on its feet.

As she took her bow, Addy looked down and saw Jonathon on the front row, a big smile on his face and a thumbs-up in her direction. She stood and stared at him for a moment, taking in his double-breasted tuxedo and brilliant smile.

"Pssst." Eric waved from offstage. "Let's go, Addy."

She tore her gaze away from Jonathon and walked back to a squealing, clapping Kara waiting in the wings.

Hank walked over and pulled her aside. "Not bad, Addy. I didn't know you had it in you."

She blinked. *Is he actually complimenting me?*

"So, are you ready to play by my rules now? I'm still willing to give you a shot."

Addy stepped back. "Your rules?"

"Don't act innocent. Your parents can give me a call and we can work something out. Here's my number." He held out a card.

"Thanks, Hank, but I don't think so." Addy refused to take the card.

He put the card in his back pocket and scowled. "I hope you enjoyed this week, then. Because it will be the last one you have here."

Addy tried to speak, but Hank cut her off. "No, no, Miss Addy. You've made your choice."

℮

Addy woke up the next morning to Kara's screams.

"Addy, Addy. You are *never* going to believe this." Kara jumped up and down and clapped.

"What in the world . . . ?" Addy croaked, rubbing her eyes.

Kara hopped over to Addy's bed and deposited her laptop on Addy's lap. "Read."

"More blogs?" Addy groaned. "I don't want to know. I'm sure I already know: 'Addy Davidson is the biggest idiot in America,' right?"

"Wrong," Kara sang in her best opera voice. "Read, Addy. *Read*." Kara was still jumping up and down.

"Fine." The headline read "America's Sweetheart." Addy looked at Kara. "What?"

"Keep going, *sweetheart*." Kara grinned.

"'Thumbing her nose at the other twenty-nine contestants, Addy Davidson triumphed with a rousing kazoo solo in last night's *Book of Love*.'"

"Honestly, Addy, if I didn't know you, I'd think you were a genius."

She pushed Kara off her bed. "Thanks, roomie."

"Seriously. *I* know you weren't using any strategy, but everyone else thinks you are, and brilliantly. Well played, my friend. You're a shoo-in for the Top Twenty-Five. I wish I could see Hank's face right now."

"There was no strategy," Addy said. "I just don't have talent."

"I know. Well, I mean, no offense, but . . ."

"None taken. I am aware of my inabilities."

"America *loves* that you don't have talent. Look." Kara grabbed the laptop and clicked to an entertainment website. "'Addy Davidson, Our Hero.'"

Addy frowned. "I don't understand. I play a kazoo and I'm a hero?"

Kara shut her computer and looked at Addy. "Pretty much. You see, the rest of us were acting like this was Miss America or *America's Next Star*. And I'm not gonna lie, we were all pretty amazing. It was like putting twenty-nine Picassos onstage with my little niece's drawing of Barney. Picasso may be great, but Barney stands out. It's cute, original, and endearing."

"So you're Picasso and I'm Barney. Is that what you're saying?" Addy asked with a crooked smile.

"No. I'm Picasso and you're my niece—she's *much* cuter

than Barney. And smaller. And less purple, and definitely not as annoying."

"Okay, okay. So people like me because I'm untalented?"

"People like you because you're not ashamed of being untalented."

Addy was still trying to understand when she heard a commotion outside her door.

"Addy Davidson! We'd like to talk with you, if y'all don't mind."

Addy looked questioningly at Kara, then walked to open the trailer door.

A mob of girls in pajamas was crowded around the little metal steps leading to Addy's trailer. A mob of *angry* girls in pajamas.

Lord, give me strength. "Yes? What would you like to talk about?"

Southern belle Anna Grace stepped forward. "Don't act all innocent with us, Addy." She tossed her short blond hair. "Do you think this is a joke?"

Addy thought of at least half a dozen fabulous comebacks, but, remembering her desire to be a light, she held back. "I'm sorry?"

"Well, you should be. We work our butts off preparing for last night, and you waltz in with that stupid kazoo and get the entire spotlight?" Anna Grace crinkled her perfect little nose. "First you act all nasty; now you're a clown. You'll just do anything to get people to notice you."

Addy massaged her temples and tried to speak but was cut off by another of the contestants—Taylor from Tacoma.

"Don't even try to deny it. We've all been watching you

and we're onto you. You're going to regret this, Addy. We'll make sure of it."

With that, the girls turned their heads and walked off. It was so perfect Addy wondered if they had choreographed the whole thing. She shut the door. *These girls are ridiculous. Last night everything was fine. Lila even told me I was creative. I thought things were finally getting better, that maybe we could all be friends.*

"How could they change so much in less than twelve hours?" Addy picked up her pillow and threw it back down.

"Don't listen to them. They're ridiculous and self-absorbed and jealous." Kara squeezed Addy's shoulder. "They were fine last night because they thought you weren't any major competition. They're upset today because they found out that you *are*. You have the spotlight they all want."

Addy took a deep breath. "I guess I'm just getting a little taste of what it's like to be a celebrity. And I'm even more convinced this life is *not* for me."

"Don't worry, kid. They mess with you and they've messed with me. And believe me, they don't want to mess with me. Now, get dressed. We have a meeting in ten minutes."

"We do?"

"Yes, ma'am. Your public awaits."

Addy groaned, dressed, and dragged herself to The Mansion's front porch. *Help me, God. I don't think I can handle any more of my "public" right now.*

Chapter 14

adies," Hank began, "and *Addy*," he spat, causing the other girls to laugh conspiratorially. "The Top Twenty-Five will be announced tonight. Jonathon is making his decisions as we speak."

"Excuse me." Taylor raised her hand, looking sideways at Addy. "Will there not be any kind of discipline for last night's *kazoo* fiasco? I mean, it's really making us all look bad." A murmur of agreement arose from the crowd. "Can't someone talk to Jonathon and make sure he doesn't make any choices that would cause him to appear less than intelligent?" Taylor leaned forward. "I'm just trying to look out for *him*. He has a reputation to maintain, you know."

Kara stiffened. "Really, Taylor? You think Addy should

be disciplined for playing the kazoo? What about you and Anna Grace and the others outside our trailer this morning, yelling and screaming? Shouldn't there be discipline for that? Or is behaving like a jerk okay? Kazoo playing, yeah, that's the real crime."

Several of the girls began yelling at once. Hank motioned for them to stop. "Kara, what happens when I'm not around is not my business. I am sure, however"—he smiled at Taylor—"that the other producers and myself want very much for the integrity of our show to be upheld at all costs." Hank glared at Addy. "And I think much of our frustration will end tonight when the Top Twenty-Five is announced."

Her stomach turned to lead.

"Now," Hank said, "I have a surprise for you girls. The world-famous Jacobson's department store is celebrating its one-hundred-year anniversary. And as one of our show's sponsors, they've invited you to come to their flagship store in New York City enjoy a shopping spree. And then"—Hank paused, his too-white teeth glistening—"off to Central Park for the announcement of the Top Twenty-Five."

The girls cheered and jumped up and down. Even Addy was excited.

"*Home sweet home,*" Kara sang.

"Quiet down, girls," Hank yelled. "The plane leaves in an hour."

The other girls ran toward their trailers, laughing and talking, making sure to shoot Addy at least one more dirty look on the way out.

"Hey, Addy, are you okay?" Kara asked, her face a mask of concern.

"I'm going to New York City." Addy smiled. "Of course I'm okay."

"Seriously. Hank was pretty brutal."

"You know what? I don't care. I get another day with you, *and* I get to go to New York City. What more could I ask for?"

"I like this new, positive Addy." Kara patted her on the back. "Let's pack."

Chapter 15

The Top Thirty girls sat in Central Park, lights, cameras, and thousands of people surrounding their live broadcast of *The Book of Love*. Jonathon, flanked by Secret Service and his Top Thirty, was perched on a huge rock, looking relaxed and gorgeous in faded jeans, blue button-down oxford, and brown blazer.

Hank—once again ultrahip in his new Armani sports jacket and three-hundred-dollar jeans—welcomed the crowd, thanked Jonathon, and urged the viewers to "Stay tuned for an exciting night."

The crowd cheered, the girls beamed, and Jonathon remained on his perch looking like royalty.

Addy was uncomfortable, to say the least. The girls'

"shopping spree" turned out to be a day of pictures with various department store executives. Afterward, each girl was given a bag with a specially chosen outfit for the evening's show. Addy had been dressed in a fuchsia sundress and jeweled sandals. She had then been forced to sit in the makeup chair and be covered in layers upon layers of foundation and powders. Her hair had been teased, curled, brushed, and sprayed.

When it was all over, Dominique, the head stylist, said, "Looks great. Very natural."

Addy would have laughed, had her face muscles not been paralyzed by the weight of her blush.

The other girls underwent similar tortures before being placed in green padded chairs surrounding Jonathon's rock. Addy couldn't help thinking it was like a teenage version of *The Lion King*.

Hank would definitely be Scar.

Addy couldn't believe how dead a "live" show was. First, there was the intro—Hank announced that the show was beginning and spent a few minutes talking to Jonathon. Addy was constantly amazed at how poised Jonathon was. He didn't look awkward and he always said the right thing. But he didn't appear to be putting on a show or even acknowledging the cameras. After spending three years surrounded by Secret Service, Jonathon had probably just adjusted to being watched every minute of the day.

After the intro came a four-minute commercial break. Television sets were mounted behind the cameras so Hank, Jonathon, and the girls could see what was happening.

"Don't look at them while you're on, though," Hank warned.

The next forty minutes were filled with the week's "packages" and more commercial breaks. Addy felt like she was watching the same interview twenty times over. After each package, Hank would spend thirty seconds talking with the contestant. "How has your time been?" "What has been your favorite part?"

Each girl, as instructed, said she loved everything and everyone and was just so thankful for the opportunity.

"America doesn't like whiners," Hank had cautioned. "Don't complain or appear ungrateful." He looked at Addy.

She deserved that so she let it go. She was committed to focusing on the positive.

Finally, it was her turn.

"So, Addy, tell us about your week at The Mansion."

"I've had a great time. Kara and I are roommates, and I can promise you, she is just as fun as she seems. Other than waking me up way too early in the mornings." Addy leaned over to smile at Kara.

"So you're not a morning person?"

"Not exactly."

Hank smiled and pulled an index card from his jacket pocket. "I have a special question for you, sent in by one of our viewers: 'Hank, could you please ask Addy if she plans on going professional with her kazoo playing?'"

The audience laughed, then clapped. Addy looked over at Taylor and saw a smug look on her face. *I bet she is the "viewer" who sent that question in.* Addy was being mocked in front of fifteen—no, twenty million people.

"Well, Addy? Will we see you with the Philharmonic?"
When in Rome . . .

"As a matter of fact, Hank," Addy said, smiling, "I'm already working on my first album—*Christmas Kazoo*. It'll be out at Thanksgiving." She laughed and the audience joined in. Nothing like a little self-deprecation to win friends and influence people.

Taylor crossed her arms and frowned.

More commercials, more talking, more packages. Then, finally, it was time to announce the five girls leaving. The vase of red daisies sat on a table next to Jonathon's chair. He pulled out the first one and announced, "Janet."

That young woman took the daisy, hugged Jonathon, and walked toward Eric, who was waiting with a box of tissues. Christina, Gabrielle, and Amy were called, each receiving the daisy, a hug, and her own box of tissues.

"One daisy left," Hank said to the camera. "Who will be the last one leaving tonight? Stay tuned to find out!"

Eric motioned for a commercial break and Addy looked around. Taylor was sitting beside her, smiling and smug. Kara was at the end of the row. Addy was sure that last daisy had her name on it.

I'm actually going to miss it here. Kara is such a good friend. She's stuck by me, even when all the other girls hate me. She's helped me. She puts up with me. She's made being here worthwhile. Addy looked at Jonathon. *I can't believe I even considered that he might be interested in me. I must be crazy. Look at these girls. Still, it feels like we have a connection. But maybe it's just me. Too bad I won't be able to stick around and find out.*

Eric got into position and motioned to Hank that the

last segment was about to begin. Hank tapped Jonathon's shoulder and brought him behind the rock. He obviously didn't realize Addy was just on the other side.

"Listen," Hank said, his voice low. "Your parents have high standards for you. Don't forget that. You need a girl who is worthy of having the privilege of being on a date with the First Son. Don't feel like you have to choose girls that America likes. We can make America like the girls you pick. That's our job. Your job is to make your parents proud. Choose girls who will reflect the dignity of your father's office. All right?"

Jonathon didn't have time to respond because Eric gave the thirty-second warning. Addy didn't need to hear the response, though.

Hank might as well have come out and said, "Don't pick Addy. You're too good for her." If she had any doubt she'd be leaving tonight, it was gone.

Addy waited as the host talked about the last week's highlights, the twenty-six girls who remained, and the exciting surprises that awaited the audience in next week's show. "And now, Jonathon, time to announce the name of the last girl to be leaving."

"The last daisy goes to . . ." Jonathon paused as the cameras panned the girls' faces. "Taylor."

"What?" Taylor shouted. Out of the corner of her eye, Addy could see Hank stiffen.

Taylor walked over to Jonathon and grabbed the daisy from his hand, glaring at Hank over Jonathon's shoulder as she gave him the "good-bye hug."

The crowd was talking, and Hank valiantly tried to speak over them, looking at the camera and inviting everyone to tune in next week for another chapter in *The Book of Love*. The crowd joined him in shouting the show's name, then erupted in squeals and "Hi, Moms" to the cameras.

"Cut," Eric shouted.

The crowd pressed in on the yellow barricades set up to keep them from getting too close to the set.

"Can we have your autograph?"

"Jonathon, pick me!"

"Your dad's a jerk. We need to get someone in the White House who knows what he's doing."

"I love you, Jonathon!"

Jonathon whispered something to the large guard standing next to him. The guard slapped Jonathon on the back and yelled for the crowd to move away. "Enough, folks. Leave the boy alone."

The girls were surrounded by bodyguards and led to the buses. Taylor walked over to Hank. Curiosity took over and Addy stayed behind to listen.

"Hank, you promised I'd make the cut. I know my parents gave a big 'donation' toward your next project—"

"Look, Taylor, this was not supposed to happen."

"You need to get Addy off and get me on, then." Taylor folded her arms against her chest, lips tight.

"This is live TV. We can't do that. The audience would get too upset. I'm sorry, Taylor. I really am. I'll keep you in mind for my next project, okay? Don't worry. This is just a setback. All performers have them."

Taylor cursed at Hank, then stalked off. Addy tried to sneak away but Hank saw her, grabbed her arm, and pulled her behind a nearby tree.

"This is the last straw, Addy. I'm tired of you ruining this show for the girls who deserve to be on."

"I didn't do anything, Hank." She waved her hands. "I didn't make Jonathon choose me. I think you're just upset because someone who didn't pay to be on has made it another week."

Hank squeezed her arm even tighter. "This is a business. *My* business. How many times do I have to tell you that *I am in charge?* I will not allow you to make a fool out of me."

Addy wanted to say that the ridiculously tight T-shirt he was wearing already made him look foolish, but that wouldn't be appropriate.

"What are you smirking about?"

"Nothing, Hank. Look, I'm sorry. I promise I had nothing to do with any of this."

"*Right*. Just get on that bus and get out of my face." He turned around to face a camera flash from the top of a neighboring tree. "What the—? Get down here!"

The tree shook and a wiry man jumped down, running toward the cover of the crowd.

Addy took his cue and made a beeline for the buses before Hank could start in on her again.

"So what do you think happened?" Addy asked Kara back in their hotel room after an incredibly awkward bus ride.

"I think Jonathon actually picked you. It sounds like he was instructed not to, but he did it anyway. How romantic." Kara sighed. "You *better* send me pictures from prom."

"Hank will make sure that doesn't happen. Did you see how Taylor was conspiring with them on the ride home?

And you know Hank won't care if she plans anything vicious. He might even be in on it with them."

"Please, Addy. Those girls are too scared they'd break a nail to try and mess with you. And Hank might be a jerk, but he's not about to do anything to jeopardize the show's success. Think of how bad it would look if word got out you were being bullied by the others. Didn't you watch all those clips from last week? The producers want to make it look like we're all best friends."

"So 'reality TV' is completely orchestrated?"

"You're learning, my dear. So let's play our parts and enjoy the ride," Kara said. "Now, as a major television star, I have work to do. Fan mail doesn't answer itself, you know."

Addy laughed and crawled under her sheets, still thinking about her evening. *Jonathon picked me. He picked me. Maybe I can handle staying here a little longer, God. If you really want me to . . .*

Chapter 16

For the first time since the show started, the girls were given an entire day off. Addy was thrilled.

Kara hung up the phone. "I just got permission to go home for the day. Wanna come?"

"Really?" Addy said.

"No, I was kidding." Kara thumped Addy with a pillow. "Duh. Yes, really. You're going to love my family."

"Tell me about them." Addy sat up in the hotel bed, looking expectantly at Kara.

Kara shifted on her bed, smiling at Addy. "Well, it's a little complicated. Are you ready?"

"I think so."

"Okay, Pop was married before and had my half brothers

Joey and Luke. His first wife died of cancer when the boys were little."

"Oh, that's so sad." Addy understood that pain far too well.

"I know. From what I've heard, she was a great lady. But if she hadn't died, Ma and Pop never would have met. See, Ma also had been married before and had my half sister Mary and my half brother Patrick. Her first husband was a loser and ran off and left her for some floozie he worked with."

"That's terrible."

"Yeah, well, Ma was obviously better off without him. He's never been heard from since. So then Ma and Pop met when Ma was working as a nurse at the hospital where his first wife died."

"Wow," Addy said.

"Kind of creepy sounding, I know. But my dad's first wife loved my mom, and nothing went on until months after she died."

"That so sweet."

"I know. My mom had a soft spot for Luke and Joey, since they were so close in age to Mary and Patrick. She'd pick them up and take them out for ice cream or just to talk. After a while, Pop starting coming along for ice cream, then later, he'd leave my brothers and take Ma out for ice cream. A year later, they were married."

"How did all the kids adjust?" Addy couldn't imagine suddenly having a family of six.

"I never heard any complaints. They had my brother Sam about a year later, then I came along when he was ten. So here we are. The typical American family."

"Whoa. So how old are your oldest siblings?"

Kara laughed. "Joey's the oldest. He's thirty-nine. Mary's thirty-eight, Patrick is thirty-seven, Luke is thirty-six, Sam is twenty-seven, and I, of course, am sixteen and three-quarters."

"Do they all live nearby?"

"We're all on the Island."

"The Island?"

"Yes, Long Island. Sorry, I forget you're not familiar with my turf. Long Island is that big piece of land that sticks out from Manhattan," Kara said.

"I know that, smarty-pants." Addy swatted at Kara. "Kind of."

"Anyway, everybody but Sammy and me are married with kids, so when the whole family is together, it's a riot. And you better believe the whole clan will be out today. So are you ready to meet a couple dozen McKormicks?"

"Are they all like you?"

"Oh no," Kara said. "*I'm* the quiet one."

The girls quickly dressed and called for their show-appointed limo to drive them the fifty miles out to Kara's home in Smithtown. Having never been to New York, Addy spent most of the drive looking out the window as Kara played tour guide.

"Look, Addy, the Empire State Building. Most romantic place in the world. Not that I'd know. My brothers scare all the boys off before they can even make it to the front door. Speaking of boys, see that hotel ahead? That's where Mary got married. And, oh, right there—no, there, to your left—that place makes the best hot dogs in the world. Gray's

Papaya. Mmm, mmm. I'd get you one, but if I fed you before we got home, Ma would kill me. And up here, Saint Patrick's Cathedral. Ma used to take me in there after we went to FAO Schwarz, just to get me to stop talking for a minute."

What Kara didn't know—which wasn't much—the driver helped with. About twenty minutes into the ride, Kara asked him to roll down the window separating him from the girls and she drilled him with questions. Joe was happy to answer Kara, and the two of them taught Addy more about the history and architecture of New York City than most people learned in a lifetime.

"This bridge, for example," Joe said, "she's named the Verrazano. Howeva, the same year she was built, President John F. Kennedy was killed."

"Was that 1963?" Addy asked.

"A history buff." Joe pumped a fist in Addy's direction. "November 22, to be exact. But the name for the bridge had already been chosen when that happened."

Kara leaned forward. "Who was Verrazano?"

"Good question, little lady. Verrazano was the very first explorer to come into New York Harbah. A great explorer."

"Makes sense," Addy said. "Name the bridge that crosses the harbor after the first man to cross it."

"Well said." Joe lifted a finger in the air. "But the people thought her name should be Kennedy to honor the fallen president. Well, there was some huge fights about it all, but in the end, she was named Verrazano. Precisely for the reason you just said. Now millions of people drive over this bridge every year. The New York City Marathon starts right here too."

Addy loved hearing Joe and Kara talk, laughing at the way they pronounced certain words—*dowg* and *coafee* being her favorites.

She was also surprised that as they drove farther east into Long Island, the high-rise apartment buildings and far-as-the-eye-could-see cement gave way to long stretches of stunning green lawns, beautiful homes, and quaint villages. Kara had Joe take the scenic route rather than the Long Island Expressway, so Addy could experience all the beauty of her native land.

Sooner than Addy expected, Joe turned off the main road onto River Street. The houses were modest one- and two-stories with lawns dotted with flowers and decorative rocks. It was a pleasant neighborhood, and Addy loved hearing about the inhabitants of each of the homes they passed until they finally pulled up to Kara's home—located at the end of a cul-de-sac.

Kara wasn't kidding about the size or volume of her family. As soon as their limo pulled up in front of Kara's house, the front door opened and people poured out, screaming Kara's name. Joe attempted to come around and open the girls' door, but he was shoved out of the way by a man Addy could only assume was Kara's father. He opened the door with one hand and pulled Kara into a huge bear hug with the other. Addy tried to step out unseen but was intercepted by another hug.

"Miss Addy," Mr. McKormick roared, almost crushing her ribs with his powerful arms. "Welcome to our home."

Addy took a deep breath after he released her, only to be pulled into more hugs from smaller but equally powerful McKormick family members.

Children of all ages surrounded the girls as well, yelling, "Aunt Kara! Aunt Kara! We saw you on TV," and squeezing whichever knees were closest—Kara's or Addy's.

Mr. McKormick yelled for everybody to get inside. "Stupid paparazzi out taking pictures again. Leave these girls alone," he yelled to the men and women holding cameras down the length of Kara's street. Kara gave one last wave, though—per Hank's orders—before skipping into her house.

Once the girls were inside, Mrs. McKormick sat them at the table and insisted they eat. Enough food to feed twenty times their number covered the spacious dining room table, the side table, and every inch of the long counters in the kitchen.

"Ralph, go out and get a few more pork rolls," Mrs. McKormick said. "I'm afraid there won't be enough for everyone."

"Ruth, we got enough food to feed all of Suffolk County. Relax." Mr. McKormick lovingly wrapped an arm around his wife's shoulders. "Enjoy our celebrity daughter being home with us for a day."

Addy looked around and enjoyed hearing the New York accents and seeing this huge, loving family interacting with each other. Twin girls were standing at the side table, eyeing chocolate chip cookies; a woman who must be Kara's sister held a chubby baby who, amazingly, slept through all the noise. Siblings took turns hugging Kara and talking about how all their friends wanted her autograph and praising her for the great job she had done at the talent competition.

"We're forgetting about Miss Addy over here," Mr.

McKormick boomed. "We're glad to have you here with us today. You okay? Want some of Mama's delicious cinnamon rolls?"

"No thanks, Mr. McKormick. I'm fine."

Kara shot Addy a "don't you dare refuse my mom's cooking" stare, and Addy amended, "Well, only if I could get a big glass of milk with them, of course."

Mrs. McKormick beamed and clapped her hands as she served Addy some of the biggest, best-smelling pastries she had ever seen.

"So is this your first trip to New York?" asked a man in a striped polo.

"My brother Patrick," Kara introduced.

"Oh yeah, sorry." He laughed. "Maybe we should all give our names so you can be thoroughly confused."

"Good idea. I already gave her all the dirt on you guys," Kara joked, her accent getting even more pronounced the longer she was around her family. "Okay, you know Ma and Pop—greatest parents on earth." Mr. McKormick gave Kara another bone-crushing squeeze and Mrs. McKormick added an extra cinnamon roll to her plate.

"I already introduced you to this guy." Kara pointed to the man in the striped polo. "Remember I told you Patrick was the one who sucked his thumb till he was thirteen?"

The McKormicks laughed and agreed. "I could tell you a few things about Little Miss Sunshine here too," Patrick said.

"Moving on," Kara interrupted. "Patrick's saving graces— his wife, Beth, and kids, Ethan and Emily."

Kara took half an hour to introduce and pick on each of her siblings, their spouses, and their kids. Addy learned that

Luke wet his pants the first time he saw Mickey Mouse, and Mary ran out of the house naked when she was five because she thought she saw a gremlin in the bathtub. One of the nieces, Sally, vomited all over Kara the first time she saw her, and her brother-in-law tricked her into eating cow tongue when Kara was just four.

Addy was trying to digest all the stories and the people. Since she was six and a half, family consisted of her and Uncle Mike. Period. She had never had this many people in her living room in her life.

This is nice, though. Addy took in their warmth. *I wonder what it would be like to have such a large family.*

"Okay, enough breakfast. Let's digest a couple hours so we can enjoy lunch, huh?" Mr. McKormick announced, moving the family into the large living room.

Kara's mom obviously enjoyed the country motif. Their living room held two large couches, covered in a stiff blue-and-pink plaid material. Beautiful pictures of old barns were suspended above each of the couches, and the coffee table held books filled with pictures of farms and more barns and animals of all kinds. Stands holding beautiful quilts surrounded the room, and the large mahogany entertainment center was filled with dozens of family pictures.

"This is a beautiful home," Addy said to Mrs. McKormick.

"Thank you, Addy. We have made a lot of good memories in this place." She put an arm around Addy's shoulder. "Come out back, let me show you Kara's old tree house. Sit back down, all of yous. Addy and me, we're going out by ourselves. All you McKormicks can be a little overwhelming. Sit and digest. We won't be too long."

With that, Mrs. McKormick took Addy's arm and guided her into the large backyard. The pair walked in silence to a huge oak tree where a faded pink tree house sat perched in the thick branches. A No Boys Allowed sign hung below the window.

"Have a seat, Addy." Mrs. McKormick positioned herself on a bench below the tree. "I can't tell you how many hours I spent out here while Kara and her friends were up there playing." She smiled and patted Addy's knee.

"I bet she was a busy little girl."

"My Kara has always been a bundle of energy. I had a hard time keeping up with her. But I wouldn't trade her for anything."

Addy felt tightness in her chest. *It's not fair, God. Kara has this huge family. A mom who cries over her and brothers and sisters who look out for her. A whole houseful of people cheering her on.*

"I don't want to step in where I shouldn't, Addy," Mrs. McKormick said after a moment of silence, "but Kara told me about your folks. I'm so sorry." She pulled a tissue from her pocket and wiped her eyes. "You're a special girl. I think your mom and pop wudda been real proud of you. It must have been hard, losing them when you were so young."

Normally Addy would have changed the subject. But Mrs. McKormick was so kind, so genuine, Addy felt comfortable. She started to speak, then realized she was crying too.

"I'm sorry." Addy took the tissue Mrs. McKormick offered her. "It is hard. I miss my parents. I wish they were here. I mean, my uncle is great. He really is . . ."

"But he's not a mama."

Addy laughed. "Definitely not."

"Well, listen, honey, if you ever need a mama to talk to, you give me a call, okay? Anytime. I mean it." Mrs. McKormick put her arm around Addy and squeezed her shoulders. "We've got a few more minutes before the gang starts yelling for us. Why don't you tell me more about yourself?"

Addy sat there for another fifteen minutes, talking to Mrs. McKormick about school, golf, her plans for the future. Addy couldn't remember the last time she had talked so much about herself.

The peace and quiet ended as soon as the women walked in the back door.

"Addy," Mr. McKormick said as she walked through the living room to the couch. "Tell me about this Hank character. Do I need to come and talk to him for you?"

"*Kara*," Addy scolded.

Her hands shot up in an "I surrender" pose. "I didn't say a thing."

"We saw a picture in the paper today." Mr. McKormick pulled up a paper from a magazine rack at his side. It showed a huge shot of Hank yelling and Addy cowering, taken the night before, right after the Top Twenty-Five had been announced. "Host or Heavyweight?" the caption read.

"Oh great," Addy moaned.

Several of the family looked at the picture and told Addy what they'd like to come down and do to Hank.

"I appreciate your concern, but he's harmless. He was just mad because of what happened."

Kara shot Addy a look. "Hey, we can't talk show stuff, remember?"

Addy remembered. Another clause in the contract they signed was that no information was allowed to leak. The girls weren't allowed to talk about behind-the-scenes anything for at least two years. The producers didn't want anyone making money off book deals or giving interviews to tabloids until the show was gone and forgotten.

"You're right," Addy said. "It's fine. Really. Kara is protecting me."

With that, the family laughed and assured Addy that she couldn't have a better bodyguard than their Kara.

The day flew by too quickly. Addy had never eaten so much in her life. But never had she laughed so hard or felt so at home with other people. She wished throughout the day that Uncle Mike could be there. She was sure he'd love the McKormicks as much as she did.

The limo came at nine o'clock to take the girls to the hotel. They were flying back to Tennessee first thing the next morning. Addy reluctantly said good-bye to Kara's family.

"You're one of us now." Mr. McKormick gave Addy one last bear hug. "You come back, bring your uncle. You're welcome anytime. We got lotsa room."

Addy thanked her hosts and walked out to the limo, thinking about how much she was looking forward to doing just that.

Chapter 17

"Okay, Addy, it's your turn to help *me* out," Kara instructed as the girls looked over the week's schedule in their trailer on Monday.

Golf.

Addy was thrilled. Finally something she could do. Uncle Mike had insisted she learn the sport from the time she was old enough to hold a club. "It's a thinker's sport," he'd assured her. "And not too many girls play. If we can get you playing really well, you could get a scholarship. Pay your whole way through college."

Because it was a sport that could be played alone, Addy loved it. No coach yelling at her, no teammates barking orders. No teammates' parents yelling from the sidelines. Just her and clubs and silence for hours on end.

Silence. Kara was already in trouble.

"And what are you smirking about?" Kara asked.

"I was just thinking about how hard it's going to be for you to stay quiet for eighteen holes."

Kara put her hands on her hips. "And what are you implying?"

"I'm not *implying* anything. You, my dear friend, are one of the loudest people I know. Having met your family, I know you come by it honestly. But golf is a quiet sport." Addy grinned and stood over Kara. "I can give you lessons, though, if you'd like."

"In what, quiet or golf?" Kara shot back.

"Both."

"Ha ha ha. Don't forget that you need me. If I'm off this show, you're moving in with one of the other girls. Anna Grace, maybe. Or Lila," Kara warned.

"Okay, okay." Addy sat on Kara's bed. "Lesson number one: Real golf is nothing at all like miniature golf."

"So no cute little windmills or purple golf balls?"

Addy spent the next hour trying to explain the sport. Kara tried to follow but got confused. Addy described the different types of clubs, how each was used, and how to know which club was best based on distance from the green and the condition of the lay.

"Okay, just to make sure I'm clear. The green is where I want to be. Sand, water, and anywhere off the grass is bad. Hitting hard won't necessarily help, and every hole will require a different strategy. Is that right?"

"Pretty much." Addy nodded.

"And how long have you been playing golf?"

"About ten years."

"Hmmm. So this is my kazoo moment?" Kara raised an eyebrow.

"You could come out dressed like a windmill."

"Very funny."

The girls were able to practice that day and the next before the cameras began rolling. Hank had reminded the girls that since Jonathon is a well-rounded young man, his date should be well-rounded also. Talented, athletic, smart. They should be able to interact with him on many levels.

Hank had been surprisingly calm since returning from New York. Kara guessed he was upset over the pictures of him yelling at Addy. He had aspirations of doing more than just this reality TV show and he didn't want his reputation tainted. So he was sugary sweet—even to Addy. But Addy could see the anger in his eyes when he looked her way.

Eric remained the only kind face on the crew. All the others cowered before Hank and obediently followed his example. Eric countered Hank's behavior by being even nicer to Addy, making sure she got first on the list for special days out—massages, salon appointments, even the best tee times for golf practice.

The others were furious at this, complaining to Hank and saying horrible things to Addy. But she didn't care. She was determined to enjoy every minute on the show. *After all, if Hank has his way, my days here are numbered.*

"Well, look. If it isn't the Bobbsey Twins," Anna Grace said as she passed them on her way to the fourth hole. "Aren't y'all just so cute?"

"Yes it is, and yes we are," Kara said. "And how are you? Having trouble with the course?"

"No," Anna Grace said. "I am doing just fine. As if it matters. This is a formality. They can't kick us off because we don't know how to play golf. It's about how we look in our little outfits. Too bad about that, Addy. Because you are sure not doing well there." Anna Grace eyed Addy's white Bermuda shorts and green polo. She was beginning to give a lecture on fashion when a stray golf ball flew within inches of her face. She turned her anger on the offending golfer—Jessica.

"Hey, you did that on purpose," Anna Grace yelled across the fairway.

Jessica walked toward Anna Grace, her finger wagging in the air. "Girl, if I wanted to hit you, I wouldn't use a golf ball. It was just a bad hit. Don't worry. It won't happen again."

"You better watch it." Anna Grace's voice got louder. She walked closer to Jessica, then saw the camera crew coming over the hill. "Well, girls." Anna Grace smiled, suddenly the nicest young lady in all of the South. "It was great talking with y'all, but I need to get to work. I'm not too good at this, you know. Toodle-oo." She waved, glanced up at the cameras to make sure they caught how wonderfully friendly and humble she was, then picked up her bag and walked toward the crew, chest out, smile on.

Addy rolled her eyes.

"Cameras, Addy, cameras," Kara reminded, her own smile in place. "Hank's already looking for ways to make you look bad. Let's not give them to him."

By the tenth hole, Kara was wiped out. "Who knew golf could be so exhausting?"

"Yes, well, having to hit the ball twenty times for each hole *can* wear a person out."

"Are you *mocking* me?" Kara said. "Just because you get your turkeys and Humphrey Bogarts doesn't mean you can laugh at *my* score. If this were bowling, I would be killing you, young lady. *Killing* you."

"Birdies and bogies, Kara." Addy shook her head at her friend's failing attempts to remember her golf lessons from the day before. "And I'm *not* getting bogies. Birdies, yes. And eagles."

"Well, I think I am doing so horribly that I deserve to make up my own lingo." Kara leaned against her club. "Twenty over par is now officially a turkey. Hitting the ball in the water at least five times is an alligator." Kara winked at Addy. "That one is for you, my Florida friend."

"*Golf According to Kara.*" Addy laughed. "You should write a book."

"Maybe I will. In fact, I think I'm going to start on it right now, while it's all fresh in my head. Think you could finish the game without me?"

"I suppose I could manage," Addy said, glad for the opportunity to move quickly through the final holes.

"Don't look so eager. You're hurting my feelings." Kara shouldered her bag and started walking back toward the waiting vans. "See you back at the trailer."

Addy looked around. No cameras, no girls, no one. She breathed a sigh. As much as she loved Kara, talking all day every day was exhausting. Addy looked forward to some silence. She was tempted to go back a few holes so the end wouldn't come so soon. She glanced at the sky. Not much daylight left. She only had time to finish the course. That must be why all the cameramen were packing up for the day.

"Hi there, Addy."

Addy knew that voice. Her toes started tingling before she even turned around.

"Jonathon." Anna Grace's face suddenly came to mind, her critique of Addy's outfit replaying in her head. What must she look like—sweaty, hair coming out of her pony-tail, grass stains from digging around trying to find Kara's stray golf balls?

"Addy?"

Addy realized this wasn't the first time he had said that. "Sorry. I was just . . ."

"Thinking?" Jonathon finished.

"Yes." Addy looked down, stomping the grass with her foot.

"You do a lot of that."

"What?"

"Think."

"Oh yes, I guess I do. I come from a small, quiet family. Lots of time to think. I guess I'm not quite used to all this."

"Must be nice."

"What?"

"Having quiet. I wouldn't know what that was like."

"No, I guess not." Addy looked for a way to try to make a fresh start with Jonathon. "Tell you what. I was looking forward to finishing the course in silence. Want to join me?"

"No talking?" he asked, eyebrows raised.

"Absolutely none."

"Really?" He sounded like a kid sitting on Santa's lap.

"Just the sounds of the clubs swinging and golf balls flying. And birds. And the wind in the trees. You'll be amazed at the things you hear when you don't talk."

"Deal." Jonathon motioned—quietly—for Addy to begin.

She wasn't surprised to discover that Jonathon was significantly better than she but was relieved to stay within a few strokes of his score. After three holes, though, he started laughing.

"I've had enough silence. Could you really have stayed quiet the whole time?"

"Sure." Addy shrugged.

"I can't do it. Even when I'm playing by myself, I listen to my iPod or talk on my phone between holes."

"Are you ever by yourself much?" Addy noted that in just the last ten minutes, he had received and responded to dozens of text messages.

Jonathon completed yet another text. "Those are mostly from friends. They want to know what I'm doing and with whom—you know, typical guy stuff." Looking down at an incoming text, he grinned. "This one's from my mom. She wants to make sure I finished my research paper for English class." His thumbs flew over the tiny keyboard as he mouthed, "Yes, Mom," then flipped the phone shut and returned it to his back pocket.

"What's your mom like?" Addy was curious to know more about the First Lady.

Having worked as an interior designer before her

husband began his political career, Mrs. Jackson had completely redone many of the rooms in the White House when the First Family moved in. She allowed a camera crew to tape the whole thing, turning it into a popular prime-time documentary three years before. Mrs. Jackson's tasteful updating had been impressive, earning her rave reviews from the public and from other professionals. Her designs were so popular, home decor and furniture stores across the country had doubled their business the following year, selling out of fabrics and decorative items that mirrored those in the White House. And like her husband and son, Mrs. Jackson was quite comfortable in front of the cameras, leaving viewers feeling more like neighbors than the American public listening to its First Lady.

"Did you watch the special about her remodel a couple years back?" Jonathon asked, leaving Addy wondering if he could read her mind.

"I did. She did a great job."

"Well, that's my mom. She wasn't acting for the cameras; she really is that outgoing and energetic. Sometimes *too* energetic." He laughed, shaking his head.

"What do you mean?"

"My mom can do a hundred things all at the same time, so she thinks my sister and I can too," Jonathon said. "And really, Alexandra is a lot like Mom, so she doesn't have trouble keeping up. But not me. I can't go like that."

"Not a multitasker?" Addy asked.

"Not at all. I'm more like my dad—slow and steady."

Addy found it hard to comprehend that she was hearing about the First Family. She listened as Jonathon told stories about growing up in Washington, DC. His father had been elected to his first term as a senator from Indiana when Jonathon was just three years old, so most of his memories revolved around famous leaders and celebrities. While Addy was home studying her times tables, Jonathon had been dining with speakers of the house and secretaries of state.

"A couple years ago, I got to go to Japan with my dad."

"Wow," Addy exclaimed.

"It was amazing. We met with the prime minister and several other leaders of the country. They treated us so well. Americans can learn a lot from the hospitality of the Japanese." Jonathon grunted.

"Have you gone places where people were rude to your father?"

"Yes, Vermont."

Addy laughed. "Really?"

"They hate Dad."

"Isn't that hard on you?"

"Sure it is." Jonathon shouldered his golf bag. "But it's part of the job. We all do what we can to help make him look good. Sometimes that's easier to do than others."

He looked at Addy in a way that made her almost forget how to hold her golf club.

Addy cleared her throat. "You have an exciting life."

"I guess. It has its drawbacks, though." Jonathon pointed behind him to the four Secret Service agents who always stayed within a hundred feet of the couple. "They go everywhere. And I mean *everywhere*. I'd trade trips to Asia for some extra privacy any day."

She could tell it was Jonathon's turn to think, so they played out the rest of the course in relative silence.

As they finished out the eighteenth hole, Addy found herself sad to see the afternoon end. They put away their clubs and walked back to the vans, then Jonathon turned to face her.

"Thanks, Addy."

She suddenly felt very warm, despite the slight chill in the March air.

"This was great. Maybe we can do it again sometime?" He paused, looking uncomfortable and nervous—the same look he'd had when she saw him in the forest. But this time, Addy knew it was genuine. No pretenses. He felt awkward. Just like she did. In Addy's mind, that made him even more attractive.

She smiled and nodded. "I'd love that."

Jonathon reached out and grabbed her hand, covering it with both of his. "Thanks."

She couldn't believe how a simple touch from this boy could make her heart race like she'd just run a marathon. But there it was. She glanced at the van waiting just a few feet away. "I guess I should be getting back to The Mansion."

"I guess so." He squeezed her hand and smiled. "Did I say thanks?"

"Yes, I think so." Addy laughed.

"Good. Because I meant it."

On the ride home, Addy relived every minute of their time together. She hadn't enjoyed herself so much in a long time. She felt energized, happy. Jonathon didn't feel like the president's son or the guy she was trying to win a date to prom with. He felt like a friend.

Addy leaned back against the leather headrest as the van pulled onto the dirt road that led to the row of trailers. She enjoyed one last minute of quiet, knowing that as soon as she stepped foot into their trailer, Kara would expect to hear all about Addy's golfing adventure.

Chapter 18

Jonathon Jackson Gives Kazoo-Playing Contestant Private Lessons?'" Addy threw down the paper and screamed. "What is this?"

"There are more," Kara said. "Some little elves left them for us this morning with a note attached. The note was so dirty I flushed it down the toilet."

Addy felt like her chest was going to explode. Apparently paparazzi had been hiding in the woods around the golf course. Her picture along with ridiculous speculation by "journalists" left Addy looking like a slutty opportunist.

"We did *nothing*, Kara. We just played a round of golf. With Secret Service guys right behind us the whole time. And these papers make it sound like I took him into the woods and . . ." Addy couldn't even finish her sentence. Tears burned her eyes. "How do I even fight this? If I say we just played golf, no one will believe me. If I don't say anything, people will just assume it's true." The tears couldn't be held back any longer, falling like fire onto Addy's cheeks. "Kara, I've never even *kissed* a boy."

She sat next to Addy, rubbing her back and nodding. "Addy, breathe. It's probably going to get worse before it gets better."

"Gee, thanks."

"But it's going to get better. These things are like a Jolly Rancher—juicy for a while, but eventually it disappears and is completely forgotten."

Addy couldn't help but laugh. "That has to be the dumbest simile ever."

"Hey, I got you to smile."

Someone banged on the girls' door, and Addy knew her life was about to get much worse.

"Get out here right now, Addy," Hank boomed.

Addy squeezed Kara's arm for support, then walked to the door and opened it. Hank was standing on the top step, almost causing Addy to stumble right into him. Less than ten feet away, the other girls and half the crew stood looking on. Addy was sure she saw fiendish glee in their eyes. Bloodlust. She pictured Hank grabbing her by the neck and throwing her on the ground, the others jumping on top, kicking and punching and pulling her hair. The coroner would of course rule it an accidental death.

"Don't you *dare* ignore me," Hank demanded.

She had been doing just that—unintentionally, of

course. But she wasn't even going to bother trying to tell Hank that. She had to choose her battles, and today's battle was named "I am not a slutty opportunist."

Hank shook a paper in his hand, the veins on his bronzed forehead looking like a map of downtown Tampa. "What do you think you're doing?" he yelled. "It's one thing to try to get attention by mouthing off or by making a fool of yourself. But how dare you pull Jonathon into your lunatic schemes."

Bile rose in her throat. She tried to explain what actually happened, but of course, Hank didn't believe a word.

"Jonathon called me first thing and insisted the story wasn't true." Hank snorted. "Sure he said that. He has a reputation to maintain. The president is so upset by this, he is threatening to pull the plug on the whole show," Hank continued, St. Petersburg now added to the forehead map. "This entire show could be demolished because of *you*," Hank yelled, the crowd behind him joining in.

Hank took another step toward her, and Addy braced herself for what she was sure to be a blow when Eric pushed through the crowd.

"Stop it, Hank. This is a seventeen-year-old girl," Eric spat, eye to eye with his boss who had stepped down from Addy's trailer. "And this is a free country. We are innocent until proven guilty here, and pictures on a tabloid are certainly not proof of guilt."

Hank's forehead continued to throb, but he backed away, walking toward the crowd and pushing aside anyone who happened to be in his way. The crowd followed him and within seconds only Addy, Kara, and Eric remained.

"Addy, I'm sorry." Eric watched Hank and the girls storm off. "Sorry for the papers, sorry for Hank. You don't deserve this. You and Kara are probably the sweetest girls we have on this show. I've watched you the past two weeks—I know." He sighed and raked a hand through his thinning blond hair.

"Thanks, Eric." Addy sniffed, barely able to breathe through her tears.

"Come with me for a minute." Eric pulled her behind the row of trailers. "I've got some news that will cheer you up, but it has to stay between us. All right?"

"Of course."

"Good." Eric spoke quietly, looking around as he continued. "I did go to film school, which is why I'm here. But I am currently a Secret Service agent working undercover."

"Wow."

"Shhh," Eric whispered. "We can't be too careful with the president's son. So no one knows who I really am. The crew just thinks I'm one of the assistant directors, and that's how it needs to stay."

"Why are you telling me this?"

"We discovered a problem with one of the show's guards yesterday."

"Oh no." Addy put her hand over her heart. "Is Jonathon in trouble?"

"No, he wasn't after Jonathon. He was selling information to the tabloids. He was the reason a photographer caught your golf date with Jonathon. No one was supposed to know any of you guys were out there."

"That's terrible," Addy said.

"Here's where the good news comes in." Eric glanced around before going on. "I spoke to my superior. He served with your uncle back in the nineties."

"Uncle Mike?"

"Yep. Small world, huh? They were both at MacDill Air Force Base."

"But how did he know Mike was my uncle?"

"It's our job to know everything about everybody who comes near the president's son."

"Oh," Addy said.

"My boss wants to bring Mike in to replace the guard we just fired."

Addy forced herself not to jump up and down and scream. "That's wonderful."

"He's coming tomorrow," Eric said. "But you can't let anyone know you're related."

"Why?"

"It's just better that way. Trust me."

"But won't Hank and the other producers know?"

"The lawyers keep all that information, and they work in LA," Eric reassured Addy. "No one here, least of all Hank, has even looked at that paperwork. Hank doesn't even know the names of the crew."

That was true. Just yesterday she had seen Hank walk up to a cameraman and lift the name tag from the man's lanyard before addressing him. Even then, Hank had mispronounced the man's name.

Addy returned to her trailer with a skip in her step. *Uncle Mike is coming!*

Jessica

BOL: Good morning. How are you enjoying your time here on *The Book of Love*?

JESSICA: How am I enjoying it? Lemme just tell you . . . no, I can't. There aren't words. I mean, just look at this place. Seriously, turn that camera around. That's it. Look at it. It rocks. It's like being in an old movie but with fancy cameras everywhere. And food. Woo, if I didn't watch it, I could eat so much you'd have to ship me out in a semitruck. I'd be squeezing myself out that door, grabbing one more jelly-filled donut on the way out.

BOL: Well, all right. So what do you do back home in Colorado Springs?

JESSICA: It's more like what do I *not* do. I am on the varsity track, basketball, skiing, and softball teams, so I'm moving all the time.

BOL: I can tell. Do you ever have any free time, and if so, what do you do with it?

JESSICA: Well, I *am* a Colorado girl (wink to the camera), so I love hiking and skiing and anything outdoors. Gimme the sun and the snow and off I go.

BOL: What do you hope to do after you finish high school?

JESSICA: I love my sports, and I plan to stick with those through college and beyond. Skiiing is my absolute favorite. My dream is to try out for the Olympic ski team. Gold medal, baby. USA all the way.

BOL: Very impressive. Now tell us about boys, Jessica. What do you look for in a guy you'd like to date?

JESSICA: Can he take me on in a one-on-one basketball game? Can he ski the black diamond, or is he on the bunny slope? Those are the questions I'd ask. I stay busy and I stay outdoors, so my guy needs to be able to keep up.

BOL: And do you think the young Mr. Jackson can keep up with you?

JESSICA: Well, I don't know. (Looking at the camera) But I'm sure willing to let him try.

BOL: Excellent answer. Well, thank you, Jessica, and good luck on the program.

Chapter 19

"Uncle Mike," Addy whispered. Addy had left her trailer an hour earlier, sneaking away when Hank had gone for his weekly collagen injection. She was sitting on her favorite stump in the woods looking carefully around to make sure no cameramen were hiding anywhere in the vicinity. Eric had promised to send Mike to her as soon as they arrived from the airport.

Mike hugged Addy, holding her longer than normal. He held her face in his hands. "Are you all right, Addy-girl? If I'd known what a mess this show would be, I'd never have made you do it."

"Oh, Uncle Mike, it's all right. Hard, but all right. God has me here for a reason. I am sure of that."

That reason is to make me depend on God more because I'm being attacked from all sides. But Uncle Mike doesn't need to know that. He's worried enough about me.

"Well, glad to hear it." He hugged her again before sitting down on the damp forest floor. He took a deep breath. "Smell that air, Addy. Nothing like it."

She smiled. She had known Mike would like the grounds. He'd probably be trying to talk Eric into letting him camp out here instead of being put up in a nearby hotel with the other security guards.

"As long as you're okay, I'm okay. I was worried for a while. We were all worried." He picked up a leaf and examined it.

"How's Lexi?"

"Shoot." Mike laughed. "You know Lexi. She'd probably be a better security guard than me. She'd just squash anyone who came near you."

"She has texted me about twenty times a day. I miss her."

"She misses you too, Addy-girl. Everybody does. The kids have Go Addy posters up all over school, and the Lawrences call every couple of days to check in and see how you're doing."

I don't think I appreciated how great my life is until I left it for a while.

"Listen, I can't stay long. I'm on the job, after all," Mike said. "I get to meet this Hank in a little bit. It's going to take all I have not to just rip his head off." Uncle Mike shook his head, and Addy knew he wasn't kidding. Mike was a full head taller than Hank and 250 pounds of pure muscle. He could easily hurt Hank if he wanted to.

"I brought you something I think you'll like." He lifted a backpack from his back and handed it to Addy, his eyes moist. "These are your mama's journals. She kept them from the time she arrived in Colombia until the day she . . . well, until the Lord took her home." He twisted his mustache and coughed. "I've been saving them for you. I knew the Lord would tell me when you were ready to read 'em. I think now is that time."

Tears filled Addy's eyes as she took the surprisingly heavy pack from her uncle, unzipping it to find half a dozen leather-bound notebooks. Uncle Mike patted her arm and walked away, wiping his eyes, leaving Addy alone with the journals.

She pulled out the first, dated over twenty years ago. She smiled at her mother's handwriting, so tiny and perfect. Her mom drew little pictures of flowers and trees and sunsets in the margins. Addy took a breath and began reading.

We're here! We're actually here. The plane ride was fine. Bumpy, but Josh and I were so excited we barely noticed. As the clouds broke through, we saw glimpses of Central and South America—rain forests. They are so green. I couldn't wait to get down there and explore them in person. Getting off the plane, finding our luggage, and using our horrible Spanish was a challenge, but we managed to get everything and meet up with the Collinses who drove us over the bumpy roads to their home in Mitú.

From there, we were on foot. Or canoe. We left some things with the Collinses and packed the rest in the big backpacks we brought. Our guide, Jose, led us into the jungle. Josh and I, I'm sure, annoyed him with all our questions and "oohs" and "aahs" at seeing the foliage for the first time.

We eventually found the village—three days later. And we saw the beautiful people God had called us to serve. Our Quechua is even worse than our Spanish, but thankfully, news of our coming had reached the people in the village so they were expecting us. They looked through our bags and tried to ask us what all the medical equipment was for, but of course, we didn't know how to explain it all to them. Then they helped us put together a little lean-to to sleep in for the night. Josh and I praised God for getting us here safely, and we prayed for these sweet people. I can't wait to know them better.

Addy closed the journal and saw the village again. But this time, it wasn't the vision of leaving her parents in the center, guns held to their heads. It was through her mother's eyes, seeing it all for the first time. Mom was going to a tribe in the middle of the jungle, and she was thrilled. Not a complaint in there. She was doing what God asked her to do joyfully and wholeheartedly.

Did she have even a fraction of the faith her parents had?

God, I didn't even want to leave Tampa. And even though I'm here, I'm still too scared to tell anyone I'm a Christian. What would my mother think of me if she were alive? I'm sure she'd be disappointed. I'm too scared to do anything that matters. Way too scared to tell people about you. She and Dad sacrificed everything for you, and what have I done? Nothing. Oh, God. Help me.

Chapter 20

Oh, Lex, it's so good to see you." Addy looked into her computer screen and the face of her best friend smiled back.

"Technology is a wonderful thing," Lexi replied. "I'm glad you finally got around to doing more than just texting me."

"Hey, it's not my fault." Addy adjusted the laptop's monitor. "Hank has kept us on a tight leash."

"And now?"

"Now he's so mad about all those pictures that came out he's decided that phone calls and video chatting aren't such bad ways to spend our time."

"Man, you guys are all over the magazines in the grocery stores." Lexi laughed.

Most of the pictures were a result of the errant guard who was recently fired, but Addy couldn't share that information with Lexi.

"Is Jonathon as gorgeous in person as he is in print?"

Addy laughed. "Our first face-to-face conversation since I got to Tennessee, and you want to talk boys?"

"Not 'boys.' Jonathon Jackson. Seriously, Addy. I'm watching this show to see him, not you. I mean, he's perfect."

"Thanks." Addy looked at her friend. "He is pretty nice to look at."

"Nice to look at? A new basketball uniform is nice to look at. Jonathon Jackson is stunning."

"Enough." Addy's face warmed. "Can we please change the subject?"

"Fine." Lexi paused. "So . . . the commercials are saying this is sports week. I know about the golf—lucked out there, huh?"

"Oh, Lexi, you have no idea."

"Is that all, though? I mean, golf is all right. But if they really want to check out your athletic ability, they need to put you guys out on the basketball court."

"We are not having this discussion again." Addy rolled her eyes. "Actually, that's not all. They're having us do some kind of 'academic competition' this week too. But it's also sports related."

"What?"

"That's all we were told," Addy said. "We're supposed to study until the competition starts."

"Well, study hard." Lexi pointed her finger toward the

webcam. "I am enjoying the popularity I'm getting here. All these years of being your friend are finally paying off."

"Glad I can help." Addy laughed.

"So what are you studying?"

"My mother's journals."

"That'll be very helpful for the competition." Lexi crossed her arms and leaned back into a stack of pillows.

"Lexi, it's amazing. It's like she's talking to me and giving me advice." Addy pulled a journal from her backpack and opened it. "She's so honest. Listen to this."

These women run around with no tops and they're tattooed all over. They use dirty needles and a strange concoction of plants and animal debris for the ink. Don't they know how disgusting that is? How unhealthy? But when I try to tell them, they laugh and say I am unlucky. Unlucky. Well, if wearing shirts and a bra and not sticking feces in my skin is unlucky, may I be cursed.

Lexi laughed loudly and Addy turned some more pages. "See? Here's one where she is really mad. Look at her handwriting: it's all big with words scratched out."

I hate this place! Tonight Josh shook a man's hand. *Shook his hand*, and the whole village went crazy. How was he supposed to know that was an offensive gesture here? He was trying to be nice. He was introducing himself, for goodness' sake. This guy was a medicine man from another village. When Josh shook his hand, the medicine man screamed at the top of his lungs and demanded Josh

be killed for the insult. But then the chief said, "Oh, do
not be upset. This is just a stupid foreigner. Forgive him."
A stupid foreigner! My Josh, who graduated at the top
of his class in medical school and could be back in the
States making hundreds of thousands of dollars a year
from people who didn't think he was the village idiot,
called a stupid foreigner. But Josh, ever humble, apolo-
gized. In front of the whole village. I know that was the
right thing to do, but I don't have to like it.

"Most of this journal is like that," Addy said. "She really
struggled for a while."

"I always thought missionaries were perfect."

"It's kind of comforting knowing they weren't. But
Mom always wrote out prayers after those kinds of entries,
asking God to forgive her. Listen."

Oh, Father, you brought me here to serve these people,
and I love it. As long as they love me. But when they
start treating me with disrespect or, worse, treating
my husband with disrespect, suddenly my calling is
gone. I'm so weak. Keep stripping away my pride, God.
I need your humility so I can love others the way you
love me. Thank you for reminding me I can't do that
on my own.

Addy wiped a tear just as Hank's voice came barking
over the intercom.

"Okay, *ladies*." Addy could just picture the sneer on
his face when Hank said, "The competition starts in ten

minutes, and it's going to be dirty. Literally." He laughed. "I'm talking good old Tennessee mud. So put on something you don't mind getting messy and meet me out back."

"Guess I have to go." Addy shut her computer as Kara walked into the trailer.

"What's this about mud?" she asked. "This must be Hank's paybacks. I thought we were supposed to have an *academic* competition. I was thinking *Are You Smarter Than a 5th Grader?* or *Cash Cab* or something."

"I have no idea." Addy shrugged. "But I guess we better get ready to go."

In ten minutes the girls were huddled around Hank, all smiles with invisible halos hanging over their heads. They were *way* too scared of Hank's temper to risk ruffling even one designer feather.

"Okay, here's what's going to happen," he began as the crew set up around an immense obstacle course surrounded by mud that looked like hot fudge. "You'll be given a topic—history, science, English, math, or 'other,' and you'll have sixty seconds to answer the question. If you cannot answer or you answer incorrectly, you'll be sent through the obstacle course."

He walked over to a six-foot-tall ladder covered in blue foam. "Climb this, then swing across the rope to the platform on the other side. The rope is covered in oil, so it won't be easy." He laughed a wicked laugh, then went on. "From there, you walk across the balance beam—also coated in oil—to the next platform. You climb down that and race to the flag all the way at the end. Any questions?" Hank's tone implied there had better be none. He continued by numbering the girls and making sure there were cameras at every station.

"By the way, ladies, Jonathon will be right over there, and he'll give a surprise announcement at the end, so be on your best behavior."

The other girls squealed and tied their already super-short, super-tight pseudoshirts in knots, revealing as much skin as was possible on a prime-time show.

"This is going to be great," Lila said. "America is going to love seeing us all down and dirty."

"What about being smart?" Anna Grace asked.

"Hank doesn't have all this mud here for us to stay clean."

"But he said—"

"I know what he said." Lila looked at the course. "But that's not what he means. Of course he wants us in all that. It's going to look great on camera."

Jonathon walked over to his seat. Half the girls ran to greet him. Addy refused to be among that group but watched to see how Jonathon reacted.

Anna Grace was the first to reach him. "Jonathon, I just love your shirt. Is that American Eagle?"

"I'm not sure, Anna Grace." Jonathon smiled at her, and Addy resisted a sudden urge to join the group of admirers.

"What's the announcement, Jonathon?" Renae tied her shirt back to reveal her flat, tan belly.

"Can't say." Jonathon turned away from Renae to take his seat. Hank yelled for the girls to get in their places.

Addy was eighth in the lineup. Lila was ahead of her, making every effort to flick her long, black hair in Addy's direction as often as she could. Addy was sure she had permanent grooves in her eyeballs from Lila's ultra-hair-sprayed locks scraping through them.

Addy thought the questions were too easy. "What is the smallest unit of an element?"

Atom, duh.

But Jennifer answered, "H_2O," and began the slimy, slick trek across the course. By the end, she was covered in mud and flanked by cameras. The other girls apparently followed her lead, answering, "George W. Bush" for "Who was the first president of the United States?" and other similarly ludicrous responses.

When Addy's turn came, she chose English, and Hank asked her to name the author of *Jane Eyre*.

"Charlotte Brontë," Addy said.

"You're right." Hank nodded. "First one today."

Addy returned to the end of a very muddy line, giving Kara a high five as she passed her.

Kara was last and had no problem identifying what continent Kenya was on.

The game continued—a total of five rounds. Addy successfully answered all her questions. Kara got stuck on the third—"What was the *Enola Gay*?"—and so was forced to go on the course. Kara took her time, though, and ended up with only her lower half muddied.

The entire competition took over three hours, with breaks for the girls and the crew, technical difficulties, and Hank's angry outbursts constantly causing retakes.

Hank was furious at the girls' wrong answers, though Addy had no clue why. She assumed he would like all the mud and falls and screams. It made much better TV than just answering questions and moving on. "America" would surely prefer the dirty dummies.

But Addy soon understood the source of Hank's frustration.

Jonathon walked over to the smiling, mud-covered young women.

"Hi, girls." He smiled. All the girls sighed. "That was a lot of fun. Some of you are definitely not afraid to get dirty." He laughed and the girls congratulated themselves on their victories. "However, my date has to be pretty smart. My parents have high academic standards for me, and they expect the same of my dates. So"—the girls winced and Hank stormed off to the front of the house—"the winner of this competition is the one who answered the most questions correctly: Addy Davidson. And, as winner, I am happy to tell Addy that she will have immunity for the week."

The girls applauded politely. That was expected of them, after all. But Addy could tell they wished their hands were hitting *her*. Eric yelled, "Cut!" and Jonathon waved a quick good-bye.

"I'm sorry, but I have to run." Jonathon looked right at Addy before continuing. "But I'll be back later tonight for our talks. See you then."

The girls watched Jonathon get into his limo. As soon as it was out of sight, they erupted in screams of outrage.

"This whole thing was fixed," Jessica said, her caramel-colored skin dotted with mud. "Girl, somebody better hold me back or so help me—"

"Jessica, don't stoop to her level." Lila put her mud-covered arm through Jessica's. "Of course it was fixed. Little Addy Sunshine never would have been able to pull this off on her own. But now's not the time to get our revenge . . ."

Hank rounded the corner and silenced Lila with a loud clap. "You girls are out of your minds if you think we fixed this for Addy to win. You idiots just dropped the ball. I gave you—" Hank must have realized he said too much. Addy and Kara hadn't been given anything.

What a jerk. Hank did everything in his power to ensure we lost. Addy smiled. *Too bad his plan backfired.*

He continued, quieter. "Addy now has immunity. She will not be getting kicked off this week." Hank breathed loudly. "I suggest you rest up for your interview tomorrow and try a little harder next time. You are competing to go to *prom* with the president's son, not be the next WWE star. You would do well to remember that."

Kara looked at Addy and winked conspiratorially, then grabbed her by the arm. "We better run back to the trailer before we're attacked."

Chapter 21

Great job today." Jonathon was in The Mansion's living room, and Addy was the last one to meet with him for their "talk." This would be aired after Addy's immunity was revealed. That knowledge made her relax a bit more during her interview.

"Thanks," Addy said. "It was interesting."

"So golf and academics. Both strong suits." Jonathon leaned forward. "What are your weaknesses?"

Being on national television? Making conversation with the president's son? Not making Hank Banner angry with me? "Too many to name, Jonathon."

"I think I know one." Jonathon smiled and Addy forced herself to keep breathing.

"Y-you do?"

"You think more than you speak. How come?"

"Don't you think that's a good thing?"

"So you're saying you have no weaknesses?" Jonathon's eyes twinkled, and Addy forgot for a moment that they were being filmed.

"No, I'm saying that whenever I do speak without thinking, I usually say something I regret."

"Like . . . ?" Jonathon's palms opened toward her, and she knew she had been set up.

"Like when I said I wanted to be the first to be kicked off the show."

"You mean that wasn't a publicity stunt?" Jonathon's eyes grew wide with mock surprise.

Hank's going to love this. "No, definitely not a publicity stunt." Addy laughed. "Just a mistake."

"So you want to stay on the show?"

"Well, I didn't say that." Addy smiled.

"Too bad, because you've got immunity. At least one more week here."

"I guess I can suffer through that."

"Thanks for your sacrifice." Jonathon winked at Addy.

"Cut," Eric yelled. "She's the last one, Jonathon, so if you want to keep talking, don't mind us. We'll just be packing up."

"Off the record, huh?" Jonathon smiled. "What do we talk about?"

"I have some questions."

"Okay, shoot."

"Your dad," Addy said.

"My dad?"

"Yes, we talked about your mom on the golf course, but what about your dad?"

Jonathon leaned back and sighed. "My dad is amazing. He works way too hard, but . . ."

"Kind of comes with the job."

"Right." Jonathon smiled, but it didn't reach his eyes. "He loves that job. But he loves us too. He's a typical dad, I guess. Overprotective, stern when he has to be. But always fair."

"He can't be too overprotective. He let you come on this show."

"Actually, the reason—"

Eric cut Jonathon off, stepping in front of him to get a wire. "Sorry, man. Go on."

"No, it was nothing." Jonathon looked at Addy. "Overprotective in the sense he's having trouble letting me grow up. I'm still his little boy."

"That's sweet."

"I guess. But I'm almost eighteen. I'm getting ready to go away to college. Sometimes it seems like he doesn't get that, that he looks at me and still sees a four-year-old who needs to have his hand held walking across the street."

"Says the guy whose dad took him to Japan." Addy raised her eyebrows. "To meet the prime minister."

"You got me there." Jonathon grinned. "And I didn't even tell you about the time he snuck me into a top-secret meeting in the Oval Office."

"What?"

"I didn't tell you that. Because that would be classified information."

"And you know classified information?"

"That would be classified." Jonathon grinned again.

"What were you saying about how tough your life is?"

Eric began turning off the lights, and Addy knew that was her cue to leave.

"Thanks for talking with me." Jonathon reached out to shake Addy's hand. He held it a little longer than was necessary, and Addy felt a slight squeeze as he finally released her hand. She carried the memory of his fingers wrapped around hers all the way back to her trailer.

Chapter 22

Talented? Check." Hank looked into the camera as the live episode began. "We saw last week that we have quite an array of talent here at The Mansion."

Hank waited as the cameras panned the girls seated in front of the massive front porch of The Mansion.

"But what about athletic and smart?" Hank walked in front of the girls. "Tonight you're going to see just how these twenty-five girls measure up. We've had two competitions this week. And I'll tell you what, they were messy."

The girls laughed, and Addy saw several peek around Hank to make sure the cameras saw them as well.

"One girl will have immunity." Addy was sure Hank had to force himself not to scream after saying that. "And five girls will be going home. Stay tuned to see all the excitement in this week's chapter of . . . *The Book of Love.*"

As the night wore on, Addy watched clips of each of the girls playing golf.

Anna Grace's segment had been edited to make her look like a pro. A sugary sweet pro.

"I just love golf," she said, eyeing the green as she prepared to tee off. "My dad and I have been playing together since I was just a little thing." The cameras quickly focused on her ball flying in the air and not on her horrible form in taking the shot.

Lila looked beautiful, as always, and made sure to let America know again where she was from and that "Hawaii has some of the best golf courses in the world."

It's like watching a commercial. She might be mean, but Lila sure is comfortable in front of a camera.

Addy found her gaze drifting to Jonathon as the segments droned on. Sitting to their left, Jonathon remained attentive the entire time.

He is so poised. So natural. Like Lila. They would look good together. They would make sense together. Beautiful Hawaiian heiress with the equally beautiful president's son. Why am I even letting myself think he'd be interested in me with girls like that throwing themselves at him?

"Don't go anywhere, folks." Hank's plea to the cameras interrupted Addy's thoughts. "When we come back, we'll see the *The Book of Love*'s Academic Mud Bowl. You don't want to miss this."

Next to Addy, Jessica let out a big "woo-hoo" as soon as they got the "all clear" from Eric. "America is going to love this," Jessica said, her back turned to Addy. "I don't know what Hank was thinking, wanting us to get the answers right. You know folks enjoy muddy girls over clean ones."

Behind Addy, Heather agreed. "You know it. Maybe there was immunity, but no one's going to remember the ones who stayed clean. Everyone will be talking about us tomorrow."

Kara leaned forward from behind Addy and whispered, "Yeah, they'll be talking about how stupid they are, missing questions that a second grader would know."

Addy didn't have the time—or the desire—to respond. Jonathon returned to his seat from a quick bathroom break, and Eric signaled that the show would continue in just ten seconds.

Hank spent most of the segment discussing the obstacle course, and, as predicted, most of the shots were of the girls who had to cross it.

Finally Hank made his way to Jonathon. He pulled up a chair beside him, and the pair chatted as if they were old friends.

"So, man," Hank said. "All that for you. Girls sliding all over an oily, muddy obstacle course just for a chance to be your prom date. You are one lucky guy."

"I know." Jonathon smiled. "They did a great job."

"Now, you're pretty athletic, right?"

"I enjoy playing sports. In fact, I'm missing a big base-ball game tonight."

"Stuck here with twenty-five beautiful girls fighting to go out with you when you could be sliding into home plate with a mouthful of dirt," Hank said. "Stinks to be you right now."

Jonathon gave Hank a playful shove. "I guess I'll live."

"So what did you think of these girls this week? Were you impressed with their abilities?"

"I was." Jonathon looked out over the girls, his eyes stopping at Addy. "I think I enjoyed this week's competition even more than last week's."

"Really? Why's that?"

"If we're talking about my date, I'd much rather know she can play a good round of golf or talk with me about what I'm learning in school than to know she can perform in front of a crowd."

Hank paused for a moment, and Addy knew he was not happy with that answer. "But being comfortable and poised in front of others is important too. After all, you're not the typical boy going to his senior prom."

"That's true." Jonathon shifted in his seat.

"And speaking of your senior prom." Hank stood and motioned toward the girls. "You've got to choose five more girls to leave. And he'll be doing that right after this."

Eric yelled, "Cut," and the girls all watched as Jonathon stood to stretch.

"Great interview, Jonathon," Jessica called out.

"Sorry you're missing your game." Anna Grace stood and waved. "I know your team is real sad to have you gone."

The other girls took their cues, and within a minute, all but Kara and Addy were trying to engage Jonathon in conversation.

Thankfully the commercial break was short. Ten excruciating minutes later, five more girls sat crying into their daisies, and Jonathon was waving good-bye to the cameras.

Addy couldn't wait for Eric to yell, "Cut," so she could go hug Kara and congratulate her for being among the Top Twenty girls remaining.

"Not that I doubted you'd make it." Addy linked her arm with Kara's as they made their way back to the catering table.

"You and me, baby"—Kara dipped a fat carrot stick into ranch dressing—"we're going all the way."

Addy laughed and went for the less-healthy option of the fried mozzarella sticks dipped in marinara sauce. A huge blob of the sauce landed on her shirt.

"You'd just better hope the next challenge isn't table manners." Kara laughed and handed Addy a napkin.

Chapter 23

The next challenge is table manners?" Addy asked Kara, hoping maybe she'd heard wrong.

"Etiquette, to be precise," Hank continued, oblivious to Addy's whispered question. "A seven-course meal at a black-tie restaurant."

Most of the girls were thrilled. Hank spent the next few minutes trying to silence them before finally resorting to an ear-splitting whistle.

"Etiquette." Hank glared at the girls. "Meaning proper behavior. The opposite of what you were just doing."

Lila raised her hand and asked in her best teacher's pet voice, "Where are we going?"

"Great question, Lila." Hank paused for dramatic effect. "You girls are going to get to go to Colorado."

"Woo-hoo!" yelled Jessica, who was immediately silenced by Hank's upraised hand.

"Last week we saw you could get dirty. And, granted, America did love that." Hank allowed a few "I told you so's" before continuing. "But now we need to show them you clean up just as well."

The girls sat silently, waiting for further instructions.

"This is a magnificent restaurant, right in the Rocky Mountains. It is one of the finest in all of America, and it's all ours tonight. Jonathon will be there too, spending a few minutes at each table."

The girls tried to contain their excitement, but a few squeals escaped. Hank again waited for complete silence before going on.

"You have a few minutes to pack your bags, then you'll meet with a stylist for hair and makeup. The plane leaves for Denver at two o'clock, so we need to leave here no later than noon."

The girls got up to leave, and Hank called after them, "And make sure to grab a jacket when you're in the wardrobe trailer. March in Denver can get chilly."

Kara and Addy walked back to their trailer. Addy jumped in the shower, praying that the water would wash away her worries.

It didn't.

Addy walked out of the bathroom, drying her hair with a towel. "Seven courses? How is that even possible?"

"Typically, it's appetizer, soup, salad, pasta, main course, dessert, then fruit." Kara stood and ticked off the courses with her fingers. "Of course, some chefs prefer having a palate-cleansing sorbet before the main course, and others serve chicken then beef, rather than pasta, before the main dish."

Addy's mouth hung open. "How do you know all that?"

"Internet research." Kara crossed her arms smugly.

"What about the silverware and all that?"

Kara sat back down and looked at her computer screen. "Always start from the outside in, and never ever use the same utensil twice."

Kara went on to try to educate Addy on how to hold each utensil, when to lay them down, where to lay them down, correct napkin placement, proper cup-holding and meat-cutting techniques, and a plethora of other seemingly ridiculous rules.

"Stop." Addy rubbed her temples in a useless attempt to fight off a headache. "You lost me at 'hold the fork like a pencil.' I feel like you're speaking in some other language. This is *way* out of my league."

Kara took Addy's hand and patted it. "It's all right, my barbaric friend." She laughed. "Just sit next to me and it'll all be fine. Ma and Pop put me in the Good Manners Camp when I was ten. They'll be happy to know they're finally going to get their money out of it."

The girls had no more time to talk because they each had to meet with a stylist to get ready for the big night.

Ruby, Addy's stylist, tried desperately to get her to wear an ultrarevealing V-neck red dress that clung to her like Saran Wrap on a chicken wing.

"It's just not . . . me." Addy found a plain blue sundress. "How about this?"

"You are goin' to a five-star restaurant." Ruby shoved the dress back on the hanger. "You have to wear an evening gown."

Finally they compromised on an elegant violet floor-length gown with a sweetheart neckline and intricate beadwork. Once the dress was selected, Ruby gave it to the wardrobe people to tailor and press. It would be waiting for her once her hair and makeup were done.

Ruby insisted on an updo. She really wanted Addy to have bangs. "Your hair is too thick to be all one length." She lifted Addy's hair and let it drop onto her back. "And you really don't have the face shape to pull it off anyway."

Addy was sure Hank had handpicked Ruby for her lack of any sort of compassion. Ruby always acted like she was being put out, having to work with Addy—such a boring, non-risk-taking ingrate.

In the end Addy won out, and Ruby pulled her hair straight back into a ponytail. She curled, teased, sprayed, and brushed Addy's hair until she rolled it all under using bobby pins and possibly staples, coating it in what was probably a lethal amount of hairspray.

Makeup was next, and that was even more unpleasant. Ruby insisted that since this was a black-tie event, Addy *must* have smoky eyes. Addy wasn't sure what that was. She discovered it meant every part of her eyes would be covered in dark shadows and pencils. As usual, a great deal of foundations, concealers, and multicolored powders were layered on first, making Addy feel like the canvas for a kid's first oil painting.

When the process was completed, Ruby stepped back

and praised herself on being so good. She took Addy to a full-length mirror.

"Wow." Addy looked like a model. She didn't look like herself at all, but Ruby's creation was fabulous.

"Addy, do not move until the van comes to take you to the airport," Ruby insisted.

"All right." She sighed, twiddling her perfectly mani-cured thumbs.

"Stop!" Ruby grabbed Addy's wrists. "You might chip the polish or make the acrylics pop off. Just sit still, all right?"

So Addy sat, feeling like a porcelain doll on display in a shop window. *I sure hope this night goes by quickly. At least I have Kara to help me.*

Chapter 24

*W*ell, look who's joining us." Lila glared at Addy as she slid her linen napkin out of its sterling silver ring.

Addy's attempt to be seated with Kara was squashed before the girls even made their way into the ornate restaurant.

"Your seating arrangements have already been made," a smug Hank said. "Just look for your name plates at the tables."

Addy had been placed at a table with Lila, Anna Grace, and Jessica.

Addy sat down, the beads in her dress cutting into her legs. She wanted to enjoy the restaurant, with its crystal chandeliers, floor-to-ceiling windows framing the Rocky Mountains, and waiters in tuxedos. But she couldn't do anything but check her phone and count down the hours until this evening would be over.

Lila's waist-length black hair had been styled and curled the way Ruby had wanted to style Addy's—soft waves, bangs framing Lila's heart-shaped face, drawing attention to her huge onyx eyes. She looked perfect. Her smile was for the cameras, but Addy saw the hatred behind it as her gaze rested on Addy.

"Split-pea soup, my favorite. Hank added it to the menu just for me." Lila took dainty sips from the sterling silver spoon. "Have I told you girls that my parents have been talking to Hank? They're going to help finance his new project. He says there's a perfect part in it just for me."

"Oh, Lila." Anna Grace batted her eyelashes, her short blond hair styled to make her look like a teen Reese Witherspoon. "You are so lucky. What kind of project is it?"

As Lila turned to respond, her knee hit Addy's. Addy had a spoonful of the split-pea soup halfway to her mouth. It spilled from the spoon onto the white tablecloth.

"Oh, I'm so sorry, Addy." Lila dabbed at the stain with her napkin. "How clumsy."

Cameras at her side, Addy smiled and tried again. This time the table shook as Addy dipped her spoon in the bowl. Looking up, she saw the three girls smiling conspiratorially at each other. She gave up and waited for the next course.

Unfortunately, the spinach-and-strawberry salad also went untouched as Addy's fork was "accidentally" knocked from her hand, and her goblet of water almost fell right into her lap when the tablecloth unexpectedly shifted.

"Jonathon's coming," Jessica announced, and the girls all sat up straighter and smiled.

"Good evening, ladies," Jonathon said. "You look beautiful."

Addy watched Jonathon look at each of the girls. *They're so pretty*, Addy thought, not for the first time. *I just blend into the background around them. Why do I even bother trying to get to know Jonathon? I can't compete with them.*

Addy spent the next thirty minutes watching each of her three tablemates interrupt and talk over each other in an attempt to garner Jonathon's attention. Anytime the young man tried to speak to Addy, one of the girls would find a reason to draw his attention away.

"Jonathon, how's your baseball team doing?"

"Where are you looking to go for college?"

"Try this filet mignon. It's delicious."

When Hank walked over to announce it was time for Jonathon to join another table, all Addy had been able to say to him was "hello." Addy thought she saw sadness in Jonathon's eyes as he was leaving.

Please. I'm fooling myself. He might be sad, but not about leaving me. No way.

As soon as he left, Addy's tablemates' sweet words and friendly banter ended. They were back to shaking the table and kicking Addy's leg and doing anything else that would cause her to look even clumsier than she already felt.

The time after the dinner flew by. The girls were given a day of skiing in Vail, a spa day in Breckenridge, then they were shuttled back to The Mansion for two days of school-work and photo shoots.

In that time, experts were brought in to comment on the tapes of their dinner. Their comments were edited in with the footage so the entire four-hour-long ordeal was a neat and tidy forty-two-minute package.

Oh, God, I would really like to just disappear right now. Addy shifted in her seat on the front lawn of The Mansion as she waited for the show to air. *I hate seeing myself on TV to begin with, but seeing the super made-over version of myself trying to act like I knew what I was doing is awful. Not even getting to see Colorado was worth having to be so formal.*

"Okay, ladies. Tonight we watch the footage from earlier in the week." Hank walked out of The Mansion like he owned it.

"After the airing, you'll all be interviewed about your thoughts on the comments made about your performance at the dinner. So pay close attention to what is said so you can speak about it."

"Great," Addy said to Kara. "Just what I want to talk about."

"And then, of course, tomorrow night, five more of you will be asked to leave." Hank looked expectantly at Addy.

"And," he added to the rest, "a very special announcement will be made."

The girls clapped even harder, plastic smiles in place just in case the cameras surrounding them were on.

Kara squeezed Addy's hand. "It'll be fine, I'm sure." But both girls knew that wasn't likely.

The introductory segment confirmed Addy's suspicions.

"Which girls demonstrated grace and poise, and which should have some private lessons with Miss Manners?" Hank's voice-over said as clips of several of the girls daintily wiping the corners of their mouths with linen napkins preceded clips of Addy dropping hers and looking confusedly at her forks.

"You'll find out tonight on *The Book of Love*," Hank said as the opening credits rolled, followed by commercials for everything from bookstores to feminine products.

The next half hour went by smoothly. The panel of experts was introduced, followed by a short segment explaining why they were chosen to be on the show. Each of them emphasized the deplorable lack of manners shown in our country and hoped that this episode would encourage a return to proper table etiquette and fine dining. Next, each girl was analyzed.

"Jessica showed great poise," one of the experts said. "But—oh dear—didn't know that the spoon was to be placed on the *plate*, not in the bowl, when she was finished. Tsk tsk."

A second expert then appeared, her pearl necklace circling a tiny neck supporting a perfect face. "Anna Grace lived up to her name, sitting up properly, nodding to the waiter in the appropriate way at the appropriate time. Bravo.

"Heather, Renae, and Kara all showed above-average etiquette. They did make a few mistakes, see there." The expert pointed to the screen behind her. "Wrong fork. But overall, I was pleased with their understanding of the rules of etiquette."

Addy thought she'd fall asleep from all the soft voices

and classical music playing under each of the video segments that night. She hadn't even seen herself since that
first clip, so she was hoping they'd just left her out entirely.
Hank's way of "getting even" at her for earning immunity
the week before.

No such luck.

After the next-to-last girl had been discussed, the teaser
right before the commercial break promised that the best
was yet to come. Circus music played beneath the promise
with Addy's face, screwed up in a "What do I do?" pose, filling the screen. The girls around Addy hooted with laughter
and clapped. Hank leaned against an oak tree looking smug.

The commercials ended and Hank said, "While most of
the girls behaved like refined young ladies who would be a
jewel on the arm of any young man, one stuck out like a bad
piece of costume jewelry."

Images of Addy asking which fork to use, waving the
waiter over, almost spilling her drink, and being told to sip
the soup from the other side of the spoon played on the screen
with pipe organ music pumping in the background and cym-
bals crashing for effect every time she made a mistake. The
whole thing made Addy look like a complete buffoon.

And to make it worse, as the night went on, her makeup
began smudging, and of course no one had told her. She'd
wiped her eye at one point and drug a finger-width line of
"deep amethyst" eye shadow halfway down her cheek. Her
lipstick was gone by the third course, making her look eerily
corpselike, and her hair began coming out of the perfectly
smooth bun, piece by teased, curled, unruly piece.

Addy's segment was last, and Hank concluded the show

laughing and shaking his head. "Well, folks, that's it for tonight. But don't miss tomorrow's show—we'll hear from each of the girls as well as Jonathon, and we'll also find out which girls' chapters have ended in . . . *The Book of Love.*"

Addy wanted to raise a white flag and declare defeat but, having had enough attention for one day, chose instead to stand quietly and make her way back to the trailer as inconspicuously as possible.

Hank caught her before she could depart.

"Nobody leaves yet, girls." He smiled like a cat that had finally gotten its mouse. "Interviews, remember? I hope you were all paying attention to your segment. Go ahead to your spot and get ready. We'll start shooting in ten."

Addy sighed. She had her own "spot" set up with a cameraman, interviewer, and crew. She was to sit in a wicker chair on the east side of The Mansion with the camera beside her so it could catch the beautiful Tennessee hills in the background, in case what she had to say was too boring.

Addy was determined to be as dull as possible, leaving no further room for humiliation. She wanted her last "package" to be circus-music free.

"Yes, I was unprepared."

"But you girls had access to information about etiquette before the dinner. Didn't you study?"

Addy knew the interviewer was fishing to get her to admit frustration or gossip about the other girls. But she refused to give him any more ammunition to use against her. She would be polite and forgettable.

"Yes, the producers did give us a packet of information. They are very kind."

"And yet you didn't even know which fork to use with the courses. Did the girls at your table not help you?"

"They did all they could." Addy smiled. "But I just wasn't prepared."

"Don't you have anything else to say, Addy?"

"It was a lovely restaurant. I am so grateful for the opportunity to have gone."

"Is that all?"

"Yes, sir."

"All right, then . . . you sure?"

"Quite."

Addy was finally released, and she dragged herself back to her trailer. To pack. So much for getting to know Jonathon better or having the opportunity to make a difference here.

She had blown it all in one excruciating seven-course meal.

Chapter 25

Addy woke up to find Kara's laptop at her feet, a sticky note attached to the screen. Addy lifted it off and read, "Midas Strikes Again."

Addy could tell by the Broadway tunes being belted in the shower that Kara had left the computer there for her on her way to the bathroom. Addy pushed the space bar on the keyboard to wake the hibernating computer and saw that Kara had Googled Addy's name, resulting in thousands of hits. Most of them were positive.

The general conclusion was that Addy remained the "real" one, not putting on airs, not acting like a perfect little lady. Addy was "everygirl" and America loved her. In fact, they loved her more the more flaws she showed.

"We don't want to see Jonathon Jackson with a perfectly polished debutante," wrote one popular blogger. "We want someone we can identify with. I would have been right with Addy Davidson last night, sipping my soup the wrong way, cutting from the 'wrong side' (how can it be wrong when it feels so right?). I can't even eat spaghetti without spilling red sauce all over my shirt."

Addy felt relieved. Then she felt guilty that she felt relieved. Was she actually starting to *care* what "America" thought? She was shaking her head when Kara walked out of the shower.

"Don't tell me you're *upset*?" Kara turned her head upside down and twisted her wet hair into a towel-turban. "They like you. They really like you."

"No, I'm not upset. How could I be?"

"Then what were you shaking your head about? You're not still wanting to get kicked off, are you?"

"Not really." Addy shut the computer and looked up at her friend. "I was just thinking that a few days ago I didn't care what other people thought and now I do. I'm already getting corrupted."

"Oh, Addy," Kara crooned, sitting down on Addy's bed. "Do we need to have the talk about the dangers of being a celebrity? You know, you people never turn out normal, so worried about what other people think you can't lead a well-adjusted life. So sad. So, so sad."

Addy hit Kara in the head with her pillow and laughed as Kara used her own words from their first conversation against her. "Ha ha, Dr. Kara. I'm just . . . conflicted. And I'm not used to feeling conflicted. I usually know what I'm doing and I do it. And no one really cares. Now I have no plan, no idea what I'm doing, and millions of people are suddenly interested."

"Tell me all about it." "Dr. Kara" smirked. "What was a typical day in the life of Addy Davidson preshow?"

Addy thought about that and raised her eyebrows. "Promise you won't laugh?"

"Of course not."

"Of course you won't *promise*, or of course you won't laugh?"

"Just go on." Kara grinned, still sitting on Addy's bed.

"Okay. Here it is." Addy closed her eyes and imagined herself in her tidy room. "I'd wake up at 6:00 a.m. and shower, then eat breakfast and read my Bible, brush my teeth and get dressed, gather my backpack and school supplies. School starts at 7:45, but I like to get there early to review for any tests or quizzes, so I get there about 7:20. School ends at 3:00. I go home, work on my homework anywhere from 1–3 hours. More if necessary. I play golf a couple days a week. I clean my room, do the laundry, eat some dinner, and watch TV with my uncle. After that, I read or sometimes go for a walk, then I go to bed." Addy felt calmer just thinking about her old life.

"Wow," Kara said, trying very hard not to laugh.

"Go ahead, you know you want to." Addy pushed Kara, causing her to lose her balance.

Kara righted herself and burst out laughing. "What are you, eighty-five? I didn't know seventeen-year-olds could be that scheduled."

"It works for me." Addy frowned.

"You write all this down, don't you? The old-fashioned way too, not with any electronic help. I'm right, aren't I?"

"Yes." Addy stood and crossed her arms.

"Is it here?"

"Yes."

"Please let me see it." Kara jumped up and clapped her hands.

Addy rolled her eyes and walked to her dresser, opened the top drawer, and pulled her planner out from under her T-shirts.

"Aww, it even has your name on it." Kara opened the leather-bound planner.

Each day had its own page and every hour its own line. Addy's tiny handwriting filled most of the lines with everything from homework assignments and tee times to housework reminders and grocery lists.

Kara flipped through months of pages, then looked at Addy, her brow wrinkling. "Where's the fun?"

"What?"

"Fun. You know, going out to the movies or hanging at the mall with friends? Don't you ever have fun? From this, it just looks like your life is all work and no play."

"Sure, I have fun." Addy grabbed the planner from Kara's hands and returned it to her drawer. "My best friend, Lexi, and I hang out all the time. Uncle Mike and I golf and bowl together. We go out to eat. I help with clubs at school . . ."

Kara raised her eyebrow.

"Okay, maybe I don't have the most exciting life, but I want to get into an Ivy League college. And my uncle doesn't have a ton of money, so I need scholarships. And good grades. And great scores on my SAT and ACT."

Kara sat still, saying nothing. A first for her.

"Okay, I'm a loser." Addy sat on her bed. "You happy?"

"No. And neither are you. But I can help you."

"Oh, I don't like the sound of that." Addy pulled the pillow from the head of her bed onto her lap.

"Come on now. Just think of me as Dr. Fun. I'm going to teach you how to have some excitement in your life—let loose." Kara grabbed Addy's planner from her dresser and tried to write *spontaneous fun* on the day's date but kept misspelling *spontaneous*, so she just crossed it out and left the word *fun* followed by five exclamation points.

"First assignment. Grab the first outfit you can see and let's go out."

"Out? We're prisoners, Kara. Or have you forgotten?" Addy crossed her arms.

"Fun Rule Number One," Kara began, throwing on her clothes and running a brush through her still-damp hair. "Fun is an attitude, not a location. Got that?"

"Got it." Addy saluted.

"Then say it."

Addy obeyed, got dressed, and walked out the front door for her morning of spontanious, spontaineous, spontaneus fun!!!!! The morning lasted exactly sixty seconds. Right up to the point that an angry mob of girls met her walking toward the breakfast tables.

"Addy Davidson," Lila spat. "Aren't you just everybody's favorite little loser?"

The other girls closed in, leaving Addy feeling claustrophobic. Kara leaned in to Addy's ear and whispered, "Fun is an attitude, not a location," and both girls laughed.

"Are you *mocking* us?" Renae piped in. "How dare you!"

"How dare we?" Kara snorted. "You're surrounding us like vultures to roadkill. How dare *you*."

Addy wanted to say something, but she wasn't sure what. Kara was being a little harsh, but so were those girls. But Addy couldn't stand up for them, not after all Kara had done for her. And she couldn't join Kara, or Addy would lose any chance of getting to talk with them. *God, what do I do?*

The mob of girls was looking at each other, not sure if they should attack or scream or run off and tell Hank.

"Oh, I'm sorry," Kara said. "Were you trying to intimidate us? And we interrupted. How rude. Go ahead now. Tell us everything you planned to say. Come on. Now I know you've got a speech or two prepared, right?"

The girls huffed and stammered but, in the end, simply walked off.

Kara glowed as she watched the retreat. "And that, my friend, is the fun way to deal with bullies."

Chapter 26

Addy returned to the trailer to rest from her morning of "fun" while Kara was off talking to her family. Addy picked up one of her mother's journals and began reading.

This medicine man is ridiculous. He has been here less than two weeks, and he acts like he is in charge. He is even going around to the men in the village saying Josh is a fake. That his medicine is just "magic." This from the man who tells pregnant women to chew a flower to make their babies smarter. Josh has prevented a spread of a nasty virus with the medicine we brought in. He saved a woman's life last month when she developed an infection from some of their "herbal" remedies. And he is the fake? I just wish my Quechua was better so I could tell this man what I really think about him and his medicine and his lies. But my Quechua is awful. The most I can do is smile and nod and say some Tarzan phrases. Somehow I just don't think, "Husband mine smart. You smell. Leave" would be very effective. Or Christlike. But I'm just so frustrated. I didn't think it would be like this. We came here to help. To serve. And we are being treated like primitive idiots.

Addy turned the page and noticed her mother's handwriting was smaller than on the previous page. More controlled.

I just read what I wrote. Am I still struggling with the same old issue? Still? My pride is hurt so I lash out. God, when will I learn? The worst thing I could do is go yell at the medicine man. In my pride to protect our reputation, I would ruin any chance we had to minister to him. Thank you, God, for making my language skills so bad that I couldn't say something I'd regret. Thank you for protecting me from my own stupidity. Again. Help me love this man, to show him grace. Help me turn the other cheek so he can see you in me and want to know more about you. You are why I'm here. Forgive me for forgetting that.

Addy shut the journal and sobbed. God couldn't have spoken to her more clearly had he come down, sat on her bed, and talked to her himself. She got down on her knees beside her bed.

Forgive me, God. Forgive me for even thinking about being mean to those girls. Forgive me for not saying anything to them, for not saying anything to Kara. What kind of friend am I? I haven't even told Kara I'm a Christian. I'm so scared, God. I don't feel strong enough to be your light here. I've barely even remembered to pray this last week or so. I've gotten so caught up in everything here. I'm sorry. I don't know what to do. Help me. Help me talk to Kara about you. Help me be kind to the other girls. Help me be like my mom. I want to show grace to the people around me. Show me how I can do that.

Chapter 27

Addy didn't get a chance to speak to Kara right away. When Kara returned, Addy was called out. The girls were being interviewed by a teen magazine, and the reporter wanted to speak to each girl individually. After that, Addy was rushed to Ruby so she could get ready for the night's episode. Five more girls would be asked to leave.

"Well, if it isn't my little star," Ruby declared. She was always happiest when Addy was in the news. It meant she'd get to "do her magic" a little bit longer. Apparently the pay for making over mousy teenagers was better than styling the desperate housewives of Rutherford County.

Addy smiled and tried to focus on showing grace to one

person at a time. For now, Ruby was that one. Addy asked Ruby questions about herself and her family and was surprised to learn Ruby was one of nine children.

"I grew up on a farm in Oklahoma," she said.

"You must have had a fun childhood."

Ruby picked up a curling iron and smiled. "I've got some stories."

"Can you tell me some?"

Ruby spent the next thirty minutes regaling Addy with stories about life on the farm. Addy enjoyed hearing about Ruby's mom shooing cows away with hickory sticks and threatening neighboring pigs with a rake.

"Your mom sounds like quite a character."

"With nine kids and a big old farm to run, she had to be tough. But she was the best mom in the world."

Addy felt tears prick her eyes, faced again with the reality that she'd never have stories like that to tell. But Ruby was on a roll so Addy didn't have time to dwell on her thoughts. By the time Addy's hair and face were all done, she was not ready to leave.

Ruby promised to come back with more stories tomorrow. "Thanks for listening, Addy." Ruby patted Addy's hand. "I haven't thought about home in a long time. That was fun."

"I enjoyed it. But I want to see some pictures next time."

"You got it, girl," Ruby promised, humming to herself and gathering her kit.

Addy looked up to see Lila walking toward her. *Oh boy. Help me, Lord.*

"Let's see how tough you are now, now that your little bodyguard is gone."

"Listen, Lila. I need to apologize for today."

"You better believe you do."

Addy closed her eyes. This wasn't going to be easy. A dozen retorts were coming to mind, none of them kind or loving. "I was rude to you this morning, and I shouldn't have been. I don't want us to be enemies. I'm sure we could find some common ground somewhere. I'd like to try."

"You bet we can find common ground," Lila spat. "We will both do anything to win this competition. But it won't work with me."

"What won't work?"

"Oh, you might have that ditzy Kara on your side, helping you win. But I'm not that gullible. I'm in it to win it, and no one is going to stand in my way. So you can just drop the 'nice girl' act."

Addy held her breath. How was it that "nasty" came so easily to her and "nice" was like a foreign language?

"Lila, I'm really not putting on an act." Addy prayed that God would help her say words that would bring healing. "I am genuinely sorry for the way I behaved this morning."

For a moment, Addy thought Lila's dark eyes were softening, but only for a moment.

"Look, Addy, just stay out of my way, all right?" Lila turned and walked off before Addy could say anything more.

Addy sighed and looked out toward the woods. *How I wish I could just escape for a while.*

Chapter 28

Welcome, ladies and gentlemen, to tonight's very special episode of *The Book of Love*." Hank gazed into the camera and informed the millions of viewers watching live that tonight five girls would be asked to leave and one very special surprise announcement would be revealed.

When the show returned, Hank introduced clips of the girls enjoying their days spent in Denver.

Jessica flew down the slopes like the pro she was. "Welcome to my house." She waved to the camera and smiled.

Kara wobbled but was able to make it down the intermediate slope. Several of the girls remained in the lodge, enjoying hot chocolate and playing board games. Addy found that snow skiing was very different from waterskiing, and she often lost her balance as she tried to navigate her way downhill.

Of course, Hank made sure to get shots of me falling. Addy watched the large screen and glanced at Jonathon in his usual spot to the left of the girls on The Mansion's front lawn.

While the shots of the girls at the spa played on the big screen, Hank walked over to Jonathon and whispered in his ear. Jonathon smiled and stared at Addy. Hank noticed the direction of his gaze and frowned. With his hands moving all over, Hank was trying to convince Jonathon of something. Hank pointed to Lila, then patted Jonathon on the back. Jonathon glanced at Hank and shrugged.

What is happening over there? Addy didn't have time for further thought, though, because the last commercial break was ending and the eliminations were about to begin.

"I loved this week." Jonathon gazed at each of the girls. "You all looked beautiful at dinner. I enjoyed getting to know you a little better there."

The girls were all facing Jonathon with toothpaste-commercial smiles.

"I know America sees it, but these girls are great. We've got champion skiers, national finalists in debate and dance, award-winning cheerleaders . . ." He went on, and the cameras stopped at each girl as Jonathon mentioned her accomplishments.

"You learned a lot about our Top Twenty this week." Hank stepped in beside Jonathon and put his arm around the younger man's shoulders.

"I sure did," Jonathon said. "In fact, I spent yesterday watching the editors compile the raw footage from their time in Colorada, so I was able to learn even more about them."

Several of the girls stiffened. Even Hank took his arm off Jonathon's shoulder and paused. "Really? Unedited? And what did you discover?"

"Heather loves bacon, Jessica loves sports drinks, Kara is very much a morning person. And Addy . . ."

"What about Addy?" Hank leaned in.

"Addy stays after each meal and cleans up the plates and cups left by the other girls. She brings water bottles to the guards, and in one clip I saw her helping one of our assistant directors tape down wires before a session."

"Look at that," Hank jumped in. "I am being told it's time to go to commercial." Addy looked around and saw no such signal, but Hank continued on. "Stay tuned, folks, because as soon as we come back, we'll find out which five girls are going home!"

During the break, the girls vied for one last shot at Jonathon's attention. They leaned forward, crossed their legs, and did everything possible to get him to notice them.

Addy looked over at Kara and saw her friend wiggle her eyebrows toward Jonathon. *He noticed me*, Addy thought. *Silly things like cleaning up and he noticed them. Maybe . . . No, I can't go there. He's just being nice. There was nothing else to say about me, after all. No awards or state championships. He had to say something.*

But as much as Addy tried to reason with herself, she couldn't stop the way her heart hammered in her chest every time Jonathon looked her way.

Addy blinked hard as she realized the show had started once again and Jonathon was standing to announce the girls who would be leaving.

Three girls Addy knew just casually were asked to leave. Each cried when given the red daisy but managed to hug Jonathon and tell Hank thank you for the opportunity to be on the show.

"The next girl I'll be asking to leave is . . . Sarah."

Sarah's face went white, then tears filled her eyes. She was genuinely shocked. Anger followed closely behind her shock, but she hid it well, turning to hug Lila and wave good-bye to her "dear friends." She then walked up to Jonathon and took the daisy from him, hugging him a little longer than necessary before walking out of the room.

"The final girl leaving tonight is . . . Renae."

Renae reacted in much the same way as Sarah, except she looked from Hank to Addy with a frown. Hank shook his head slightly, and Renae took her daisy and hug from the president's son and walked off.

Jonathon sat down and Hank again commanded the cameras. "This chapter isn't over yet, folks. We have a shocking twist coming just after this commercial break."

The girls were talking all at once. Hank said nothing but smiled haughtily, and Addy wondered what "shocking twist" he had planned.

She didn't have to wait long. The show was running later than scheduled, so the commercial break was only one minute long. Hank was told he had forty-five seconds to make the announcement. He smiled at the camera as if he had all the time in the world.

"Until now, *Jonathon Jackson* has chosen the girls who will be asked to leave *The Book of Love*. But the producers have decided that, from now on, that choice will be made by"—eyebrows up and big smile—"the viewers."

The girls cheered. Lila made sure to send a smug smile Addy's way.

Addy looked at Jonathon. He was as surprised as the girls. She could tell by the set of his jaw that he was not happy with this announcement. She followed his gaze to Hank, who shrugged and turned back to the camera.

"Next Tuesday, you'll see each of the girls in her hometown, at her school and with her family. And then *you* will choose which girls deserve a chance to go to prom with Jonathon Jackson and which girls need to have their chapters ended in . . ." He motioned for all the girls to join him.

"The Book of Love."

Chapter 29

Addy bit her fingernails and looked out the window of her trailer. She thought her heart would jump right out of her chest when Hank announced they'd be going home this week.

What am I going to do? Everyone's going to know Mike is my uncle. Eric said it's better to keep that a secret or we could be in trouble with the producers.

Addy tried to pray, but her nerves wouldn't allow it. Her mind was racing, all kinds of scenarios running through it—Mike would lose his job and they'd end up homeless; or even if they did get to keep the house, all of America would be so upset that Mike and she would be forced to move to another country and live incognito for the rest of their lives.

The last of Addy's nails were gone when Mike knocked on her trailer door. Addy could barely keep up the pretense of guard-escorting-contestant as they rounded the corner and walked to the car that would take Addy to the airport, headed for Florida.

As soon as the car was loaded and the pair were sure they were far enough from The Mansion to avoid being seen by the paparazzi, Mike began laughing.

Addy hit her uncle on his arm. "How can you be so lighthearted when I'm scared to death?" Addy rubbed her temples. "I mean, really, Uncle Mike. What are we going to do? We can't let people know we're related. But we can't lie because everyone in Tampa will know it. I thought about having you wear a disguise, but someone at home would say something. Besides, we can't lie. I know we're not telling the whole truth right now. But we're not *lying*. Not exactly, anyway . . . Say something, Uncle Mike. And stop laughing."

"Addy-girl, I don't think I've ever heard you say that much in one breath before." Mike grinned. "Relax. God saw this coming and he has it all worked out."

"What are you talking about?"

"Well, I hadn't told you because I didn't know if you'd even still be here this week . . ."

"Hadn't told me what?"

"This is one of my weeks to go with the National Guard," he explained. "I was just going to cross that bridge when I came to it. I was afraid if you knew I'd be gone, you'd be upset. But I'd already told Eric, and he agreed before I came on. It's on the books and everything. Official."

Addy let the news sink in. Mike would be gone for a week. It was planned. When asked, she could truthfully say her uncle was off in the Georgia woods, working to protect his country. No one back home would question it because Mike, a retired sergeant in the U.S. Army, had been training young soldiers with the National Guard for the last twelve years.

He had retired from the service when Addy's parents died, choosing to stay in Tampa near MacDill Airforce Base, where he had served his final term with the military. He had easily gotten a job with the Tampa police force, but because of his expertise in outdoor survival, he had been requested to spend two weeks a year training soldiers in rural Georgia.

Mike winked at Addy. "No need to lie or worry or break our cover. How about that?"

Addy took a deep breath. *How about that?*

She looked out at God's beautiful creation—the gray rocks bordering the highway, water trickling down from high above, green trees and shrubs on the hillsides—and realized how little she appreciated God's majesty. That he could create the beauty around her and yet still be involved in the seemingly insignificant details of her life was astounding.

"Amazing," she said.

"I'm going to ride with you into the Tampa International Airport. My stuff is already at MacDill, thanks to my buddies at the precinct, so I'll get a cab and go straight there. The Lawrences have agreed to pick you up and take you home. They'll take over from there."

Addy was excited to see her principal and his wife, Addy's fourth-grade teacher. Mr. Lawrence was a talker, but Mrs. Lawrence had always understood Addy's need for privacy. Between the two of them, Addy would be cared for and protected. They weren't Uncle Mike, but they were familiar and kind.

"And," Mike continued, "Eric just happened to be the assistant director assigned to your trip. He'll arrive tomorrow."

Addy didn't think things could get any better.

"And if you can handle more excitement, I have something else for you." Mike pulled a cell phone from his pocket. "This is from Jonathon. An official White House phone." He looked over at Addy and twisted his mustache. "I like that boy, Addy."

Addy felt her ears get hot and bent forward, her hair covering them so Mike wouldn't notice. *I am not having this conversation with Uncle Mike. That is way too embarrassing.*

"Now I know you'd probably rather not talk to him in front of me, but I think this car will be about as private as you get the next four days. So I'll just sit here and drive and pretend I don't hear a thing."

Addy opened the ultraslim phone, pressed the Phonebook button, and immediately saw Jonathon's name. She pressed Send and waited, her stomach in knots as she heard the phone ring.

"Addy?" Jonathon whispered. "I can't talk right now. But I want to talk. Can I call you back in ten?"

Addy assented, her heart thumping. An incredibly long ten minutes later, the phone rang and Addy willed herself to wait until at least the second ring before she picked up. No sense letting Jonathon know how anxious she was to hear his voice.

"Addy." Jonathon sighed. "I'm so glad you called. I was afraid you might not."

"Are you kidding? I feel like an international spy. I would have preferred the phone come in a shoe or something, though. That would be more exciting."

Jonathon laughed. Addy thought it was the cutest laugh she had ever heard. Then she winced. She really *was* turning into one of those silly girls she had always ridiculed.

"Addy? Don't think when you're on the phone. I can't see your face. I just hear breathing. I feel like I'm in a horror movie."

"Sorry. Where are you?"

"I'm in my favorite place—the cutting room. I love watching all the uncut footage and seeing how the guys edit it. It's unbelievable, Addy. I mean, these guys are so detailed. They have to make sure whatever cuts they make line up. If a girl's head is on the upper left side before the commercial, that's where it has to be afterward. And with computers, they can do a little work and—boom—it's there. I've seen them playing around and making you guys say all kinds of things—one word here, another there, from different times. It's hysterical. They've been teaching me too. I'll come in sometimes and watch, and every once in a while, they'll let me help."

"Wow, it sounds like you really love that. Is it something you'd like to do one day?"

"President Jackson's son a *film editor*?" Jonathon said. "Not likely."

"Why not? 'Do what you love,' right? That's what my uncle has always told me."

"Unfortunately, not everybody gets the freedom to do what he loves," Jonathon replied, his voice sad. "I'm expected to go to law school and enter politics. Period."

"What if you don't?"

"There is no 'what if.' It's not an option."

"Well, that stinks," Addy said.

"No kidding. Everyone thinks I'm so lucky to live in the White House and travel all over and meet famous people and all that. And yeah, it's exciting, I guess. But it gets old sometimes. I am constantly told what to do and with whom to do it. And I'm never left alone for a minute."

"Secret Service?"

"Them, the paparazzi, even lobbyists will come up to me, trying to get me to talk my dad into voting for their bills. It's crazy. I'd give anything to just live like we did that day on the golf course," he said. "That was great. I mean, sure, there were Secret Service guys in the woods, but they kept out of sight."

"I barely even noticed them."

"Neither did the paparazzi, apparently." Jonathon sighed. "I'm not left alone for a minute. There's always the possibility of potential assassins when you're a member of the First Family."

"Have there been any attempts since your dad has been in office?"

"I don't know. My dad tries to keep Mom and my sister and me in the dark about the threats he receives. But we know. Being president isn't the safest job in the world. And as much as I hate all that comes with being his son, I know my dad loves this country and he takes his job seriously. His passion is what will force me to follow in his footsteps, but it's also what I love most about him."

Addy teared up as she heard Jonathon's soft voice praising his dad. Pity and envy battled in her heart. She wished her dad were still here to talk to, but she was glad she didn't have to live with all the pressures Jonathon had.

"Addy? Are you still there? The phone didn't die, did it?"

"No, sorry. I'm here. I was just thinking."

"About what?"

Addy wasn't ready to divulge her thoughts, but she didn't want to hurt Jonathon's feelings. "I was thinking that your dad should open a new position: White House editor. Forget the biased news stations putting their spin on what happens in there. Make it an inside job. You get a crew to film cabinet meetings, overseas trips, state dinners, and edit it all together for the public."

"You know, that's not a bad idea." Jonathon chuckled. "Maybe I'll pitch it to my dad once this show is over." He paused. "What about you, Addy? What is it you want to do? Be a pro golfer?"

"I wish." She laughed. "I'm not really sure. I know I want to go to an Ivy League school, but from there, I don't know. I love English. I've thought about journalism or even law—but the research side, not the actual standing-in-front-of-huge-crowds-of-people side. I would hate that. Sitting home reading and writing, though . . . that would be great. With some occasional golfing breaks, of course."

"So maybe we'll end up in some classes at law school together then, huh?"

She wasn't sure if his tone was mocking or serious. "I doubt we'd run in the same circles."

"I'd like to," he said, his voice soft, vulnerable. "I don't have a lot of people I can just talk to, Addy. Everyone around me has expectations of what I should be or say or do. Except you . . . Thanks."

Her heart started beating so fast she thought she would pass out. But she had no idea how to respond to him. She could talk academics, golf, even make small talk. Flirting, though, was not something she knew how to do.

Addy looked up to see the sign welcoming people to the Nashville International Airport.

"I'm sorry, Jonathon," she said, her voice shaking from nervous excitement. "I'll have to go—we're at the airport. Talk to you later?"

"Sure," Jonathon said, and Addy could hear the confusion in his voice. She felt bad, but she pressed End anyway.

She hoped he would still be interested despite her inept response.

Chapter 30

The hour-and-thirty-minute flight back home went by in a blur. Addy enjoyed the silence and spent most of the time with her eyes closed, replaying that last conversation with Jonathon in her mind. She hoped she'd get another chance to talk to him while she was in Tampa.

Grabbing her carry-on, Addy stood to leave. Since she and Mike were seated in the first-class cabin, Addy hoped to be the first off the plane.

Preteen girls rushed forward, crushing that hope. Three of them babbled on simultaneously. Addy had no clue what they were saying, but she caught her name, Jonathon's, and something about being the greatest. The whole thing ended with pleas for an autograph. On their shirts. Addy felt strange, but she obliged as the girls turned their backs to Addy and she scrawled her name across their shoulders.

By the time she finished, Addy was surrounded.

"Can I have your autograph?"

"You're a jerk. I can't believe you've made it this far."

"You look a lot prettier on TV than you do in person."

Afraid to say anything, she just smiled, turned around, and walked forward.

Trapped in the tram going from the gates to the main terminal, Addy tried to answer as many questions as she could without breaching either contract or dignity.

"Yes, Jonathon is very handsome."

"No, we haven't kissed. We're just friends."

"Well, the other girls are certainly . . . enthusiastic."

"Yes, I actually *am* that clumsy."

Addy was exhausted before the doors even opened. But as she walked from the tram to the main floor of the airport, she saw a wall of people. Some faces were familiar, but most were not. Everyone was screaming. Dozens of signs were up. Addy's face was plastered over most of them with slogans like Tampa Loves Addy and Jonathon Loves Addy 4-Ever. Camera crews from all the local television stations were present; reporters had their microphones out as they pushed their way through the crowd.

Mike shot a "gotta run—wouldn't want us identified as relatives on camera" look and Addy was left alone to face the throng.

"Addy, how does it feel to be the most popular teenager on TV?"

"Addy, did you really beat up the other girls on the show?"

She shook her head at the reporters and sighed when she spotted Lexi shoving her way past the crowd.

"Look out! Best friend coming through." Lexi crushed Addy in a hug.

The Lawrences were right behind Lexi. Mrs. Lawrence grabbed Addy's arm and whispered, "Just let James take care of everything. We'll run out to the car and wait for him there."

Mr. Lawrence turned toward the cameras and began answering as many questions as he could, saying over and over how proud he was of Addy and how glad he was to have her back home again. "Tampa has come out to celebrate our favorite hometown girl," Mr. Lawrence said. "Now we're going to take her home for a *real* celebration."

The crowd cheered and Addy felt a thrill—it was good to be home.

Chapter 31

D ad's got the boat all gassed up and ready." Lexi had given Addy just enough time to lay her suitcase down in the living room. "You looked awful on the mountain trying to ski. We need to show America real skiing, and you need to redeem yourself."

Addy laughed. "What are you, my manager?"

"It looks like you need one." Lexi looked down at Addy, her hands on her hips. "You can't go all the way if you have another boring week like that. At least mouth off again or something."

"Lexi Summers, you know how terrible I felt about that."

"I know. I'm just saying . . ."

"Since when do you want me to win? I thought you wanted me to come home."

"What's another three weeks away?" Lexi said. "I mean, you win this show, go to prom with Jonathon, and you can get me all kinds of connections. I need a basketball scholarship, you know."

"You want me to win so you can get scholarships?" Addy laughed at her best friend.

"That may be the reason God has you on that show. To help me."

"I'll see what I can do." Addy pushed past Lexi and sat on the couch. "Boy, it's nice to be home." Addy glanced around and frowned. "Look at this place."

"What?"

"The couch is faded; Uncle Mike's recliner is about a hundred years old. The coffee table is all scratched up."

"So?"

"I don't know. Cameras are going to be in here tomorrow. It's a little embarrassing."

"Addy Davidson." Lexi sat beside her friend. "Since when do you care what your house looks like?"

"Since I was on a TV show trying to win a date with a guy whose mom is an interior designer."

"Who cares?"

"I thought you did."

Lexi looked around. "How about we put up one of those pictures of dogs playing poker? Right there, over the couch."

"Yes, Lexi." Addy rolled her eyes. "That would really make this place look classy."

"I know, right?" Lexi leaned back. "So skiing tomorrow?"

"Definitely."

"What else?"

"Eric wants to get some shots at school."

"Ooh, how about we go to the gym, and they could get some shots of us shooting hoops together?"

"Lex, you know I won't play basketball with you."

"Come on, just because you can't win doesn't mean you shouldn't try."

"We'll probably go to the golf course too."

"And the beach," Lexi said. "What if you snorkeled and had some of those underwater cameras with you? That would be cool."

Addy agreed. Lexi might make a pretty good manager after all.

Chapter 32

"A-D-D-Y," the cheerleaders chanted. The rest of the school, all 517, were sitting in the bleachers in the gym, chanting along with them. "A-D-D-Y."

Eric and his crew were set up in front of the makeshift stage, and Addy followed Mr. Lawrence out. The crowd erupted in cheers and screams.

"Thank you all for coming." Mr. Lawrence silenced the crowd with his hands. "I know what a sacrifice it was for you to have to miss class this morning."

The crowd laughed.

"We have been watching *The Book of Love* for the last few weeks, and we're so happy to have Addy Davidson representing Tampa Christian School."

Everyone on the bleachers stood to applaud, and the cameras panned the audience, who clapped louder and waved "Hi, Moms" as the cameras passed by.

Mr. Lawrence waited for the crowd to sit, then announced the morning's lineup: songs from the choir and the band, speeches by some of Addy's classmates and teachers, and then a special presentation for Addy from the school.

"So sit right here, Addy"—Mr. Lawrence pointed to a chair on the stage—"and enjoy the show."

Addy looked out over the crowd. *I never would have imagined this. Not in a million years. My whole school out for me? A month ago, most of them barely even knew my name.*

The morning flew by as her classmates sang and played for Addy. At the end, one of her favorite teachers came up to the podium.

"I have had the pleasure of being Addy's math teacher for the past two years," Mrs. Stevens began. "She is an amazing young woman. She works hard to keep up her grades, but she also works hard to be a good example to the other students."

Addy blushed as Mrs. Stevens talked about how she tutored younger children in her free time, and how she and Lexi led a Bible study once a week.

Addy swallowed hard. *Great, all of America is going to know I lead Bible studies. I'll get all kinds of hate mail from people who can't stand Christians. Oh, God, just when I was starting to feel a little comfortable with all this. Help me.*

"I know you were nervous about going on *The Book of Love*." Mrs. Stevens looked at Addy. "But I think we'd all agree that you are doing a fantastic job, and we are so, so proud of you."

The crowd once again stood and cheered. Mrs. Stevens hugged Addy and, wiping tears from her eyes, whispered again how proud she was.

"We're not done yet," Mr. Lawrence yelled into the microphone, motioning for the students to sit. "Addy, we have one more surprise for you."

He motioned for Addy to join him, and as she stood, Mrs. Hawthorne, the very overweight band director, was wheeled out on a dolly. A huge golden harp was in front of her, and she was dressed as a modest but comical cupid. Playing the song "The Book of Love" in a classical style, Mrs. Hawthorne was wheeled to the center of the gym while smaller "cupids," children Addy recognized from the first and second grades, walked in behind her throwing petals from bright red baskets.

"Addy Davidson," Mr. Lawrence said over the howling laughter of the students and faculty, "we have brought our very own cupid out here this morning just for you. You have all of our hearts, and we believe you'll have Jonathon Jackson's as well."

The crowd cheered again, and Addy tried to stop laughing long enough to appreciate it.

"And we want you to know that you are the winner in our 'Book of Love.'"

Two more children came up on the stage with a bouquet of flowers and a crown.

"And you are our prom queen."

Balloons dropped from the ceiling, and everyone in the

bleachers ran up to the stage, throwing confetti and shouting. Addy accepted the flowers and the crown from the children with tears in her eyes.

Oh yes. It's good to be home.

Chapter 33

"He wanted to drive the boat," Lexi said.

Spencer Adams was walking down the dock toward her.

"You can drive the boat," Addy whispered.

"But I'm not nearly as easy on the eyes as Spencer." Lexi laughed.

"Hey, Addy." He grinned. Not as perfect a smile as Jonathon's, Addy noted. *Even Spencer Adams looks plain after spending time with Jonathon.*

"Thanks for letting me come."

Addy, Lexi, and Spencer put on their life jackets as Eric and his crew set up their cameras on the shore of the lake.

"Nice place," Eric said. "What do you call those trees?"

"Cypress," Addy answered. Having grown up around this lake, she knew she took its beauty for granted. The green water sparkled as the sun hit its surface, and the large trees surrounding it looked like their branches and trunks were melting into the ground.

"Want to try?" Addy asked Eric, lifting up a ski.

"Not a chance." Eric looked through the camera lens. "There are alligators in that lake, right?"

"Sure," Lexi said. "But they don't bother us."

"That's a relief," Eric said.

"They're too scared of the boats to come near us. They like to stay near shore."

Eric's eyes widened and Lexi laughed.

"Lexi, stop scaring him," Addy said. "Don't worry, Eric. My uncle always says the alligators are just as scared of us as we are of them."

"Well, that's good." Eric leaned on his camera. "Because I am very, very scared of alligators."

Spencer started the boat. "Do you want to start on shore or in the lake, Addy?"

"In the lake."

Within minutes, Addy was jumping out of the boat into the water.

"Cold?" Lexi asked.

"A little." Addy worked her feet into the plastic boots on the water skis, grabbed the handle at the end of the rope, and positioned herself behind the boat.

"Ready?" Lexi asked.

Addy put her thumb up and Spencer hit the gas. Addy leaned back, knees bent, letting the rope pull her into a standing position. Moving outside of the wake, she easily jumped the waves the boat made. Another thumbs-up sign, and Spencer knew Addy was ready for more speed.

Addy pulled on the rope and within seconds was beside the boat.

"Show-off," Lexi yelled.

Addy pulled back, crossed the wake behind the boat, then pulled up on the other side, this time dropping one of the skis and positioning her right foot in front of her left.

Addy and Lexi had spent hours on this lake, and water-skiing came as naturally to Addy as walking. Lexi wasn't quite as accomplished, and the running joke between the girls was that Addy took pleasure in her superior abilities.

Lexi moved Spencer out of the way, and Addy knew she was in trouble. The boat made a sharp turn to the left, and she bent her knees in response, following the curve of the boat. Lexi looked back and pushed the boat even faster. Knowing she had no chance to win this battle, Addy waited until she was right in front of the dock, let go of the rope, and the momentum carried her back to shore.

"That was amazing." Eric came out from behind the camera. "How'd you do that?"

"How'd I do what?" Addy removed the ski and sat on the shore to catch her breath.

"You just came right back here," Eric said.

"I don't like falling in the lake," Addy said. "When I was little and I'd fall, I'd hear the humming of the boat's motor under the water, and I thought it was a snake. It scared me so much I didn't even want to keep skiing. So Mr. Summers taught me how to get back to shore when I was done so I didn't have to stay out there. That's how I've come back ever since."

Addy waved Lexi and Spencer back to shore. "Except when Lexi makes me crash." Addy laughed.

Eric packed up. "I'll meet you at the beach in the morning, Addy."

Spencer pulled up next to the dock and stood. "Ready to get Lexi back?"

With a gleam in her eye, Addy ran to the boat, ready to do just that.

Chapter 34

That was a bad fall." Spencer watched Lexi limp back to her house.

"She really wiped out," Addy said.

"Are you sure you shouldn't go with her?"

"No way." Addy draped a towel around her shoulders to protect herself from the chilly April breeze. "Lexi hates for anyone to see her hurt. She'll patch herself up and be back in just a few minutes."

Spencer sat beside her. "I was actually hoping for some time alone with you, Addy."

She looked at Spencer's profile. His olive skin, dark hair, and ebony eyes revealed his Hispanic heritage. Until recently, Addy thought Spencer was the best-looking boy at school. *And until now, he never even gave me a second glance.*

"I know you're getting a lot of attention and all that. And I have no doubt you're going to win that competition." Spencer turned to look at her, leaning closer.

Nice cologne, Addy thought. *But not as nice as Jonathon's.* "I don't think that'll happen. But I'll stay on as long as God wants me there."

"That's what I've always admired about you, Addy. You have such a strong commitment to God."

"Thanks."

"Listen." Spencer paused for a minute, looking out over the lake. "Like I said, I know you'll be going to prom with Jonathon Jackson. But I was wondering if . . . maybe . . . you'd go to our school's prom with me."

I did not see that coming. She leaned away from Spencer. *Seventeen years without any boy giving me a second glance, and now the cutest boy in school is asking me to prom?*

"You are going down, Addy Davidson." Lexi ran up from behind Addy, lifted her up, and carried her over her shoulders down the dock. Addy's thin frame was no match for Lexi's bulk, so Addy surrendered and prepared herself for the inevitable.

Lexi dropped Addy into the water. Bobbing up, Addy said, "Are we even?"

"Maybe." Lexi held out her hand to help Addy up. Using all her weight, Addy grabbed Lexi's hand with both of hers and pulled the larger girl into the lake beside her.

Both girls were laughing when Spencer walked down the dock.

"Hey, Addy," he said. "I have a baseball game tonight, so

I need to go . . . unless you'd rather I stay. I mean, I can miss this one game. I don't mind."

Addy squeezed the water out of her hair. "No, that's fine, Spencer. The team needs you—you're their best player."

He beamed and waved good-bye. The girls climbed up the ladder to the dock and Lexi handed Addy her towel.

"Spencer and Addy, sitting in a tree," Lexi sang.

"Very funny." Addy slapped Lexi with the end of her towel. "He did just ask me to prom, though."

"Spencer Adams asked you to prom?" Lexi whistled. "Dreams really do come true. The president's son and the most popular boy in school. Where do you go from there?"

"Home to get ready for bed." Addy stood to walk back to her car.

"Wait a minute, young lady." Lexi walked beside her. "I know you're a star and all that, but Spencer Adams just asked you to prom. What did you say?"

"Nothing. Right after he asked, you came up and threw me in the water."

"I saved your sorry behind yet again. First, I get hurt so he has the time to ask you. Then I come back just in the nick of time so you don't have to answer him. Who's the best friend ever?"

"Or the worst." Addy opened her car door and grabbed a dry towel from the backseat.

"What?"

"I can't go to prom with Spencer."

"Why not? You've had a thing for him since you were twelve."

"What about Jonathon?"

"Jonathon Jackson? The president's son?"

"Do you know another one?"

"Addy, you're on a TV show with him. Even if you win—correction, *when* you win—it's just prom. But Spencer is . . . he's Spencer."

"But, Lex, I really think I like Jonathon."

"Jonathon Jackson? The president's son?"

"Lexi, will you stop?"

"Sorry, but seriously, Addy. He's the president's son."

"I know. But I think we might be friends."

"So be friends with Jonathon and go to prom with Spencer."

"That just doesn't feel right," Addy said. "I don't date around."

"You don't date at all."

"I can't lead Spencer on when I like Jonathon."

"Jonathon is currently 'dating' fifteen girls, Addy. You're just thinking about going to prom with one."

"But what if Jonathon really likes me? What if something could happen there?"

"And what if nothing happens with Jonathon and you throw away your chance with Spencer?" Lexi leaned against the hood of Addy's car. "You'll be one of those little old ladies who never marries and has a houseful of cats. And then you'll die, but no one will find your body and it'll just melt into the floor next to the cat carcasses."

"That is disgusting." Addy pushed Lexi off her hood.

Lexi spread her hands. "I'm just saying."

"God is not going to force me to be the crazy cat lady because I choose not to lead one boy on when I like another."

"You hope." Lexi grinned.

"You'll be the one to find the body."

"All the more reason to talk you out of refusing Spencer."

Addy laughed. "Good night, Lex." She pulled out of her friend's driveway.

God, what do I do? I like Jonathon. But I don't know if there's any chance with him. Even if there is, I don't know if he's a Christian. And Lexi is right; he is on a show where he's dating fifteen girls. What does that say about him? Of course, I'm on that show too, so what does that say about me? Oh, Lord, this is so complicated.

Chapter 35

ddy!" Addy hadn't even entered the trailer when Kara flung open the door to welcome her roommate back to Nashville. "What took you so long? I came from New York and got here two hours ago."

"My flight didn't leave until three," Addy said, trying to hug Kara with her arms full of suitcases.

"So tell me all about your week while you unpack." Kara took Addy's smaller suitcase and put it on the bed.

"It was great. Too short."

"Of course," Kara said. "By the way, Pop says hi and that you are required to come visit this summer."

"Tell him hi back, and I'd be happy to."

"Back to Florida."

"I went water-skiing, played golf, hung out with my friends."

"Boring," Kara said. "Tell me the good stuff. I know you've got some good stuff."

"Well . . . I got asked to prom by a guy from school," Addy said.

"He must not be just any guy from school." Kara leaned forward. "Tell me about him. What does he look like? What's his name? How did he ask you?"

"Slow down." Addy held up a hand. "His name is Spencer . . ."

"Spencer," Kara repeated in a British accent. "Very proper. I like it."

"Actually, he's Cuban American."

Kara assumed a Spanish matador pose. "Spencehrrrrrr. *Que bueno.*"

Laughing, Addy continued, "He has dark hair and dark eyes."

"Is he tall?"

"I guess. Why?"

"Tall, dark, and handsome. *Muy bien.* Go ahead."

"Anyway, he asked me to prom."

"Where?"

"By the lake after we went skiing."

"Romantic." Kara danced around the trailer with Addy's brown sundress.

"But I turned him down."

Kara stopped dancing. "You did what?"

"I just couldn't." Addy took her sundress and hung it in the closet. "I like Jonathon."

"I like Jonathon too, but it didn't stop me from telling four different boys I'd go to prom with them."

"What? Four?"

"Different schools, different nights. And don't change the subject."

"It just didn't feel right," Addy said. "But he understood."

"Sometimes I just don't get you, Addy. But I'm glad you're back. I have been so bored."

"You mean in the two hours you've been back?"

"Yes, in the two hours I've been back." Kara laid a hand on her forehead. "It has been torture."

"I've missed you too." Addy put the last of her clothes away. "Now let's go find some food. I'm starving."

Chapter 36

"Addy, over here."

She heard the voice but couldn't tell where it was coming from.

"Addy," she heard again.

Looking toward the sound, she only saw a row of trailers. From the door of the farthest trailer, a hand motioned for her to come in.

"Go on." Kara pushed Addy toward the door. "But I want to hear all about it."

Kara walked toward the catering tables and Addy walked forward. Jonathon greeted her from inside.

Addy stepped up into the trailer and looked around. The room was dark, with a large portable screen at the far end. Below the screen sat a table that held equipment Addy had never seen before. Knobs and dials and little computer screens, flanked by larger computer monitors and speakers of every shape. A huge whiteboard calendar hung to her left, the words written on it completely illegible. Crushed soda cans, half-empty pizza boxes, and yellow Post-it notes covered every surface in the room.

"What is this place?"

"The editing room." Jonathon stood. "Nice to see you too."

"I'm sorry, Jonathon. It is nice to see you. How was your week off?"

"Not exactly a week off." He motioned for Addy to sit down. "I had some major tests to take and several baseball games to play."

"How did it all go?"

"Really well. But I'm glad graduation is just a couple of months away." He stretched. "I'm getting too old for this."

"So this is where you come to relax, huh?" Addy remembered their conversation on her way to the Nashville airport.

"I love this stuff." Jonathon flipped a button and all the moniters in the room came on. He keyed in a few commands, then Addy saw a clip of herself skiing at the lake with Lexi. And Spencer.

"Impressive." Jonathon watched the screen as Addy dropped her ski and jumped the waves. "Do you think you could teach me how to do that?"

Addy's heart raced. "I don't know if I'm a very good teacher. I've tried to show Lexi how to do that, and she still can't do it."

"And Lexi is . . . ?"

"My best friend." Addy pointed to the screen. "Right there."

"I see." Jonathon pointed to Spencer. "And that? Who is he?"

"He's . . . a friend."

"Would this friend mind if you taught me how to ski?"

"What?"

Jonathon blushed, and Addy thought it was the cutest thing she'd ever seen. "I mean, is he a boyfriend or just a friend friend?"

Is Jonathon Jackson actually acting shy around me? *Is he jealous?* Addy tried to take a deep breath so she wouldn't hyperventilate.

"Just a friend. Really, more of a classmate than a friend. There's nothing to be . . . I mean . . ."

"Good." Jonathon leaned closer to Addy. "Because I spent a lot of my week thinking about you. When I saw this footage, I thought that . . . Well, you're a great girl. A guy would be crazy not to be interested. But I was hoping I still had a chance."

Oh, Lord, please let this not be a dream. I will be so upset to have to wake up from this. Jonathon Jackson is actually interested in me? Me?

"Addy?"

"Yes, yes, you definitely have . . . I'm . . ." *Just one sentence. Can I just speak one complete sentence here? He's going to think I am an idiot.*

"So you'll teach me how to ski with one ski?"

"Slalom," Addy said.

"What?"

"It's called slalom skiing."

"Okay. So will you teach me to slalom?" Jonathon was so close Addy could see the stubble on his face. *He is beautiful.*

"Yes, I'll teach you how to slalom." *You just might have to remind me to breathe.*

"Great." Jonathon sat back up and Addy exhaled. "But let's keep this between us, if that's all right."

"The skiing lesson?"

"No, this talk." Jonathon looked into Addy's eyes and smiled.

"Yes, this . . . sure . . . I'll see you later." Addy stood to walk away and, for a moment, feared her legs would give way beneath her.

Chapter 37

"Good evening, ladies and gentlemen, and welcome to tonight's special episode of *The Book of Love*." Hank looked into the camera and smiled. Addy and the other girls sat, once again, in their spots on the front lawn. "Tonight we'll see each of the Top Fifteen in their hometowns. And when the show ends, the phone lines will open for you to vote for Jonathon Jackson's Top Ten."

The girls clapped as Hank walked in front of them. He continued to talk about the week, and Addy replayed her time in the editing room with Jonathon.

Best. Day. Ever.

Addy looked up to see the first of the packages being shown. Each girl would have a ninety-second package. *That sounds so short*, Addy thought. But after seeing the first few, she knew a lot could be fit into a ninety-second clip.

Jessica was first, smiling and crying as she showed America her hometown of Colorado Springs, Colorado.

"This is where my sisters and I used to spend our days in the winter, sledding down this hill over and over again, until our mom made us come in to get warmed up."

A parade was given in her honor and the mayor of Colorado Springs named Jessica its citizen of the year. Jessica's home—a huge ranch with a view of Pikes Peak— was filled with friends and family who were thrilled to see her.

"I have the best family in the world," Jessica cried for the camera. "I don't know what I'd do without them."

After the package, Jessica, once more wiping tears from her eyes, expressed how grateful she was for all the people in Colorado Springs who loved her and came out to support her last week.

"Is there anything else you want to tell them?" Hank urged.

"Oh yes." Jessica looked straight into the camera and folded her hands together. "I almost forgot. Vote for me. Please!"

Lila was next. Wearing a traditional grass skirt, she led the cameras around a luxurious luau given in her honor. Pigs were roasted, women danced, and the beach was filled with fans chanting Lila's name.

"No one deserves to win as much as this Hawaiian jewel." Lila's cousin hugged the beauty and the crowd around the luau roared their approval.

"Thank you, Lila," Hank said to the camera. "Next we have Kara McKormick, returning to her hometown of Smithtown, New York."

Kara's homecoming was as fun and dramatic as Kara was. Her family met her at the airport in a limo and drove her all through Long Island, her torso hanging out the sunroof as she waved at the people lined along the streets of her hometown.

Kara's classmates threw a party in her honor at Theodore Roosevelt's vacation home.

Mr. McKormick even earned some airtime there.

"Look at this." He pointed to the turn-of-the-century mansion. "We are here at a former president's home celebrating our current president and his son. Fitting, I think. Jonathon, I know you're watching this. You can't do better than my girl here."

"Pop, America picks now, not Jonathon." Kara laughed as her father pulled her into an even tighter hug.

"Then, America, you pick my girl Kara. She's the best daughter a man could ask for."

The camera cut away, but not before Mr. McKormick produced a handkerchief and wiped his eyes.

Addy, seated next to her friend, squeezed Kara's leg. "I love your dad."

"Me too," Kara said.

Addy's package was twelfth in the lineup. *Not very exciting. Mrs. Hawthorne stole the whole show with her cupid getup, though. Even Hank had to laugh at that.*

Out of the corner of her eye, Addy saw Lila yawning. *So maybe my life isn't the most exciting. But I love it. I love it, God.*

Thank you for taking me out long enough for me to see how wonderful it is.

The evening's show finished and the girls stood in a semicircle around Hank.

"Call or text your votes tonight, and tune in tomorrow for the next chapter of . . ."

The Top Fifteen all leaned in and shouted, *"The Book of Love."*

Chapter 38

On Friday, having been given the morning and afternoon off, Addy decided to sneak away to her favorite spot in the woods. Uncle Mike had just returned from his trip, and she had sent word through Eric for him to meet her there.

"Over here!" Addy watched as Mike stomped through the forest, removed his backpack, and sat down. He pulled out a couple of sandwiches, a bag of chips, and two huge bottles of water, then spread a plastic red-and-white-checked tablecloth on the ground.

The two prayed, and Addy began to eat her sandwich— turkey with Swiss cheese and spiced mustard. Her favorite.

"Looks like you had a nice trip home," Mike said.

"You saw the show last night?"

"Are you kidding?" Mike wiped mayonnaise off his mouth. "When I told those recruits I worked with whose uncle I was, they insisted we make it home in time to watch it."

"You watched *The Book of Love* with a bunch of soldiers?"

"Sure did. And they loved every minute of it."

"I missed you at home."

"I missed you too, Addy-girl." Mike patted Addy's leg. "Everything going all right? Any more problems with Hank?"

Addy shook her head. "He hasn't spoken much to me in the last week or so. I know he's still upset that I'm here. He hates that."

"Why do you think that is?"

"He wants to be in charge of everything," Addy said. "Can you believe he allowed some of the parents to pay to have their daughters put on this show?"

"I can believe just about anything about that man." Mike finished off his sandwich. "He is one piece of work. And it seems like we both have the same effect on him. He hates me too. Must be something in our genes."

"I thought no one was supposed to know we're related?"

"No one does—don't worry," Mike said. "But I got off the van for my first day of work and went up and introduced myself to Hank. He looked at me like I was from another planet. Asked me if I was aware he was the host. I said I was and I was happy to meet him." Mike shook his head and snorted. "Later, one of the guards told me no one talks to Hank. 'Speak only if spoken to,' I was told. Can you believe that? He thinks everyone around him should cower in his presence, like his job makes him a better man than the rest of us." Mike was getting mad now. "I can't stand it when people think that."

"Calm down, Uncle Mike. It can't be that bad."

He looked sideways at Addy with an "Are you kidding me?" stare. "Hank's made sure to ridicule and patronize me every day since. Treating me like some ignorant little rookie."

"Be good now, Uncle Mike. You're here to help *me*, remember?" She laughed.

"I know. But I'm human too, girl, and that guy just rubs me the wrong way. Do you know he walked up to me in the cafeteria when I was praying and started speaking to me? My eyes were closed. He didn't care. He just picked up my name tag and started telling me what to do. I was so mad. I kept my trap shut, but that was just by the grace of God. Wouldn't look good to punch a man right after you say 'Amen.'"

"You know"—Addy put her arm around his shoulder— "a wise man once told me it's the meanest ones who need love the most."

He kissed the top of Addy's head. "Using my own words against me, huh? Well, all right. You got me. I'll try to be nice. But it sure isn't easy."

"You're telling me."

"Ah, well, I don't think things can get worse, right?"

Addy started packing up their things. "You'd better be careful, Uncle Mike. Those sound like famous last words."

Chapter 39

Later that day the Top Ten would be announced. Nausea swept over Addy in a wave, and she ran to the bathroom, barely making it in time. As she weaved her way back to bed, Kara looked up, frowning.

"Addy, what's wrong?"

"I don't feel well." She collapsed onto her bed, pulling the covers over her in an attempt to warm her freezing body.

"Hang on." Kara jumped up from her bed and placed a cold hand on Addy's forehead. "You're burning up." She grabbed her cell phone from her nightstand. "I'm calling Eric to get you to a doctor."

"No." Addy was shaking, every inch of her body hurting. She just wanted to curl up in a ball and sleep. Forever.

In ten minutes Kara had dressed Addy and handed her off to Eric, who "happened" to request Mike guard Addy for the day.

Kara had found a bucket for Addy to bring with her in the truck on the way to the hospital. Mike tried desperately to weave in and out of mid-morning traffic on I-24 so he could get Addy to the hospital as quickly as possible. The motion made Addy feel worse, but she barely had the energy to raise her head to the bucket. The open window next to her didn't help at all. Addy felt as if she were moving in slow motion, on the bottom of an icy ocean with weights tied to her feet.

Voices and faces floated in and out, but Addy couldn't focus on any of them. She fell asleep and woke up, each time in a different place—on a stretcher, in triage, and finally, in a hospital room. She heard machines beeping and felt herself being touched and pricked, but she was barely aware of what was happening. At one point, she felt her leg being pulled up and something cold applied to her thigh.

The next time she woke up, the room was quiet and Mike was sitting next to her, smiling.

"'Bout time you woke up, girl."

Addy looked around. She was in the nicest hospital room she'd ever seen. Soft blankets covered her, and the walls were painted a warm yellow, with framed Monet prints above the oak dresser and between the two large windows. Her leg was propped up on pillows, and an IV led from her arm to a bag at the head of her bed. Uncle Mike was sitting back, still smiling.

"This is *funny*?" she asked.

"It will be when you find out what put you here. I want you to guess first, though, to make it fun."

"I'm lying in a hospital bed, Uncle Mike. I do not feel like playing guessing games."

"Come on. Just a couple of guesses?"

Addy's body was still too sore for her to slap her uncle, but the thought definitely crossed her mind.

"Spider bite," Mike said, his hands slap-slapping on his thighs.

"What?"

"Yep, a brown recluse. Bit you right below your rear."

Addy closed her eyes and moaned. "Please tell me you're kidding."

"Nope."

"What time is it?"

Mike looked at his watch. "Three o'clock."

"In the afternoon?"

"Yep."

"What have I been doing all this time?" Addy asked.

"Sleeping, mostly. And groaning."

Addy moaned.

"Yep, just like that." Mike laughed. "You came in pretty dehydrated. That's why you were so tired. Then they pumped you full of Benadryl and Tylenol and some other stuff, and the combination of all that just knocked you out." Mike put his hand on Addy's arm and squeezed. "I was getting a little worried."

"Please tell me you didn't hurt any of the doctors or anything?"

"I didn't hurt anybody," Mike said. "I just made sure

they knew you were a special case, and they needed to find out what was wrong and fix it. Fast."

"How did they finally figure it out?"

"You kept getting sicker and sicker, and all the doctors knew was what you *didn't* have. Finally one of the nurses turned you over because you were complaining about your leg, and that's when they saw it."

"But they dressed me in this." Addy picked at her tan hospital gown. "How did they miss it then?"

"Well, they weren't looking for it. When we brought you in, the docs all thought you had a bad case of the flu, so they just started treating you for that. But you didn't get better, so they went to work. Like I said, the nurse finally caught it just a couple hours ago. Looked bad too." Mike shook his head. "Some of the skin around the bite was starting to look nasty, so they raised your leg and kept putting ice on it."

"What do you mean my skin looked nasty?" Addy asked.

"Relax." Mike stood to pace in the small room. "It happens in rare cases. The spider's venom causes the skin tissue to die." He walked over and patted Addy's leg. "No worries, though. They caught it in time, and the doctors say if you keep it elevated for a few days, you'll be fine."

"A few *days*?"

"Either that, or the skin dies and you have to get it surgically removed and new skin grafted back." Mike sat back down. "Your choice."

"Fine," Addy said.

Mike held Addy's hand. "Don't you do anything like that to me again, Addy-girl, you hear me?"

Addy squeezed her uncle's hand in return.

Mike's cell phone rang and he answered, "Yes . . . yes . . . . okay," and hung up.

"Who was that?"

"That, little girl, was Jonathon. He's been calling every half hour since he found out you were here. He's managed to get his Secret Service guys to sneak him in through the back hallways so he can see you. He'll be up in a couple minutes." Mike winked and stood.

Addy was frozen. Jonathon was coming *here*? To see her in a hospital bed, laid up because a spider crawled up her pants and bit her? Could anything be more humiliating?

Bedhead and morning breath sprang to mind, and Addy pulled the blankets over her head.

"Oh, stop complaining," Mike said. "You know you're dying to see him."

There was a knock at the door and Jonathon came in. Mike slapped him on the back, then left. As the door opened, Addy saw Secret Service men flanking the hallway.

Jonathon's eyes were wide with concern and Addy felt her face flush. How embarrassing.

"I'm fine, really." Addy tried unsuccessfully to smooth her hair into a makeshift ponytail as he came in and sat in the chair beside the hospital bed. "I just feel like an idiot."

"Addy, you got bit by a poisonous spider. You were really sick. We were all worried. How could you feel like an idiot?"

"I'm in the hospital because of a *spider* bite. It's so stupid."

"Hank's been telling me you're a pain in the butt for weeks," Jonathon said. "Little did I know how right he was."

"Ha ha," Addy conceded. "You didn't need to come,

though. I'm fine. Just resting to make sure my skin doesn't fall off and die."

"That would make bathing suit season uncomfortable, huh?"

Addy laughed again, then held her stomach. All the vomiting had left her muscles sore.

Jonathon sat up straight. "Are you okay? Do you need me to call a nurse?"

"Yes. Tell her your jokes are making me sick."

He rolled his eyes. "Nice to see you're back to your old self."

They talked for almost an hour. Addy couldn't believe how comfortable she was around Jonathon. She completely forgot she was lying in a hospital bed, probably pasty white and smelly.

A knock on the door signaled it was time for Jonathon to leave. The Top Ten names were being announced tonight with or without Addy. Jonathon had to be at The Mansion dressed and ready to go by seven o'clock.

"Thanks for coming, Jonathon." Addy smiled. "I really appreciate it."

"No problem." He returned the smile, his perfectly straight, perfectly white teeth sparkling beneath his perfectly formed lips. "I'll be here all week. Try the veal."

"So lame," Addy said as Jonathon was escorted out of the room and down the hall.

A nurse came in before the door closed. "Excuse me," the nurse said with a smile. "Is our celebrity ready to have her blood pressure and temperature taken?"

Addy nodded, but was sure both would be quite elevated at the moment.

Chapter 40

"Not that I want to be bitten by a poisonous spider ever again," Addy said after taking a sip of her strawberry smoothie, "but this is a much better way to watch the show than having to sit through it on the lawn of The Mansion."

Mike was on her left side, and Lexi's face filled the computer screen at her right side. Addy was propped up on pillows and given her choice of items on the "black market" hospital menu. Addy chose a smoothie and a grilled chicken sandwich.

A camera crew was dispatched to the hospital. Hank had made sure they brought a red daisy along—"just in case."

Ruby had come too, trying to make Addy look presentable

while only being allowed to take a sponge bath and change into a robe.

"Honey, I've had to do with less," she said. "A little powder and a whole lot of hair spray, and voilà." Ruby surveyed her work with a smile.

Addy watched Hank welcome the girls and recap the episode from the night before. He spoke about Addy's spider bite—as little as possible and without even a hint of sympathy.

I'm sure Hank thinks I did this on purpose, just to get attention. Love your enemies, love your enemies. Oh, Lord, that is so hard.

Heather was the first to receive the good-bye daisy, then Hannah.

"Uncle Mike, I haven't really thought much about whether or not I'll stay on," Addy said during the next commercial break. "But with America voting, I don't know if I will. I mean, I love Tampa, but my life looked pretty dull next to the other girls'."

"Who put you on this show, girl?"

"God." Addy nodded, knowing where her uncle was going.

"And who will keep you on, if it's his will?"

"God."

"So who needs to worry?"

"Not me." Addy smiled. "You're right. Red daisy or not, this has been amazing. I could leave now and not have one regret."

Except that I haven't actually told anyone I'm a Christian. I've made a couple of friends, but have I really done what you brought me here to do, God? Addy knew the answer to that question.

The commercial break ended and two more girls were asked to leave. Hank's favorites, Lila and Anna Grace, were still there, as was Kara. And Addy.

"I just have one more daisy for you to give away, Jonathon." Hank looked at the girls and paused as the camera panned the faces of the eleven who remained. The red light on the camera in Addy's room lit up, and she saw herself on TV, watching TV.

"Tonight," Hank began, "the last girl going home is . . . Tricia."

That young woman clutched her chest and cried as she walked over to where Hank and Jonathon were standing.

"And these"—Hank motioned to the girls beside him—"are your top ten choices for *The Book of Love*."

The red light came on again, and Addy looked at the camera and smiled.

"We're just two weeks away from learning who will be our First Son's prom date." Hank sat next to Lila. "So tune in next week for more excitement, more drama, and another chapter of . . .

"*The Book of Love*."

Chapter 41

Addy spent Friday night in the hospital reading some more of her mother's journals.

We have finally started to make some headway with the medicine man. Last week, one of the little girls in the village was sick. Kie is a beautiful little doll the whole village just adores. The medicine man was sure he could cure her with a mixture of herbs, but she just got worse. Her mother came to us, crying. Kie was lying in her arms, completely limp. She was burning with fever and could barely even open her eyes. Her mother begged us to help. Josh had a vial of antibiotics, and he was able to give her a shot. Kie's mother was nervous about the needle. If I had never seen one before, I would be too. But she let us help sweet little Kie, and by the next day the fever had broken. Praise God. The little girl was well, and the entire village began to see that we weren't the crazy people the medicine man wanted them to believe we were.

Josh went to the medicine man yesterday and asked if he could show Josh around. Josh is interested in learning more about the herbal remedies of the medicine man, so the two of them have gone off together to find roots and berries and who knows what else. Josh is so good. He could have been angry at that man. Like I was. But he was faithful to God and what God called us to do, and now we have an ally instead of an enemy. If we can only get them to listen to what we have to say about Jesus.

Addy wanted to know more about how her parents shared their faith. Skimming through a few more pages, she found an entry that talked about that.

We will have our first Bible study tonight! Of course, they don't know it's a Bible study. Their belief system is so different, we have to start at the beginning, in Genesis, then go on. The villagers here believe in many gods, and they believe those gods can be manipulated by people. Helping them understand that the true God is one to serve, not to manipulate, will be a difficult hurdle to overcome.

Intrigued, Addy picked up another journal and flipped through.

We have gotten to Jesus! Finally! And our friends were so ready. As we walked through the Old Testament, they recognized the sacrificial rites. They understand that we are all sinners. They also saw that, even with all the sacrifices the Israelites gave to God, they were still not completely righteous. Last week, Pichka said, "They need a savior." My heart sang. I have been praying all week that as we get to this portion of Scripture, our dear friends will see that they need a savior. And that they see they have a savior. Father God, prepare their hearts for the truth.

Addy noticed there were times when several months went by without her mother writing.

We had malaria. Again. Thankfully I was over it before Josh returned. I don't know what we'd do if we were both sick at the same time. Dito would help, I know. But he still doesn't believe in all of our medicine. Nor does he know where we keep the pills for malaria outbreaks. God knows, though, and never gives us more than we can handle.

A few pages later, Addy read a heartbreaking entry, just a few sentences in length.

Lost the baby today. There are no words. I knew carrying a child here would be hard. We told no one. I didn't even write it down here because I was afraid. And now those fears have come true. Will I ever have a child, God?

Uncle Mike walked in as Addy finished reading.

"I had an older brother or sister." Addy handed him the journal.

"I know." Mike nodded. "Your mom came home not long after that."

"Was she sick?"

"Not exactly. But the grief on top of the malaria and other physical hardships had just worn her down. She came home to rest and get some help."

"I had no idea," Addy said.

"Life is hard, baby. Jesus never told us otherwise."

"But he promised to be with us."

"That's exactly what your mama said after she came out of that dark time. 'If God is for me, who can be against me?'" Mike wiped a tear from his eye. "She went back and saw dozens of people come to Christ. She was even able to help some of the other women in the village who had lost children."

Help me, God, to be half the Christian my parents were. Show me how to be a missionary to my "tribe." Tell me what to say.

Chapter 42

Order whatever you want, Addy-girl. You deserve it after all that hospital food." Mike opened the stained menu and looked over the breakfast options.

Addy adjusted the baseball cap on her head, feeling like a movie star in disguise. Mike had told her the only way they could get in and out of a restaurant would be for her to conceal her identity and go someplace only the locals would go. Addy liked the choice. It reminded her of their favorite diner back home, Dinah's. But she hated eating while wearing a baseball cap. Especially one as bright orange as the one Mike had found for her. She had been sure she would stick out. Looking around, however, she saw that as a Tennessee Volunteers fan she blended right in.

Within minutes the pair had plates piled high with biscuits and gravy, scrambled eggs, bacon, and a sliver of an orange.

"Garnish," Mike explained. They took their time eating, neither in a hurry to return to The Mansion. They were just about to pay their bill when a group of three men slipped into the booth on the other side of the wall from them. Greenery separated the tables. From her seat, Addy could see the men, but because of their height, they wouldn't be able to see her.

"You sure this is a safe place?" a man in a hooded sweatshirt asked.

"Look around, moron," another man, wearing a gray sweater and knit cap, said. "Only local yokels come here. We couldn't be safer."

Curiosity taking over, both Addy and Mike put down their napkins and leaned in toward the table where the men sat.

"Okay, here's the deal: The kid always takes the plane back to DC on Sunday. Same routine, same plane. I got a guy on the inside. He's gonna get us in as airport personnel. We wait until the kid is on the plane, then we take him down."

"But I thought we were getting paid to hit the president," the guy in the hooded sweatshirt said.

Addy sucked in her breath so loudly, she was sure the men at the other table would hear. The *assassins* at the other table. Men who wanted to kill Jonathon, then kill his father. Addy thought she was going to pass out. Mike's hand on her knee warned her to remain quiet. He leaned in closer and pulled out his phone, activating the voice recorder.

"Yes, we're getting paid to hit the president," the man in the gray sweater said in a hoarse whisper. "But first we get the kid—we don't kill him, just hurt him. That puts him in the nearest hospital, where we also have a guy on the inside. That's how we get the president."

"What about Secret Service? Won't they be all over him? Especially if his son was just attacked?"

"That's why we set this up as a crazed fan attacking the kid. Nothing at all to do with politics. The kid gets hit because he's on that dumb show. Perfect cover. The dad is too worried about his son to beef up his own security, he goes into the hospital, and wham! We got him."

"All right." The guy in the hooded sweatshirt shoved the silent man next to him. "Got it, Georgie? This is all you once we're in."

Georgie grunted and the men's waiter came up to take their order.

Mike turned off his recorder, hit the wrong button, and was answered with a loud beep. The men jumped up and peered over the bushes at Addy and Mike. Addy's heart began to beat so quickly, she could barely catch her breath.

Mike looked down at his phone and drawled, "Dang cell phone. I just got her yesterday and I can't do a thing with her. I'm trying to get ahold of my boss, and it keeps beeping on me. I'm gonna go deaf. You boys know any-thing about these kinds of cell phones?" He held his phone out to them.

The men looked at Mike, at each other, then sat back down without saying a word. Mike, staying in character, made a snide comment about "rude Yankees," paid the bill, and walked—slowly—out of the restaurant.

Addy followed Mike's lead, her head down with the bright orange bill from her cap hiding her beet-red face. She forced herself to breathe in and breathe out as they made their way to Mike's car.

Once inside, Addy exploded. "Mike, they're going to—Jonathon—the airport—tomorrow is Sunday." She couldn't continue. Mike squeezed her shoulder as he pulled out of the parking lot and dialed Eric's number.

Ten minutes later a plan was in place. Addy and Mike were on their way to a secure location to give the recording and their statement to the Secret Service. Eric was meeting with the security officers at The Mansion.

The place was empty because the girls were all in Dallas for the week's shoot. Addy hadn't been able to go because of her spider bite.

You even orchestrated that, God. If I hadn't been in the hospital, Mike and I never would have been in the restaurant today, and this plan may have actually taken place.

"Now, Addy, listen to me," Mike said as they made their way inside. "This has to stay quiet. You can't tell anybody. Not Lexi, not Kara, especially not Jonathon."

"But why?" Addy bit her lip. "Shouldn't the First Family know about this?"

"The president knows. But he doesn't want to worry the others. And he doesn't want word of this to leak. This is top secret. Got it?"

Addy nodded and did the only thing she could think might help—pray.

ᕲ

"Can you hear me?"

Addy coughed—the signal that Mike told Addy meant yes—into her mouthpiece.

"Okay, good. Now just act natural."

Addy tugged at the long blond hair in the wig she had been forced to wear, straightened the shiny green polyester shirt and white jeans, and tried not to laugh. She felt about as far from "natural" as she could get. Rectangular glasses emphasizing her heavily made-over eyes completed her disguise, ensuring that no one in the world would know she was Addy Davidson.

Addy herself had to look twice when the Secret Service wardrobe team had finished with her. Since she already knew about the planned attempt on Jonathon's life, the Secret Service wanted to use her to help fill in the small airport where Jonathon's private plane was to take off. They knew the assassins would be suspicious if the only people there were middle-aged men, so Addy was planted as a "typical teen" reading a gossip magazine—with her face on the cover—and texting on her cell phone as she waited for the next flight out.

Because of Mike's years in the military and as a police officer, the Secret Service had allowed him to be armed and ready as backup in case any part of the takedown went wrong. Addy had prayed all night that the assassins would be caught and everyone would be safe. She had never been so scared in her life.

"No autographs, please. Just let us through." This was

Addy's cue. The Secret Service agents on either side of the Jonathon decoy passed her. Addy looked up, surprised to see how closely this young man resembled the real Jonathon.

"Jonathon Jackson!" Addy tried her best to sound like a naive young southerner. "Oh, please, sirs, just one autograph. I'm your biggest fan. Really." Addy dug in her purse while standing directly in front of "Jonathon." This, she was told, would keep the assassins from seeing his face clearly and also serve as a distraction while the Secret Service men hidden on the plane prepared to make the arrests.

"No autographs, young lady."

"No, really, it's fine." The Jonathon decoy took the magazine from Addy and pulled a pen from the agent's pocket. "Thanks for watching the show. So who do you think I should take to prom?"

This was the cue for Addy to move to the side, blocking the ticket agent's view. Addy had noted earlier that the ticket agent was actually the man in the hooded sweatshirt from the restaurant.

"Oh, Jonathon." Addy giggled, thinking surely everyone around knew she was faking. "I think you should take me."

She tried to hug the decoy when the Secret Service agents squeezed him between their two sets of broad shoulders and said to the ticket agent, "We've got to get him on this plane. I'm just going to take him straight back."

"Oh, no problem, sir." The would-be assassin watched the men make their way down the ramp and onto the small private plane.

She turned to leave, knowing her instructions were to hide out in the bathroom as soon as her part was finished, when she heard a commotion from inside the plane. Men shouted, then a gun went off.

Addy was glued to the floor when she saw Eric out of the corner of her eye. He was holding a small video camera with one hand. With the other, he motioned for her to get out of the gate.

Addy ran to the bathroom. She pushed the button on her earpiece and screamed Mike's name. She clamped a hand over her mouth, embarrassed that she had been so loud.

"Addy, I'm fine. Relax," Mike said. "I'm in the same spot I've been in. They didn't even need me."

"But the gunshot . . ." Her heart pounded. She cracked the bathroom door open as several Secret Service agents exited the plane, each holding a cursing, handcuffed, would-be assassin.

"No one was hurt," Mike said, leaving the counter. "You can come out. It's all over."

Addy's knees gave way beneath her and she fell to the ground.

Jonathon was going to be all right.

Tears stung her eyes. Maybe it was time to admit just how important he was to her.

Chapter 43

Addy woke on Wednesday morning in her trailer. The girls would not return till tomorrow. Mike still had jobs he had to perform at The Mansion, so Addy was left to spend her day in silence.

I've forgotten what quiet is like. Addy laughed to herself.

She spent her morning reading her Bible. She found a Bible study online and was enjoying learning more about the book of John. Though she had read through the book before, she felt like she was seeing it with new eyes. Throughout the book, Jesus told people who he was, he showed people who he was, and yet they still rejected him. And the worst offenders of all were the religious.

Addy saw herself in those Pharisees. *God, please help me be more like you and less like those hypocritical religious leaders.*

In the afternoon Addy completed her schoolwork. She took breaks to stretch and walk around the grounds. She tried to call Lexi but her friend was working.

I'm so bored.

Out of the blue, Uncle Mike pulled up in his truck.

"Addy, come with me." He opened the side door.

"Where are we going?" Addy jumped in, not even caring what the answer would be.

"Top secret." Mike pulled out of the long driveway and onto the street. "I don't even know what's going on. I just know I'm dropping you off and someone else will take over from there."

Twenty minutes later, Mike stopped on what appeared to be a road to nowhere.

"All right." Mike walked around to Addy's door and opened it. "You're here."

"What?"

"Just get out."

Addy stepped out and peered around Mike's truck. A black SUV pulled up beside Addy and the front window rolled down.

"Come on, then," a very stern-looking man said, motioning with his head for her to get in.

Addy wanted to run. Were these friends of the assassins who discovered she was behind the plot being discovered and they were out to "take care of her"?

"I said, get in." The man leaned a huge black arm out of the window. Addy looked toward Mike. He was already back in the truck, driving off. She looked toward the road in the direction they had just come. Could she outrun the guy in the SUV? She doubted it.

"Is there a problem?"

"Um, I-I think I'd rather just go back. If you don't mind. Please." Addy backed up.

"Hey, man, she's really scared. We'd better drop the act." The stern-looking man got out of the SUV and opened its back door, revealing Jonathon laughing hysterically.

"That was classic." He wiped tears from his eyes but couldn't stop laughing. "Classic. You should have seen your face. I haven't laughed that hard in a long time."

"What is going on? What are you talking about?"

Addy was too confused to feel any of the other emotions vying for a spot in her brain.

"Just get in, I'll explain," Jonathon said.

Addy hopped into the backseat of the vehicle and buckled up.

"What is going on? And why are you laughing? I don't see anything funny at all about this."

Jonathon sobered and looked at Addy. "I wanted to see you, but I couldn't just show up at The Mansion. I had to get you in secret."

"Why did it have to be in secret?" Addy asked.

"Because he's the president's son and everything he does has to be in secret," the man from the front seat interjected.

"Meet Bull, my favorite Secret Service agent." Jonathon gave Bull a fist bump and the driver grunted.

"I like you too, Jeff." Jonathon patted the driver's

shoulder. "But Bull and I go way back. He's guarded me since we moved into the White House. He's really more like a mean older brother than an agent."

"Hey, watch it, pip-squeak. I've been trained to kill a man with one hand." Bull flexed his arm and Jonathon pushed it away.

"Anyway, as I was saying, I wanted to see you, but I wasn't sure how. So I talked to Bull. He said no one could know my location, so Mike could only drive you part of the way out. So I came up with the idea . . ."

Bull coughed. "What?"

"Bull came up with the idea that we meet out here and keep it all a secret from you. Like a spy movie. Remember how you said you wished that phone I gave you was in a shoe, like in a movie? So I thought you'd enjoy this."

"You thought I'd enjoy this?" Addy said. "I was scared to death. I have heart problems, Jonathon. I could have had an attack out here."

"Heart problems? I had no idea. I'm so sorry." Jonathon's face turned white and Addy leaned back, crossing her arms in victory. Bull started laughing.

"She got you!" Bull put a fist up in Addy's direction and she bumped him back.

"No heart problems?"

"None at all." Addy smiled. "No kidnapping?"

"Just a little First Family fun," Jonathon said.

"So no one can know your location . . . ?"

"Right. Top secret, you know. Plus, I'm supposed to be in DC right now, but my plans got changed for some reason. So I left Dallas and came here this morning. I heard you were out at The Mansion all by yourself. And I'm out here all by myself."

"Excuse me?"

"Sorry, Bull. I'm not by myself. But . . ."

"But Bull isn't a pretty little girl you want to flirt with?"

Jonathon turned red and punched Bull in the arm.

"Did you hit me, or did a little butterfly just land on my arm? I can't quite tell the difference."

Addy laughed and Jonathon continued. "Anyway, I was bored and I thought you might be too, so I decided we might as well hang out together than be bored apart."

"Aw, now, Jeff, isn't that sweet?" Bull said.

Jeff grunted.

"So sweet."

Jonathon didn't say much more until the SUV arrived at his "compound"—a large ranch-style house surrounded by a gate and several agents wearing black suits.

"Come on in the kitchen. We ordered in Chinese. I hope you like that."

As the pair settled in, Bull and Jeff retreated into the living room—close enough to protect but far enough to give the couple a semblance of privacy.

Addy scooped some fried rice onto her plate. "So what have you been doing this week?"

"Like I said, I just got back from Dallas. It's one-hour date week, and I had to go all over the Metroplex so the dates wouldn't all be in the same location. It might have been fun if we could have actually looked around some. I think the girls got to, but I was shuffled from the West

End to the stockyards to Six Flags so fast, I barely had time to even notice where I was. What about you?"

I can't tell him what I really did. What do I say?

"Well, I—"

"How about some horseback riding, kiddos?" Bull rounded the corner, phone to his ear. "We just got the all clear. There's a great trail not far from here and it's secure. This place has some beautiful horses just sitting out in the stables doing nothing. What do you think?"

"That sounds great." Addy finished the last of her orange chicken and stood. "But my spider bite. Give me a minute to add an extra layer of bandages to it."

"I forgot about that." Jonathon stood. "Forget it. We can do something else."

"No, no. I've never gone horseback riding before. I don't want a little bite to stop me. I'll just be a minute."

Addy took out all the gauze in her purse, went to the bathroom, and plastered it to her bite. When she was sure she was well protected, Addy returned to the kitchen. "I'm ready," she announced.

"Well, let's go." Bull walked toward the door.

"Wait." Jonathon stopped. "Let me check my fortune cookie. Hmm, it says, 'Bull who ride horse can sometimes be a little chicken.'"

"Hey, now," Bull said. "I can kill a man with—"

"With one hand, I know." Jonathon smirked.

"Good thing you're not a man," Addy chimed in, earning her yet another fist bump from Bull.

Thirty minutes later, Jonathon, Addy, Bull, and Jeff were mounted on horses and trotting through the woods.

Jonathon, of course, was completely comfortable and confident on his horse. Even the Secret Service agents seemed at home. Addy, on the other hand, was trying desperately to stay on. Her horse's saddle kept tipping to the side, and she twisted in her seat every five minutes, trying to right herself. But when she did that, she pulled the reins in the direction she was going, and the horse walked that way. Once, she almost ran into a tree. Another time, her horse walked right into the side of Jeff's, who only grunted and moved his horse farther away.

"Ready to gallop?" Jonathon nudged his horse and took off into a meadow. Bull followed him and Jeff stayed behind, trotting along beside Addy.

"I'll just catch up," Addy called out, absolutely sure that the only time she wanted extra horsepower was when she was behind the wheel of a car, not on the back of an actual horse.

After an hour and a half of riding, a very sore Addy dismounted. "I can't straighten my legs." Her entire lower half was in rebellion against her. Her bandages had shifted as much as her saddle, leaving her spider-bitten bottom quite sore and making walking that much more difficult.

"Give it a few minutes." Jonathon gave his horse to the lady waiting at the stable, then reached for Addy's.

"I like golf better. And golf carts. I really like golf carts."

After a light dinner, Bull announced that Mike was on his way to the meeting spot.

"I guess you have to go," Jonathon said.

"I guess so."

Neither moved. Finally Bull walked over to Jonathon's chair and shook him out.

"Boy, stop acting like she's going off to the moon. We're just taking her back to The Mansion. You'll see her again."

Jonathon's face turned red. "Thanks, Bull."

Addy said her good-byes with more hope than she'd had before.

The president's son might actually like me. Me!

Chapter 44

I missed you." Kara hugged Addy. "Don't leave me all alone with those girls again, all right?"

"I'll do my best," Addy said.

"And no more going into the woods." Kara pointed her finger in Addy's face. "Mom said people have died from brown recluse bites."

Here's the opening I've been praying for, God.

"Do you want to know the reason why I'm all right?" "Sure, Addy, I'd love to." "It's because God was protecting me. You see, I'm a Christian, Kara." "Wow, really, Addy? Could I be one too?"

Right. That's exactly how it'll happen. Oh, Lord, why is this so hard?

"Addy? Did that bite mess with your brain?" Kara waved her hand in front of Addy's face. "Hello. I'm still here."

Addy laughed. "No. I just need to tell you something, and I'm nervous. So I was planning how I was going to say it."

"Wow, you really do think too much." Kara shook her head. "You can tell me anything."

Kara sat on her bed, and Addy lowered herself next to her, her heart hammering in her chest. *Why am I so scared, God? Help me. This is my friend, and what I'm going to tell her is the good news.*

"I'm a Christian." Addy held her breath and waited for Kara's reply.

"Okay." Kara looked at Addy, her eyebrows knit together. "I kind of thought so. I mean, you read a Bible. Who does that? And your parents, they were like missionaries, right?"

Addy nodded, her stomach still in knots.

"Why are you acting like it's such a big deal? You look more scared than you did right before your kazoo solo."

"I was worried it would change our friendship."

"Only if you're going to start treating me like a project instead of a friend," Kara said, her perfectly tweezed eyebrows arched.

"A project?"

"Yeah, once I had this friend who was a Christian, but she didn't really care about me, she just wanted to 'save my soul.' She kept coming at me with Bible verses and horror stories about hell, but when she finally saw I wasn't interested, she was done with me." Kara used her long arms to punctuate her story.

"I'm sorry your friend did that. That's not how Christians should treat people."

"I know you're not like her, Addy." Kara smiled. "You're just about one of the most amazing people I've ever met."

"Thanks, Kara." Addy looked at her friend. "I believe God has a plan for your life, and that his plan is so much better than anything you could ever imagine. I don't want you to miss out on that."

"I'm just not interested, okay? I'm happy with my life the way it is."

All right, God. What do I say? "If you're right, no big deal, but if you're wrong, huge, enormous, horrible deal"? No, I can't scare her into believing. I've got to just keep praying for her. I don't want to be like that friend she had. "Okay."

"That didn't sound like an 'okay' okay. That sounded like an 'I don't like it, but I have to say okay' okay." Kara nudged Addy with her shoulder. "We're still friends, right? You're not going to drop me because I don't believe the same as you, are you?"

Addy reached over and hugged her friend. "Never. But I will be praying for you."

"I guess I can handle that," Kara said. "Will you pray that I make it to the Top Five?"

The girls laughed, then Addy asked to know about the week she had missed. Kara told Addy about the fun she'd had in Dallas, her favorite part being the two days the girls spent at Six Flags.

"The roller coasters were amazing. But I wish you could have been there to go on them with me."

"No, you don't." Addy stood and paced the length of the trailer. "I don't even ride merry-go-rounds. No way would you get me on a roller coaster."

"Oh, well, then it was a good week for you to miss, I guess."

"Interesting how God worked that out, huh?" Addy smiled.

"Or just plain old good luck," Kara retorted. "Oh, I almost forgot—there was some major drama this morning." Kara crossed to the bed, her eyes wide.

"Lila?"

"No, none of the girls, actually. One of the guards. Yours, as a matter of fact," Kara said.

"Mike?"

"Apparently Mike has been making Hank mad for a while. But when we all got off the bus, Hank was giving us orders and Mike turned to walk away. I don't know why. But Hank tore into him like you've never seen. And we've seen a lot from *him*."

"He yelled at Mike?"

"At the top of his lungs," Kara said. "Hank told Mike the only reason he was still here this week was because his replacement couldn't come in yet. But he swore to not only fire him but also make sure he never worked anywhere ever again."

I'm sure Mike wasn't too intimidated by that. But still, Hank has no right to treat Uncle Mike that way.

"I think Hank would have hit the guy if he wasn't so big. Hank probably worried that Mike would mess up his pretty face." Kara laughed but stopped when she saw Addy's face.

"Addy, what's wrong? I know he was your guard and all, but . . ."

"He's not just my guard. He's my uncle."

Kara stood, her hands over her mouth. "What? Why didn't you tell me? I can't believe . . . I mean . . . what?" She sat back down, waiting for an explanation.

"It's a long story," Addy said, trying to regain her composure. "Eric called him the second week. He's a cop."

"But how did you guys keep it secret? Didn't Hank know you two were related?"

"Hank doesn't read our files, Kara. He leaves that to the 'little people.'"

"True." Kara grabbed Addy's hand. "Wow. I'm sorry. I had no idea."

What do I do, God? Uncle Mike came out here to help me and instead gets screamed at and treated like dirt. He doesn't deserve that. Why was Hank so angry? She could tell he was miserable. He wanted control so badly he lashed out at anyone he thought was trying to take that control from him. But why?

Kara, noticing Addy wanted some time to think, left the trailer. On a whim, Addy flipped open her laptop and typed in "Hank Banner." There were dozens of hits.

As Addy skimmed the various articles, blogs, and websites, she learned that Hank hated God. Dozens of websites revealed his hate, the source of his hatred, the reasons and rantings about it.

"I am my own god," he announced in a webzine article. "I have finally realized that it is a waste of time to serve some fabricated deity. My time is better spent devoting myself to me."

Addy thought of Hank's tirades and constant pandering to the press and wished that he could see how useless a life devoted to self really was.

Addy shut her computer, feeling overwhelmed.

Hank isn't just a mean guy; he hates the God I love. The God who created Hank, whether he believes in him or not. No wonder he interrupted Uncle Mike while he was praying that day. That's probably why he doesn't like Mike to begin with.

Addy wasn't sure how to pray, or what to do to help her uncle. Even after her talk with Kara, Addy still worried about sharing her faith. She especially feared sharing her faith in public. But she sensed that, somehow, she would need to do just that.

Fear tore at the pit of her stomach. She needed to walk around to clear her head.

Chapter 45

A ddy had walked only a few steps when she saw a very angry Hank walking toward the guards' trailers.

I guess now wouldn't be a good time to talk to him. He looks so mad. I hope he's not going off to yell at Uncle Mike again.

"Addy, over here."

Déjà vu.

Jonathon stood at the door of the editing trailer, motioning Addy in.

"You'll never believe this." Jonathon pulled out a leather chair for her before sitting in one himself. "I had to tell someone. This is unbelievable."

"What's unbelievable?" Addy said, intrigued by Jonathon's excited demeanor. "Tell me."

"Okay." Jonathon paced the trailer. "I woke up early this morning. I couldn't sleep. Not sure why. Anyway, the guys in editing have been sending me the raw footage of the show, and I have it all saved on my laptop. So I decided to take some of the 'throwaway' footage and play with it. I may not be able to be an editor for a living, but it can be a hobby, right?"

Addy nodded and motioned for him to continue his story.

"So I found this file under Trash marked Top Secret. I'm not even sure how it got to my computer. I'm sure it was accidently sent. But I couldn't resist, you know?" He laughed. "At first, I thought it was a TV show. Then I realized what it was." Jonathon leaned forward, his eyes bright. "Addy, a few days ago there was an attempt on my life, and the Secret Service guys found out and stopped it."

Addy tried to look surprised as she saw on-screen the scene she had viewed from the bathroom door: the would-be assassins being taken off the airplane by Secret Service agents.

"Eric just happened to call as I was watching it, so I asked if he knew about it and he said he did, but that I wasn't supposed to."

Addy remembered Eric had been filming the takedown.

"I said I had just found out and I wanted to thank the person responsible. He told me your guard, Mike, had discovered the plot. Mike! So I asked Eric to find Hank so he could help me get something together for Mike."

Addy was beginning to piece things together. Jonathon's excitement coupled with Hank's earlier anger suddenly made sense. Addy laughed at God's sense of humor.

"You think this is funny?"

"No, no, of course not. You're just so animated."

"Well, if you'd discovered some terrorists were trying to kill *you* and your life was saved, you'd be pretty animated too," Jonathon said. "Now, can I finish my story?"

Addy nodded.

"So I found Hank and told him I had a big favor to ask. Someone had done something great for me and I wanted to repay him. Hank was really listening and agreeing with everything I said about rewarding this guy."

Sure he was. Hank assumed you were talking about him.

"So I asked him what he thought we should do for the man on staff who had proven himself so invaluable. Hank started clapping and racing around the trailer, saying the guy should get a special segment at the end of next week's show so America could see a little behind the scenes. Most people don't know all the work that goes into making one of these shows, you know?"

Addy agreed, smiling so broadly her cheeks ached.

"I thought that was brilliant. I told him I wanted to edit it myself, as part of the thank-you. Hank was thrilled at that idea. But then, it was weird . . ." Jonathon shook his head. "I told him the guy I wanted to thank was Mike, and Hank's whole face just fell. I guess he was thinking of someone else. I don't know. He shook it off, though. So I told him to grab Mike and get some shots of him at work and interview him about the plot."

Addy wanted to jump up and dance. But she controlled herself, focusing instead on Jonathon and his story.

"Wait a minute," she said. "Are you sure you're allowed

to discuss an assassination attempt on TV? I mean, doesn't your dad want to keep that kind of thing out of the public eye?"

"I called him this morning, right after I found the footage. He said the Secret Service guys do like to keep that stuff quiet, and that he didn't tell me because he thought it would scare me. I reminded him that I *am* seventeen."

Addy raised her eyebrows. "I'm sure he loved being reminded of that."

"We actually had a great conversation. At first, he didn't want me to make this public. But I told him that America needs to know about the brave men working behind the scenes to keep us safe, and he agreed. After some intense discussion, of course."

"Wow, sounds like a great talk." Addy smiled.

"It was." Jonathon pulled out his phone and scrolled through his messages.

"Oh, look at this." He showed her his phone. "Since we didn't get our one-hour date, Eric says he needs a shot of us talking for the show tomorrow."

"It's terrible that we didn't get that hour." Addy laughed.

"Too bad no one was filming you on that horse," Jonathon said. "I'd like to see that again."

"Very funny. Why couldn't someone have filmed that?"

"The other girls would be very angry, for one." Jonathon stretched his back. "And second, if someone recognized any landmarks, our security would be compromised."

"You really do have to be careful about everything."

"Tell me about it."

"I'm sorry."

Jonathon sat next to Addy. "Yes, it's too bad I have to spend another hour with you."

"So where are you taking me?"

Jonathon looked at his phone. "Eric said he's pressed for time, so he just wants to film in The Mansion. How about we meet up there in half an hour? I have some more work I need to do on this package for Mike."

Addy left, her heart lighter than it had been in days. Mike was going to be spotlighted on national TV, earning the praise he deserved for uncovering the assassination plot. And she was getting more time with Jonathon.

Walking back to her trailer, the morning sun making the dew on the grass sparkle like diamonds, Addy thought of how amazing it was that God was involved in every detail of their lives.

What were the chances that Jonathon "just happened" to find that particular piece of footage? Or that Mike and I "just happened" to be in that diner at the same time as the assassins? You had this all planned, God. Every bit of it. You are looking out for Jonathon's life and Mike's reputation. How could I ever doubt you?

Chapter 46

So, Dallas." Kara met Addy at the catering table, and Addy insisted on hearing all about her week away. "It was pretty fun. Although the other girls kept trying to pull me to the dark side."

Addy nodded. "I'm sure. Do I even want to know what they're saying about me now?"

"You planned the whole thing, of course." Kara bit into a granola bar. "The spider bite, the hospital stay. All planned. Maybe not even real. You're just so desperate for attention, you'll do anything."

"Of course." Addy grabbed a Diet Coke and sat on the lawn. "The pictures of me throwing up in the van on the way to the hospital were just the kind of press I was hoping for."

"Those were pretty disgusting."

"They think I faked all that?" Addy asked.

"It's Hank, really." Kara finished off a bottle of water. "He's got some kind of deal going with Lila and her parents. He is doing everything he can to make sure she wins, and you are messing that up."

"Look at these." Kara pulled up the Internet on her phone, showing Addy pictures of Lila. "Here she is cutting a ribbon at a store's grand opening. Do you think any of the rest of us got to do that?"

"No?"

"No." Kara scrolled down and found more pictures of Lila. "We are supposed to be keeping up with our school-work or calling home. Meanwhile, little Miss Hawaii goes anywhere she wants."

"You sound upset." Addy nudged her friend.

"Wouldn't you be?" Kara looked at her friend. "What am I saying? Of course you wouldn't."

Kara scrolled through her phone again and then handed it to Addy. "I do have something Lila doesn't have. Randall."

Addy looked at the tiny screen and saw a teenage boy staring back.

"It's a YouTube video," Kara explained, pushing the Play button. "Seventy-five thousand hits in the last three days, and it's all for me."

"Kara," Randall rapped. Very badly. "Yo, yo, wassup. This is Randall. Yeah, that's my handle. If that Johnny don't choose you, he's a foo', I know that's true. But, girl, I got your back, and I'll take you wit' me. Don't ya see? Randall and Kara are meant to be."

Randall flexed what Addy guessed were supposed to be his muscles. But because Randall had no body fat to be seen, the move was laughable.

"Girl, you make me crazies. I'll buy you lots of daisies." Those flowers filled the screen, then Randall's face appeared in the center.

"Is this for real?" Addy laughed as the next video paused to load.

"Oh, it gets better," Kara said.

"Kara McKormick, I've been on the floor sick, my love for you is not dormant. Oh, Kara. I love you. Go wit' me to the prom. You and me, we'll be the bomb. I'll bring a flower for your mom if you go wit' me to prom."

Addy wiped tears from her eyes as Randall knelt in the dirt, wildflowers in his hand, singing loudly and off key. "Ka-a-a-r-a. I'll be your prom date. Your prom date. Oh, girl, I'm here for you . . ." The last note was so high Addy was sure Kara's screen would break.

"And that's just the first one." Kara giggled.

"What?"

"Oh yes. Randall has posted a new video every day for the last three days."

"He really wants to take you to prom," Addy said.

"I'll go too."

"What?"

"Why not?" she argued. "We'd both get tons of publicity. And then maybe next year I could be on *Book of Love 2* choosing *my* date to senior prom."

"But he's crazy."

"I'm not going to marry him," Kara said. "Besides, he's

probably just doing it for the attention. Maybe we'll both get our own shows."

"I hope you'll be very happy together."

"Don't worry." Kara patted Addy's back. "I'll let you be on the show with me. You can be my conscience, making sure I don't make any bad choices."

"No thanks. I've had all the reality TV I can handle."

Chapter 47

"You may have noticed that Addy here wasn't in Dallas with us." Hank looked into the camera with a mock frown at the end of the evening's episode of *The Book of Love.*

"While the other girls were having a great time in the Dallas–Fort Worth Metroplex, Addy was back here in Nashville. Our first hospital visit of the show."

Shots of Addy being wheeled into the hospital filled the screen behind Hank.

Maybe it's not circus music in the background, but it is definitely comical. Hank must have supervised this edit himself.

"After taking a walk in the Tennessee woods, Addy was bitten by a poisonous brown recluse spider. The great team of doctors at Nashville Medical Center was able to find and treat the bite, and now Addy is back with us, safe and sound."

Hank turned to Addy, microphone shoved in her face. "How are you feeling now, Addy? All better?"

"I am. Thanks, Hank."

"It's amazing that you recovered so quickly. Just in time to be back on the show tonight."

Addy looked around and saw the other girls smirking in her direction. "Actually, I was released—"

"Sorry, Addy, your time is up." Hank pulled the microphone away and gazed at the camera. "Before we open the phone lines so you can vote for your favorite contestant, though, we have a special surprise tonight, put together by the star of the show himself: Jonathon Jackson. I don't want to give anything away, so, Jonathon, come on over and tell us all about it."

"Thanks, Hank. And, Addy, I'm glad to see you back. I spoke to your doctor when I visited the hospital, and he told me how serious that bite was. I'm so grateful for the great medical team here in Nashville."

Jonathon Jackson, I could kiss you right now.

"But Jonathon isn't here to talk about the doctors." Hank motioned for Mike to come forward. "Are you, Jonathon?"

He looked at the camera. "No, Hank. But I am here to thank someone who has saved lives. My life, as a matter of fact."

The camera panned to Mike, who looked uncomfortable in khaki slacks, a polo shirt, and a required-for-the-cameras layer of makeup.

Hank looked like he was about to be sick. Only until he was on camera, of course. At that point, he smiled his extra-bright smile and patted Mike on the back. A little harder than necessary.

"Ladies and gentlemen, I want to introduce you to Mike Scott." Jonathon put his arm around Mike's shoulders. "He is responsible for uncovering a plot against my family. Had the plot succeeded, my father, the president of the United States, would have been assassinated." Jonathon let that fact linger before continuing. "But thanks to his bravery, and the help of Secret Service agents, the assassins were discovered and imprisoned."

A short segment followed with Jonathon's voice-over detailing Mike's years of service to his country, ending with a moving rendition of "God Bless America" playing behind the footage of the assassins being captured.

"Thank you, Mike," Jonathon said as the cameras once again faced him. "I thank you as an American, and I thank you as a son." The two embraced and the cameras turned to Hank.

"Thank you, Jonathon." Hank smiled. "And thank *you*, Mike. Aren't we grateful for men like him?" The girls stood and clapped, Addy leading the way.

"Now, don't forget to vote tonight for your favorite contestant. The phone lines open in just a few minutes and voting will continue for two hours. Those votes will be tallied to reveal our Top Five! So vote tonight and tune in tomorrow for the next chapter in"—Hank motioned for the girls to join in—"*The Book of Love.*"

Chapter 48

Eric yelled, "Cut!" and the top ten girls, relieved at having their "sit in the living room and talk" time over, all gathered their things to leave.

"I've got an interview today with the producers of a new TV show." Lila tossed her long hair in Addy's direction. "That's my second interview this week."

"Congratulations, Lila." Addy pulled her hair back into a ponytail.

"What's that supposed to mean?"

"Just that." Addy looked at Lila. "You are talented. I think a show would be lucky to have you."

Lila paused. "Addy Davidson, don't try to get on my nice side now that you know you're on the way out."

"What?"

"You heard me." Lila walked closer to Addy. "I know you'll do anything for attention. But I'm not Kara. You won't get any help from me."

Lila walked away, a trail of girls in her wake.

"Addy, why do you keep trying with her?" Kara shook her head. "She's terrible."

Before she had a chance to respond, Eric walked up to Addy and whispered, "Your uncle is upstairs."

Addy didn't want to tell him Kara already knew, so there was no need to whisper. So she simply waved good-bye to her friend and walked up the beautiful, curved staircase and down the hallway until she came to a sitting room, complete with chaise longue, two couches, and an armoire.

"Addy-girl." Mike stood from the longue and hugged her.

"Look at this." Addy motioned around the room. "You get presidential treatment now?"

"Pretty much." Mike pointed out the window. "This is where all the guards want to be stationed. I can sit here, listen to Pastor Brian's sermons on my iPod, and watch the gate."

"Celebrity has its privileges, huh?"

"Yes, it does." Mike bounced his knee. "So, what are you thinking about, Addy-girl?"

She looked at the rug. "I was just wondering what Jonathon is doing right now."

"You like that boy."

Addy blushed and Mike asked, "Does he share your faith?"

"I don't know. But I'm going to find out."

"You better." Mike laughed. "And you better pray he

does, or I'm going to have one heartsick little girl on my hands. And you know I don't do well with that."

"Don't worry, Uncle Mike. I'll be fine."

Mike smiled and slapped his hands against the longue.

"I can tell you who doesn't share my faith, though." Addy leaned forward. "I spent some time researching Hank last week. He really hates Christians. I wonder if that's why we've rubbed him the wrong way so much."

"He surely does hate us. You weren't there the other morning, but he yelled and screamed at me like nothing you've ever seen before." Mike shook his head. "I don't even know what I did. If Jonathon hadn't found out that I discovered that assassination plot, I'd be on my way home right now."

"What about the other guards?" she asked. "Is he nice to them?"

"Hank is a mean cuss to everybody. The only time I've seen him treat anyone kindly was when the cameras were around."

Addy nodded. "That's the Hank I know."

"He's so caught up in himself, he can't even think about anyone else." Mike looked out the window. "It's sad, really. But you know what? I've known guys like that before, self-centered and miserable. My guess is that he's been hurt pretty badly by people who claimed to be Christians. Nobody makes Jesus look so bad as those who say they're following him."

"That's true. He did have a lot to say about hypocrites in what I read." Addy sat back in the longue. "But what do we do?"

"I don't know. Neither of us is on his list of favorite people. Let's just try to show Jesus to him, change his opinion of who Christians are and what we do."

"But how? He hates us. I doubt he'd talk to either of us even if we tried."

"Then we should give him something he can't resist." Mike smiled, his mustache twitching.

The pair leaned forward, a perfect plan falling into place.

Chapter 49

I've never been this nervous at one of the shows before, Addy thought as she sat on the lawn of The Mansion, waiting for the Top Five to be announced. *Before now, I was all right either way. But now, God, I want to stay on. For the plan to work, I have to stay on.*

"America, tonight we will announce your choices for Jonathon's Top Five." Hank walked the length of the lawn so the camera would pass each girl.

"You have watched them perform live onstage." Images of the first week's competition filled the screen.

"You have seen their academic and athletic abilities."

The girls laughed as shots of them in the mud played out in front of them.

"You have marveled at their grace and poise."

Please, please, don't show me . . . whew.

"You've met their families, and they have met you."

Music played as the screen showed the girls on their trips home and then in Dallas, signing autographs and hugging fans.

Kara nudged Addy. "See all those shots of Lila?" she whispered.

"And tonight, it all comes down to this. The Top Five. The last set of girls to be chosen before next week's exciting finale. Don't go anywhere, folks. The first elimination will begin in just two minutes."

As soon as Eric yelled, "Cut," the girls began calling for their stylists.

"I know you don't want this." Ruby walked over with a tube of lipstick. "But you just need a little touch-up."

Addy smiled and puckered her lips. "All right."

"Now, don't let these other girls intimidate you." Ruby placed the top on the lipstick, returning it to her makeup case. "You've got my vote, plus the votes of all my family. And that's about half the folks in Muskogee, Oklahoma. We're behind you 100 percent. So sit up straight and smile. Don't look so nervous."

"All right, ladies, we're back in thirty seconds," Eric called.

"I'm goin'," Ruby called as she hurried back to her spot behind the cameras.

All right, God. Help me calm down. I can't stand being this nervous. Help me trust you. I want Hank to see you in me. I want a chance to talk to Jonathon about you. I need to be here another week for that to happen. I really don't care if I win, God. Really. I just want another week. Please.

Thirty minutes later, Addy was one of six remaining. Each time a name was called, she held her breath, beginning to feel light-headed. *Breathe, Addy. Breathe.*

"The final girl going home tonight is . . ." Hank paused and the camera stopped at each girl. Suspenseful music played in the background. No one made a sound. "Is going to be announced right after this break." Hank smiled and Eric yelled, "Cut."

"I can't stand this," Kara said. "The eliminations seem to last longer every week."

Lila looked down the row to Kara. "You have good reason to be nervous. I saw your numbers. Not good."

Kara moved forward and Addy grabbed her hand. "Don't, Kara. It's not worth it."

"Of course," Lila said, looking at Addy, "your numbers are better than Little Miss Muffet's, so you might have a chance."

Kara looked at Addy and raised her eyebrows. "Little Miss Muffet. That's actually pretty good."

"Oh no." Addy laughed. "Please . . ."

"Sure, go back into your little world," Lila interrupted. "It won't be around for long."

Neither girl had time to respond because Eric was back with a "five, four, three, two" and silent "one."

"We started with one hundred hopefuls," Hank began. "One hundred of the best and brightest America had to offer to her First Son. We've watched girl after girl receive her daisy and leave The Mansion, her dreams crushed, her heart broken. Tonight, America, you have narrowed the choices down to five."

Can he possibly drag this out any longer?

"Kara, Addy, Jessica, Anna Grace, Lila, and Dawn." Hank waited for the camera to pause on each face before moving on. "One of you will be leaving tonight."

Jonathon walked out of The Mansion, down the stairs, and over to the girls, the dreaded red daisy in his hand.

"Jonathon, you're the only one who knows which girl that daisy is for," Hank said.

Right. Jonathon and all the producers and the people who work the computers and tally the votes. Everybody around here knows but us. Please, God, speed this up.

"Kara," Jonathon began.

Addy sucked in her breath. *No, not Kara. Please, God. Don't take Kara.*

"You're in the Top Five. Go ahead into The Mansion."

What? Addy watched Kara leave. *They didn't tell us about this. More suspense? At least Kara's safe. Focus on the positive. Focus on the positive.*

Addy tried to catch Jonathon's eye, but he was focused on the job at hand. *Or he's like the juries that come out with a guilty verdict.* Addy thought back to the lawyer shows she'd seen. *They won't look the defendant in the face because they know they're about to send him into prison for the rest of his life. That's what's happening, isn't it? Look at me, Jonathon. One look. Come on.*

"Addy." Jonathon looked at her. And smiled. "You can join your friend in The Mansion. I'll see you next week."

She jumped up from her seat and had to stop herself from hugging Jonathon. He still had a show to do, after all.

"Yes, yes, yes," Kara screamed as soon as the door shut behind Addy. "We're in, Addy. Woo-hoo."

She returned Kara's hug. "I was nervous."

"You were. I've never seen you that nervous. You really want that date, huh?"

"No, I have something I want to do, and I could only do it if I made the Top Five."

Addy

BOL: Welcome, Addy. How are you enjoying your time here at The Mansion?

ADDY: It has been great! I've never been around so much excitement in my life.

BOL: You are from Tampa, Florida, correct?

ADDY: Yes.

BOL: What is something folks down there in Tampa like to do?

ADDY: There's a lot to do—the beach, lots of golf courses, and we have major league football, baseball, and hockey teams. Never a dull moment!

BOL: And which of those is your favorite?

ADDY: Oh, golf, hands down.

BOL: Not the beach?

ADDY: Not really. I guess I take it for granted because it's so close.

BOL: Tell me about golf. How long have you been playing?

ADDY: My uncle bought me my first set of clubs when I was seven. We'd go out on the driving range and hit balls for hours. By the time I was nine, I'd play eighteen holes, right alongside him.

BOL: Impressive. Do you hope to pursue a career in golf?

ADDY: No, I'm not that good. But I hope to be able to keep it up. It's such a relaxing sport, with so many great courses all over the world.

BOL: If you could play any course you wanted, what would it be?

ADDY: Augusta National in Georgia where the Masters Golf Tournament is played.

BOL: You didn't even need to think about that one, huh?

ADDY: No, sir. That's my dream course.

BOL: I sure hope you get there someday. Now before we go, let's talk about Jonathon. Why would you like to be his prom date?

ADDY: Honestly, I'm not sure if I want to be his prom date. That's a lot of pressure! But I do want to be his friend. Jonathon Jackson is a great guy.

BOL: You heard her, folks! Thanks, Addy, and good luck.

Chapter 50

You're inviting Hank out on your date with Jonathon?" Kara shouted as the girls walked back to their trailer. "Are you out of your mind? Of course you're out of your mind. This is your date. Time alone with Jonathon Jackson. Time for America to see you're perfect together so they'll vote for you. If Hank is there, he'll hog the camera. You know what he's like whenever cameras are around."

Addy waited for Kara to breathe, then smiled. "I know what I'm doing. And I know what I'm *not* doing."

"Okay, Yoda," Kara said, assuming the voice and characteristics of the tiny, pointy-eared green philosopher. "Understand you not do I."

"I did some research and found that Hank hates Christians. Mike and I think he's had some bad experiences with them—like you had with that friend at school. I want him to see we're not all that bad. Jesus said to love your enemies, so that's what I'm doing. Giving Hank airtime is the best gift I have to share with him. If nothing else, it'll show him I'm not a selfish little brat looking to win no matter what. And hopefully, he'll be willing to at least listen to what I have to say about my faith."

Kara looked at Addy for a long moment. "I don't know. It seems like you're throwing away the date of a lifetime—your first date, if I'm not mistaken—all for a jerk who probably won't even listen to anything you have to say anyway."

"I'm not throwing away my first date, Kara." Addy leaned forward, thinking. "I'm giving it to God."

"I don't even know what to say to that." Kara pulled Addy's ponytail. "I don't get it. But I admire you. Your faith is real, Addy, no doubt about that. If more Christians were like you, there might be a lot more Christians in the world."

❧

"There he is." Addy spotted Hank walking toward his limo. She ran up to him and asked him to join Jonathon and her on their date.

"What are you trying to pull this time, Addy?" He narrowed his eyes. "I'm done with your little games. Look, you've won. You're in the Top Five."

"I hate that you feel so much animosity toward me,

Hank. I want you to know that I am truly sorry for having frustrated you." Addy smiled and looked up at him, his glare a little less fierce. "Think of this as a peace offering."

"Wait a minute." Hank smiled a knowing smile. "You heard about my next project and you want in. That's what this is about."

Addy laughed. "Not even close. No offense, but one thing I know for sure is that being in the spotlight is not for me."

"So what's the deal, then? What's in this for you?"

Addy's mouth went dry. "I-I'll tell you tomorrow. Okay?"

"Suit yourself." Hank shrugged and walked off.

All right, God. He's coming. Now I'm even more nervous than I was before. What am I going to say? How am I going to explain this to Jonathon? Maybe I should have just dropped a Bible in his chair or something less . . . dramatic.

Addy tried to listen as Ruby recounted the story of how she helped her younger sister win the Miss Corn Cob pageant in 1991.

"She wasn't the prettiest girl up on that stage," Ruby drawled. "But I sure made her look better than those others. Even then, all I wanted to do was to make people pretty." She stood back to survey her work. "And look at this. I've done it again."

Addy took the mirror. While she never thought she'd get used to all the makeup and hair spray required for television, she couldn't deny Ruby's words. "A new coat of paint sure helps the old barn look good."

"Thanks, Ruby." Addy walked out.

Uncle Mike rounded the corner and whistled. "You look beautiful, Addy."

She adjusted the straps on her sundress. "Thanks, Uncle Mike. I was hoping I'd get to see you before I left."

"This is my girl's first date." Uncle Mike smiled. "Of course I'm here. Not even that old Hank could keep me away."

Hank turned the corner as Mike was finishing his sentence.

"Well, well, if it isn't the national hero."

"Good to see you too, Hank."

"Mr. Banner." Hank glared.

Mike nodded.

"I'm going to be a few minutes late, Addy. I like to make a grand entrance, you know." Hank laughed, oozing "Big Brother Hank" charm. "See you around twelve thirty."

"What time do you have to go?" Mike asked.

"The limo picks me up in half an hour."

"Nervous?"

"Yes," Addy said. "I know this is what God wants me to do. I think this is the whole reason he brought me here. But that doesn't make me any less scared."

"Boy, do you sound like your mama." Mike hugged Addy.

"Be careful. If you mess up my hair, Ruby will kill you."

Mike laughed and walked in silence with Addy back to the trailer.

Her mother's journals peeked out from under Addy's bunk.

I've got time for one more. Addy reached for one from the year she was born. She was surprised to learn her mom had chosen to deliver her in the village rather than go into the local hospital at Mitú. Addy's dad had some supplies brought in, but overall, the delivery was to be much like those the other villagers had. Both parents had prayed over every aspect of the pregnancy and trusted that God would help them do what they felt he was asking by having the baby in their home.

Little Addy is such a joy. The whole village loves her. The delivery was perfect. Josh was amazing. I was in labor less than ten hours, and Ula was by my side the whole time. She was such a help. She had me doing things my friends in the States never would have done. But they worked. Labor was painful, of course, but not as bad as some of the horror stories I had heard. And then Addy was there in my arms. Neither of us could speak, we were so happy. A beautiful little girl. God is so good to us.

Once I had healed enough to leave the hut, we took Addy to our little makeshift chapel and dedicated her to the Lord. The whole village came out to join us as we gave our Addy to God, praying that she will know him and serve him and that he will do great things in and through her.

What an awesome responsibility to raise a child. Sometimes I don't feel worthy of this precious little gift from God. I know I will fail. I fail every day. But I am more challenged than ever to live a life that pleases God so Addy will want to follow my example. I look at her sweet face and beg God to help me be the mother he has called me to be so I can train her to be a young woman after his heart. That is my greatest desire for my Addy— to love God with all her heart and serve him with all her life. Nothing else matters.

Addy dabbed at her eyes with a tissue, not wanting to mess up her makeup, but unable to stop the tears from falling. She held the journal to her chest and allowed her mother's words to wash over her.

Nothing else matters . . . God, help me to be the young woman my mother prayed for.

"It's time," Eric called through Addy's door.

"Yes, it is," Addy said.

Cameras followed Addy from The Mansion's lawn into the limo, and another camera was positioned in the front seat, ready to catch her thoughts as she rode to her destination. Eric sat beside her, prompting her with questions so they'd have before and after date footage for her package that week.

"How do you feel about this being the last week?" Eric asked.

"I don't know. I'm ready to be back home, to sleep in my own bed. To get back to normal after five weeks of this." Addy gestured at the limo.

"So you think your first impression was right?"

Addy groaned. "No. I'm so embarrassed about that. I was just so overwhelmed."

"Why is that?"

"All these people," Addy said, thankful that Eric was so good at making her feel relaxed in front of the camera. "I live in a quiet neighborhood, I go to a small school. My extracurricular activities are . . . well, pretty boring to most people."

"And what has it been like for you here?"

"Not quiet." Addy laughed. "Not with the Amazing Kara for a roommate."

"You guys certainly seem to have bonded."

"She's the best." Addy looked into the camera. "I can't imagine what this experience would have been like without her."

"Do you want to talk about the rumors that have been circulating about your relationship with the other girls?"

Eric, I know what you're doing. You're giving me a chance to defend myself against some of what those girls have said about me. Their comments in the magazines that I faked the spider bite and that I'll do anything to win.

"Addy?"

"Actually, Eric, I wish I had gotten to know the other girls better. I know more than anyone how wrong first impressions can be. I think that maybe if we'd all given each other more of a chance, maybe we could have been friends. Maybe we still can be. Anything is possible. I believe . . ."

Eric put his hand on Addy's shoulder. "I'm sorry, Addy, but we're here. We can get more later, though, if you'd like."

God, was that you stopping me from saying something about you, or did I miss an opportunity by not talking about you at the

start of the interview? I feel like I keep blowing it. Help me to say
what you want me to say.

As soon as Addy stepped out of the limo, she was
whisked into the empty restaurant, through French doors,
to a table surrounded by lights and cameras and waiters
being made up for their moments of fame. Jonathon hadn't
arrived yet, but that was part of the plan. He was to walk
through the doors and greet Addy so the cameras could get
a full-body shot before he sat down.

"He's here," one of the waiters said, moving to open the
doors.

Addy stood and Jonathon entered, looking gorgeous as
usual in khakis and a red-and-blue-striped shirt.

We match. She looked down at her blue sundress.

"You look great, Addy." Jonathon hugged her.

Addy's stomach went into full-blown butterflies and
she worried she wouldn't be able to eat anything.

"A perfect dress for going fishing."

"Fishing?"

Jonathon chose each of the dates' locations based on what
he knew of the girls. There had been endless speculation
online about where they would go and what they would do.
Maintaining a "squeaky clean" image, the producers promised the couples would be supervised at all times and only
the highest moral standards would be in place. But America
was still excited to see their president's son out on a date.

"You like fishing, right?" Jonathon's laugh revealed his
joke. "You would have gone, wouldn't you?"

Addy relaxed. "It'd be better than horseback riding." She
took a sip from her water.

"Don't put that line in the package," Jonathon said to the cameraman.

I keep forgetting that date was a secret.

"May I take your order?" the waiter asked.

Jonathon placed his hand on Addy's. *Just when I started to relax . . .*

"You need protein," he said. "We have a full afternoon ahead of us."

"Fishing really takes it out of a person, huh?" Addy ordered lemon pepper chicken and sautéed vegetables. *I'd really rather eat a cheeseburger and fries, but that wouldn't look good.*

"I'd like a cheeseburger and fries," Jonathon said.

He is perfect, God.

"So if we're not going fishing, where are we going?"

"Where would you like to go?"

"If I tell you and it's different from what you planned, we'll both be disappointed."

"Just try me."

"Tell me about the other dates so far." Addy changed the subject.

"Okay, Lila was first."

Addy knew that. She had overheard Hank tell the crew to get Lila's segment "edited to perfection" while Ruby was finishing Addy's makeup that morning.

"I took her to New York to see a Broadway musical."

"How exciting."

"The play was amazing." Jonathon sipped his iced tea and shot Addy a look that said far more than he could verbalize with the cameras around. "Afterward, we went

287

backstage to meet the cast. They gave us a tour of the theater. Lila even got to wear one of the lead character's costumes and sing a song from the show with the orchestra accompanying her."

"I heard her saying something about that at breakfast," Addy said. "So you had a good time?"

Jonathon looked at Addy again and rolled his eyes, making sure his back was to the camera.

"Your lunch, Mr. Jackson, Miss Davidson." The waiter lowered their plates and Addy's mouth watered over Jonathon's juicy cheeseburger.

Addy closed her eyes to pray, and when she opened them, Jonathon was staring at her with wide eyes.

"There's a lot about you I don't know," he said.

Is that a good thing?

"Okay, guys. I'd like a few minutes to have *actual* conversation with Addy, if you don't mind," Jonathon said. The crew happily obliged, most discussing which items on the menu they were planning to try.

"Alone at last." Jonathon smiled.

Did Jonathon know when Hank would be joining them? She had texted him about the change but wasn't sure he had received it.

"Where's Bull?" Addy asked.

"Right here." The big man poked his head through an opening in the French doors.

"Bull," Jonathon said. "Just a few minutes of privacy. Please?"

"Jeff and I are just standing outside these doors. We're not listening to anything."

"Then how did you know Addy asked for you?"

"Sixth sense." Bull pointed to his temple. "I just know things. All kinds of things. You have no idea what's stored in here."

Jonathon lifted his hands in surrender. "Can you read minds?"

Bull closed his eyes, then jumped forward. "Jonathon Jackson. That was a mean thing to think. All right, then. I'll go."

Bull closed the door and Jonathon shook his head, laughing. "So what do you want to talk about?"

"I was going to ask you the same thing," Addy said.

He smiled. "Hmmm. What do I want to talk about?" His smile grew serious, then he glanced to the door. "Actually, there is something I've wanted to tell you for a while. It's a secret, but I think I can trust you with it."

"A bigger secret than you wanting to be an editor?"

"An even bigger secret than Mike being your uncle."

"You know that?" Addy dropped her napkin and looked at Jonathon in surprise.

"I did my homework for the segment I edited, Addy. It didn't take much to find out. But don't worry. Your secret is safe with me." He winked and Addy's toes began to tingle.

"And your secret?" Addy prompted.

"Much bigger and much more secret." Jonathon's solemn demeanor intrigued Addy. He really *was* being serious.

"Tell me," she whispered, leaning forward.

"I didn't want to be on this show."

"What? It's *your* show. I thought it was your idea. Money and publicity and all that."

"Addy, don't you know me well enough by now to know that I don't go in for all that?"

She hadn't really considered that before, but as she reflected on Jonathon she realized he never did try to do anything to draw attention to himself. He didn't shy away from the spotlight, but he wasn't like Hank, constantly trying to be seen. "So why did you do it?"

"My dad." Jonathon shrugged. "His approval ratings were low, and with his reelection bid coming up in the fall, he needed some help."

"And you were that help?"

"Yes. All the publicity for the show has really helped Dad's ratings. I wasn't kicking and screaming about coming on . . ."

"Like some people we won't mention?" Addy finished.

"Well, I wasn't going to say that." Jonathon laughed. "I love my dad and he loves his job. I wanted to help him, and this was how I could do it. But it wasn't my idea. I'm a senior in high school. I was just hoping to finish out my year, play baseball, and get ready for college."

"Instead you're stuck here, having girls throw themselves at you so you'll pick them for prom."

"I picked my prom date the first week of the show."

Addy's heart thumped wildly as she felt Jonathon's knee brush hers under the table.

"I tried to tell you all this that day I saw you out in the woods," Jonathon said.

"And I thought you had hidden cameras, so I treated you like you had the plague."

"Hidden cameras?"

"I assumed you were just like—"

"Get in there so you can catch me walking in," Hank demanded, interrupting Addy and Jonathon's conversation.

The crew rushed in, lights turned back on and cameras perched and ready to go.

Hank beamed his newly whitened smile as he walked slowly from the French doors to the table, stopping to greet Jonathon with a handshake and Addy with an air kiss on her cheek. When he became European, Addy wasn't sure. Sitting down, Hank unrolled his napkin and glanced through the menu.

Jonathon, poised as always, shot Addy a "What is *he* doing here?" look. Addy responded with a halfhearted smile and mouthed, "Check your phone." He did, scrolling through messages until he found her text. Still confused, Jonathon shrugged and bit into his cheeseburger.

Determined to let Hank have what he wanted, Addy asked, "So, Hank, how did you get into show business?"

"I have always loved it. I love stories, I love the glamour and the excitement."

"So you've wanted this since you were little?" Addy asked.

"From the time I was eleven or twelve, I'd sneak out to go to the movie theater—strictly forbidden in my family," he said derisively, "and watch whatever was playing. I didn't care if it was comedy, romance, action, or horror. I just loved being caught up in a great story, being whisked away from reality and placed into someone else's life."

What about Hank's early life could have made him so anxious to escape? Addy wondered.

As they were finishing up lunch, Hank excused himself for a moment. Jonathon asked the cameras to be turned off and pointed toward the door where Hank just exited. "Is this payback for the other day on the road?"

"No, but that's not a bad idea. Actually, it's a little complicated. Can I tell you later?"

"Is it because we're supposed to have a chaperone? Because I promise you, my Secret Service guys, the crew, and Eric would definitely qualify as chaperones."

Addy laughed. "No, it's not that. It's just . . ." Addy searched for the right words but just wasn't sure how to tell him yet. "Give me a little time. Trust me." She looked into his eyes and melted just a little bit.

"I trust you. But I sure don't understand you."

Hank returned, the cameras were again turned on, and Jonathon announced where he was taking Addy.

"Augusta, Georgia." He smiled and sat back, smug.

Hank was confused. Addy jumped up and yelled.

"Augusta National?" she asked, sitting back down, barely containing her excitement.

"Yep," Jonathon replied. "Our tee time is at three o'clock, so we just have time to get to the airport and get down there. They have clothes and clubs waiting for you."

Addy jumped up again. Hank took his time, obviously not thrilled with the location but perking up when he heard that a senator was a member and would take the couple around, not to mention a few famous golfers would be playing there.

The threesome flew in a private jet down to Augusta. A local camera crew was waiting for them, filming them as they left the plane and took the limo to the golf course. When they arrived, Addy went into the locker room to change.

"Lexi," Addy said into her phone, moving it around the ornate locker room for her friend to see. "Look at this place."

"Look at you, Cinderella. That golfing getup is better than any fancy dress."

A full outfit had been laid out for her, complete with brand-new custom golf shoes and clubs.

Addy picked up the shoes. "And these are way better than any glass slippers too."

"Turn them to the side," Lexi said. "Look at that. The blue stripe in the shoes matches the blue stripe in the outfit. Man, they spent a fortune on you."

"Hang on, I need to get changed." Addy laid the phone down on a burgundy couch.

"Great. I love staring at the ceiling."

"I can turn the video chat off." Addy stepped into the blue athletic skirt.

"Are you dressed yet?" Lexi asked. "I'm bored over here."

"Bossy." Addy picked up the phone and carried it to the bathroom. Sitting it on the shelf above the mirror, Addy put her hair up into a ponytail and applied a little lip gloss. "Do I look all right?"

"You ask the girl whose makeup of choice is ChapStick?"

"Seriously." Addy looked at her friend's face on the tiny screen. "I am about to play the greatest golf course in the world with the greatest guy in the world. Help me out a little."

"You look great," Lexi said. "Now stick the phone in your pocket so I can hear everything."

"No way." Addy laughed. "I'll call you later."

She walked out of the locker room into the spacious lobby. Hank walked through the side door.

"Hank, will you be joining Jonathon and me on the course?"

"I think I'll stay here." He turned to a cameraman setting up and said, "But I'll be around if you need me."

"Ready?" Jonathon came up from behind Addy and put his hands on her shoulders.

Will I ever stop melting into a puddle every time Jonathon gets close?

"Ready to play the Masters golf course?"

Addy turned and looked into Jonathon's eyes, trying not to completely lose her focus. "You better believe it."

Jonathon and Addy walked out on the greens, a camera crew walking backward in front of them, capturing their first glimpses of the famous course.

A senator met the pair at the first hole. "Even I need an escort here," Jonathon whispered to Addy. "But he's really busy, so he'll just be around the first couple of holes. Long enough to get on TV." Jonathon waved at the senator.

"Hey, Jonathon." The senator took a golf club from his caddy. "Good to see you."

"You too, Senator Ray."

The senator made his shot and walked away. Addy prepared to tee off.

This course is unbelievable. The greens were in the best condition she had ever seen, with trees lining the borders. The sand traps were gleaming white and perfectly raked.

The water was glassy, with stone bridges over some of the waterways leading from hole to hole.

"Are you all right?" Jonathon asked.

"I've never been so nervous to hit a golf ball. I watched this on television when we went home. And now I'm standing here. It's unreal."

"I've never played here either." Jonathon looked around. "I've seen a couple of tournaments, but it's different to be standing right here where the pros stand."

"How about if you go first?"

Jonathon took a practice swing. "All right. Here goes. I am teeing off at the Masters." He winked at Addy. "Can I just say this is so much better than Broadway?"

Jonathon hit the ball, its arc perfect, landing right in the center of the fairway about three hundred yards away.

Addy's first shot wasn't quite as good. "Not the sand, not the sand, not the sand."

"Your ball follows instructions well," Jonathon said as the ball landed just a few yards from the sand trap.

"The pros make it look so easy."

Jonathon made it to the hole in five shots. It took Addy six.

"Not bad for a par four at the Masters," Jonathon said.

At the third hole, Addy glanced up to see David Sillet walking toward them. The runner-up at this year's tournament, Sillet was one of Addy's favorite players.

"Jonathon," David said. "I was hoping I'd get to meet you. I'm David Sillet."

"I know." Jonathon took David's outstretched hand. "I'm a big fan, Mr. Sillet."

"Call me David." He faced Addy. "And you're Addy Davidson, right?"

David Sillet knows my name.

"My daughters watch *The Book of Love* faithfully. All three of them are rooting for you."

"Thank you." Addy smiled.

The camera crew adjusted their positions, forcing Addy and Jonathon to wait a few minutes before teeing off.

"Do you have any advice for us, David?" Jonathon asked. "We've come in way over par on both holes so far."

"This is the shortest hole on the course. But don't let that fool you. It's tough. See there?" He pointed to the first green. "You want to hit that just right because the second green is much narrower. Even the pros have trouble getting past it."

David helped Addy and Jonathon choose the best club for their shots. Both managed to get their golf balls near the spot David had suggested.

"Par." Jonathon pumped his fist and pulled his golf ball out of the hole. "Yes."

"Hey, quiet on the course." David laughed. "We still have a ball in play."

Addy held her breath as she prepared to putt. *Please, God, let me get this in. I'm so close.*

"I did it," Addy shouted. "I made par. That's it. I can leave now. This is perfect."

"No way," David said. "This is just the beginning. You haven't even made it to Amen Corner yet."

Addy knew that spot was where the eleventh, twelfth, and thirteenth holes were visible.

"All right," Addy said. "But this is taking longer than I expected. It might be midnight before we get that far."

David left the pair at the fifth hole, and by the eighth hole, Addy realized that she and Jonathon had barely spoken since he left.

Addy looked up after choosing the club for her next shot. "I don't think we're giving the editing crew much to work with. We're not saying a whole lot."

"They've got us talking with Senator Ray and David Sillet. That's plenty. Besides, it's kind of nice." Jonathon smiled. "We're getting more comfortable around each other. Remember our last golf game?"

"I'd rather not." She groaned, reliving the awful pictures in the newspapers and speculations about what they had been doing off the course.

"Remember how we said we were going to play without talking but we couldn't?" he reminded her. "We weren't comfortable enough with each other to stay quiet. Now we are."

Addy hadn't thought of it that way, but Jonathon was right. The silence this time hadn't felt awkward at all. She had been able to focus on her golf game because she wasn't concerned about needing to make small talk with Jonathon.

"It's getting dark already." Jonathon grimaced. "I don't think we'll make it to Amen Corner, after all."

"I agree." Addy sighed. "This has been amazing, but I'm wiped out."

"Not too wiped out, I hope. We still have to eat dinner."

Back in the locker room, Addy wrapped a towel around her and called Lexi.

"You're not finished with your date yet?" Lexi asked.

"Nope, we still have dinner. A fancy dinner too. Look at this."

Addy turned her phone toward the dress that had been laid out for her.

"Wow," Lexi said. "Look at that thing. It's beautiful. My mom would love it."

It was a soft pink gown that looked like a prom dress—thick satin straps at the shoulders, the bodice layered in tulle with tiny pearls sewn on vertically to the waist. A satin ribbon, matching the shoulder straps, lay at the waist, tied into a perfect bow in the back. The rest of the gown floated out in a tulle-over-satin skirt. Full, but not too full.

"So where's the fairy godmother, Cinderella? And can I get one?"

"No godmother." Addy picked up a piece of paper. "But it does come with instructions: 'This dress is on loan from Nordstrom's. The jewelry is on loan from Burnham and Lacy. Please wear with care.'"

"You're like one of those celebrities at the Oscars."

"I know." Addy nodded.

"What kind of shoes do you have? Glass slippers?"

"Close." Addy picked up a pair of silver sandals with delicate rhinestones and—she breathed a sigh of relief—low heels.

"Don't turn into a diva on me now," Lexi said.

"Not a chance." Addy stepped into the dress. "I'd rather be in the golf outfit than this thing any day." She looked at herself in the full-length mirror and turned. "But it is kind of fun to dress up."

A knock sounded on the door. "Miss Davidson? I'm your stylist. May I come in?"

Addy opened the door to a woman who looked like she walked off the page of a fashion magazine. Ending her phone call with Lexi, Addy sat and let the stylist put on her makeup and fix her hair.

"All done" were the only words the young woman spoke to Addy, but her work was impressive.

Ruby would be quite pleased with her hair and makeup. Not too much, but enough. Addy looked herself over in the mirror and stared.

I can hardly believe how much I have changed, God, both inside and out, in the last month. You've forced me out of my shell, you've taught me more about you, you've stretched me in ways I didn't know I could be stretched. And you're not done.

She shut the door behind her stylist and sat on the couch.

She still had to find a way to tell Hank the real reason she invited him. Which also meant letting Jonathon know she was a Christian. Addy knew he and his family attended church, but what did he believe? They couldn't have anything more than friendship if he wasn't a Christian.

Addy sighed and took one last look at herself in the mirror.

But I do like him, God, Addy admitted to herself. *A lot. If this isn't your will, help me not lose my heart.*

A knock on the door shook Addy from her thoughts.

"Addy?" Jonathon asked from the other side of the polished oak door. "Are you ready?"

"Yes, sorry." She grabbed the silver clutch purse and threw in her lip gloss and powder. "I'm coming."

Addy opened the door and felt a pang of disappointment. Jonathon was prettier than she was. In a tailored, double-breasted black suit and gray tie, Jonathon looked perfect. Addy was speechless.

"Wow, you look beautiful." Jonathon grinned, offering Addy his arm.

"I was thinking the same thing," Addy replied as they began walking to the restaurant.

Jonathon laughed and Addy noticed that the cameras had caught that interchange.

Great. They would be here for that.

Hank waited for them at the table and the three ordered dinner. Hank grilled the pair on their golf game. He worked hard to maintain a look of interest, though Addy could tell he had no idea what they were discussing. But Hank nodded and smiled at just the right moments, overjoyed when the conversation turned to his own afternoon. He regaled the pair with stories about the people he met, emphasizing how kind and gracious they were to sit down "with a nobody like me."

As the salads were laid on the table and the cameramen took a break, Hank turned to her.

"All right, Davidson. Enough of the game. Why am I here?"

"Actually"—Jonathon laid down his fork—"I was wondering the same thing."

Addy's throat tightened. *This is it, God. Help me. Please, please, help me.*

Chapter 51

Both pairs of eyes glued on her, Addy wanted nothing more than to slink out of the room and never return.

Why is telling people who I am so difficult? Why can I talk about my aspirations to go to an Ivy League school with no qualms, but freeze up when it's time to discuss my faith?

Addy cleared her throat and looked down at her half-eaten Caesar salad.

"Well, Hank. I did some research on you," Addy began quietly, eyes still glued to her salad bowl. "I saw that you really hate Christians." Addy looked up at Hank, who shifted in his seat.

"I do," Hank said. "So?"

"Could you tell me why?" Addy's heart was hammering in her ears so loudly she could barely hear Hank's reply.

"You invited me here to find out why I hate Christians?" Hank wiped his mouth with the red linen napkin.

Addy remained silent, so Hank continued. "All right. I grew up in a home with all rules and no freedom. And the rules all came from something they called the 'Good Book.'" Hank grimaced. "That Good Book kept me from enjoying life. My parents dragged us to church three or four times a week to listen to a preacher who would yell and scream from the pulpit, then come down and yell and scream some more. He was awful. And whatever the preacher told our parents to do, they did. He'd yell and scream about the love of God and then treat us with ridicule and contempt. I never heard that man say one kind thing in my life, and his attitude carried right over to my parents. My childhood was dark and dull and incredibly stifling. I left and never came back."

"And you blame Christianity for that?" Addy asked.

"Religion in general has caused more trouble in the world than anything else." Hank leaned forward. "Did you know that? More wars, more genocides, more destruction has been caused in the name of 'God' than anything else. And for what? What good has it brought? None.

"Belief in God is destructive. It's a superstition that belongs in the Dark Ages, not in the twenty-first century."

Addy waited. Hank was shaking with anger, and Addy felt herself soften toward this man who had been so injured by people who claimed to know Christ.

"Hank." Addy swallowed past the lump in her throat.

"I think Jesus would agree with a lot of your thoughts. Religion in itself *is* destructive, but the terrible things that have happened in God's name were not done by God. They weren't condoned by God. Preachers like the one in your church don't reflect the character of Christ."

"What do you know about that?" Hank asked.

"I know because I am a Christian," Addy declared, feeling a calming peace wash over her as the words spilled out. "I have seen God work in my life. I have felt him. I saw it in my parents. They were missionaries and they went to Colombia to help indigenous people. They helped meet physical needs, but they also brought spiritual healing. They told the people about Jesus, that Jesus is God in the flesh, that he came to earth to pay the punishment for the sins we've all committed. They told them Jesus rose from the dead so we can know those sins are forgiven—once and for all. They taught them that Jesus offers the free gift of salvation to anyone who is willing to believe. And Jesus changed their lives."

Addy took a deep breath and looked from Jonathon to Hank. "My parents were killed because they obeyed God's Word. They didn't yell at people or treat them harshly. They just loved them and lived like Christ before them." Tears began to fall down Addy's cheeks, but she had to continue. "And I'm so, so proud of who they were. I'm proud to be their daughter. Honored. I hope that my life is just like theirs, that I love others and show that love, that I give grace and hope to the people around me. Christianity isn't about following a bunch of rules, Hank. It's about life. Amazing, full, exciting life."

Hank looked at Addy with a mix of confusion, anger, and helplessness on his face. The men were silent. Addy wiped her eyes with her napkin and took a drink of water to calm her nerves.

"You invited me here to tell me that?" Hank asked quietly. Addy wasn't sure if she heard rage or resignation in his voice.

"Yes." Addy gazed into his eyes so he could see she was telling the truth.

"I don't know what to think, Addy," Hank said. "You've got some nerve, I'll give you that. And you're not yelling at me or even telling me what I'm doing wrong. That's different. Not the kind of thing I've seen from the Christians I know."

Addy looked hopefully at Hank, remaining silent so he could finish.

"But one good apple doesn't mean the whole bunch isn't still rotten. I can't forget all I've seen in the name of God just because one little girl turns out to be halfway decent."

"I'm not the only one, Hank," Addy assured him. "There are others like me. Better than me. Don't assume people who do things in the name of Christ represent who he really is." Addy bit her lip and continued, "Would you do me a favor?"

Hank nodded, skepticism lining his face.

"Try reading the Bible. The book of John. I know you like stories, and that's a story—about Jesus, written by one of his friends."

"I've read it," Hank bit out.

"Read it again. Not because you're forced to, but because

you want to. See who Jesus said he was, then you can accept or reject what he taught."

Hank was silent, but Jonathon spoke up.

"I'll read it." He smiled. "Even if Hank won't, you've convinced me. I've always gone to church, but I haven't ever thought much about what any of it means. I've definitely never thought about Jesus all that much."

"You've sure got your parents' genes, Addy," Hank admitted. "Who'd have thought we'd have a little missionary in the Top Five?" He laughed. "Tell you what, no promises, but maybe. I might look into the Bible. If I can find a copy in LA," he joked.

Addy marveled at what had just happened. She shared her faith, Hank hadn't blown up at her, and Jonathon wanted to read the Bible. And the whole thing happened in a formal gown and heels.

Hank decided to stay behind in Augusta until the following day. He wasn't needed at The Mansion right away, and he had made some connections he wanted to follow up on. So Addy and Jonathon were the only passengers in the small plane flying back to Tennessee. Bull and Jeff were also there, but she had gotten so used to them, they seemed to just blend into the background.

"That was really something, Addy," Jonathon said as the plane ascended into the inky black sky.

"What?"

"You back there, saying all that to Hank. It really got me thinking. I'm going to start reading John as soon as I get back home. I may have some questions, though. Think you could help me?"

Addy smiled. "Absolutely."

Jonathon turned in his seat so he could look Addy in the face, placing his hand over hers. "Even if America votes another prom date for me, I want you to know that you're *my* choice."

Her heart felt like it would explode right out of her chest.

So much for trying to make sure I don't get too emotional over this guy.

Jonathon turned to face the front, his hand still holding hers. Both were exhausted from the day, and Addy was surprised when the lights came on and the pilot announced they had arrived in Nashville in what seemed like just a couple of minutes.

As soon as the plane landed, Jonathon was sandwiched between Secret Service agents and deposited in his limo before he could even say good-bye. Addy grabbed her luggage and exited the plane, falling asleep again as soon as she was buckled in her seat. Eric was in the front seat, and he tried to ask her about her date. But Addy was too tired to do anything but give a thumbs-up sign.

Addy woke the next morning, barely remembering walking into her trailer or climbing into bed but knowing that the day before had been one of the most amazing of her seventeen years.

Chapter 52

ere we are, ladies and gentlemen." Hank spoke to the camera as he walked through the front door of The Mansion into the living room. "Tonight is the night we have been waiting for—the night all of America finds out the lucky girl who will be Jonathon Jackson's date to prom."

Hank droned on about the show, clips from each of the episodes playing in the background.

"We started out with one hundred hopeful girls from all over the country. And now we are down to five: Lila, Kara, Jessica, Addy, and Anna Grace. Which four will go home with red daisies and broken hearts? Who did America pick to be the First Son's date?" Hank smiled and winked at the camera. "Stay tuned, because tonight is a night you won't want to miss."

Each of the girls was interviewed "one last time." Hank asked them their favorite parts about the show, its star, and their experiences.

"It's been wonderful," Lila said. "I've made such great friends, and I'll miss them all so much." Addy tried not to roll her eyes. Lila, seated beside her, held Addy's and Kara's hands as she spoke.

Kara agreed that the experience was great. "But I'm ready to get back home to my family. I've been away way too long." She blew a kiss to Ma and Pop before Hank came to Addy.

"This has been amazing," Addy said, smiling at Hank. "Jonathon really is as nice as he seems, this mansion really is as beautiful as it seems, but I agree with Kara, I'm ready to get back to my normal little life in Florida."

Brief shots of the girls followed from their performances that first week, to the fancy dinner, to the academic competition, and finally, to their dates. Full packages of those dates filled the show the night before: Lila singing her heart out on the Broadway stage, Jessica skiing with members of the Olympic team, Anna Grace at Disney, and Kara in Los Angeles meeting some of her favorite celebrities.

As Addy expected, her package wasn't all that exciting—from a marketing perspective. Just she and Jonathon. And Hank. Eating and playing golf. Much of her package featured Hank talking about his next project, chatting with celebrities in the restaurant. Addy noticed he wasn't as happy as he normally was when watching himself.

God, please work in Hank's heart. Help him to see who you really are. Help him understand that your plan for his life is so much better than anything he could dream up for himself.

There was nothing in Addy's package about her talk with Jonathon and Hank, but she carried the memory of that in her heart as the crowning moment of her time there.

"I have here in this envelope"—Hank waved a square, white envelope to the cameras—"the names of the first three girls voted off."

Kara's knee was bouncing up and down. Addy looked at her friend and winked.

"But before I make the announcement, we have a very special guest . . ." Hank motioned to the cameras and the face of the president of the United States appeared on the screen behind him. The camera panned out to show the First Lady, both sitting comfortably on a couch in the Oval Office.

"Good evening, Mr. President." Hank waved to the screen. "Welcome. And, Mrs. Jackson, looking lovely as ever. Thank you for coming on tonight."

"You're very welcome," President Jackson said. Addy noted he had the same proper way of speaking that his son had. She smiled. "We've enjoyed the show, and we're both waiting to find out who won."

"You won't have to wait much longer, sir," Hank promised. "But before I tell everyone the names of the first three girls going home, do you have any predictions? A favorite?"

Mrs. Jackson spoke this time. "Jonathon has been keeping us updated the whole time, and of course, we have been watching. Each of these girls is something special. We have enjoyed seeing them all. I don't know if we can say we have a favorite, though. Do you, dear?" Mrs. Jackson looked at her husband.

"No. They are all wonderful girls. These five and the other ninety-five. We have been so proud to see what the next generation of our country has to offer. And we know there are so many others just as accomplished. It is exciting."

"So you're not going to pick a favorite?" Hank egged.

"Not gonna do it," the president answered, laughing.

"Well, all right," Hank said. "What about expectations? What do you hope to see in your son's prom date?"

Mrs. Jackson looked at her husband and smiled. "As America has seen, Jonathon is a wonderful young man. And as long as Jonathon is happy and healthy, we're happy. We will welcome his date into our home and treat her like one of our own. This is a special time in our son's life. A senior prom only comes once. And we want his to be memorable."

The president nodded and squeezed his wife's hand. Addy noted that Jonathon's eyes were moist as he watched his parents. *They really do have a great relationship.*

Hank finished out the interview, thanking the First Couple again, and returned his attention to the cameras. "Five nervous girls, two proud parents, and one young man—all waiting to find out the same thing: who has won *The Book of Love*? The wait is almost over."

Hank stretched out the opening of the envelope an impossibly long time, reminding the girls how lucky they were to have gotten this far, how exciting this whole experience had been, how no one would walk away tonight a loser.

"The first girl to go home"—Hank motioned for Jonathon

to stand behind him and pick up the daisy—"is . . . Anna Grace."

She stood, tears in her eyes, and hugged Jonathon after receiving the good-bye daisy. Jessica was the next to be asked to leave.

"Only three remain," Hank announced. "And we will soon be down to the Top Two. Lila." He paused. "You're one of those Top Two." Lila squealed, then composed herself as Hank turned to Kara. "Miss McKormick, I'm afraid you're not."

Addy's heart sank as Kara stood to receive her daisy. She hugged Jonathon and whispered something in his ear. He smiled and looked at Addy. Kara turned and smiled at her friend, waving to camera one, as instructed, before leaving through The Mansion's front door.

"Lila and Addy. Addy and Lila," Hank said. "Two very different girls with one thing in common—a wish to be Jonathon Jackson's date to prom."

For the first time, Addy realized how insignificant a high school prom was.

Even if my date is the president's son. A month of testing and showing and fighting and missing home for the chance to do something that would be little more than a fond memory in years to come just doesn't seem all that exciting.

Addy looked over at Jonathon. They would still be friends. Maybe more. If Jonathon was a Christian and if they ended up near each other, and if the plans God had for them coincided, then maybe. But those were a lot of "ifs."

Suddenly Addy knew she didn't want to win. She didn't need to win. God didn't have her there for that purpose.

You brought me here to glorify you. I've learned more about you in the past month than I have ever learned before. You helped me to tell people about you. With you by my side, I survived the lions' den. And that's all that matters.

Addy sat up straighter, feeling lighter and happier than she had all night. She didn't need to worry about whose name was in that final envelope. In fact, she hoped it was Lila's. Lila wanted that date. She'd love all the attention that would come from going to Jonathon's prom and from meeting the First Couple. And she would be stunning beside Jonathon. A beauty worthy of a guy like that.

"And now, I have in my hand the winner of this competition," Hank said, looking at the cameras. "Lila or Addy? Who does America think belongs on the arm of Jonathon Jackson? The wait is over. And the winner is . . ."

Chapter 53

ddy and Mike spent two days getting back to
Tampa.

"I want to get home in the afternoon," Mike
had explained the day before. So they spent the night at a
hotel in Atlanta, rising early to make the seven-hour drive
home.

Addy slept most of the way, thinking through all that
had happened in the last several weeks.

She had lost the competition.

She hadn't been surprised when Lila's name was called.
She wasn't even upset. She was happy for Lila and her con-
gratulatory hug was heartfelt. As she returned to her trailer
to pack, Jonathon had caught up with her. He didn't have

much time—the crew had to get shots of Lila and him together, planning their date.

"This isn't good-bye," he insisted. "You've got my number. And you know where I live. Once all this"—he motioned behind him—"dies down, I want you to come up and visit me."

"Come to your house?" Addy said. "The White House?"

"Don't think of it as the White House. It's just the place where I live. Besides, my mom really wants to meet you." Jonathon smiled.

Addy's eyes widened. The First Lady wanted to meet her? She was speechless.

"I'll be in touch," he promised, then pulled Addy into a long hug. Addy closed her eyes and breathed in. She loved the way he smelled. She didn't notice until Jonathon pulled away that her eyes were watering.

I'm going to miss this boy.

Saying good-bye to Kara had been even harder.

"You have to come visit," Kara said. "No, wait. I'll come visit you first. You can take me to the beach."

"It's a deal." Addy grinned. "And you have to meet Lexi. You'll love her."

"Of course I will. And you've got to bring Mike up to Long Island."

"Definitely." Addy put the last of her belongings in her suitcase and snapped it shut. "I am already craving your mom's cinnamon rolls."

"I'll have her mail some down," Kara promised.

"What are you smiling about, Addy-girl?" Mike asked as he eased the truck off I-75 onto their exit.

"I was just thinking about Kara and her family and how much you'll love them." Addy filled Mike in on the complexities of Kara's large and boisterous family.

"She's a good kid. Stood by you when she could have easily flocked to Hank like the other girls."

"What do you think is going to happen to Hank?"

"Eric told me one of the girls . . . Taylor, I think, filed a complaint against him. Her parents have apparently gotten the ear of some bigwigs down in Hollywood. His sins are finding him out. I don't think he'll be doing any more producing anytime soon."

Mike's phone rang and he responded in "yeps" and "mm-hmms" and with a "you got it."

"Who was that?"

Apparently her uncle hadn't heard Addy, because he just turned up the radio and began singing to another of his favorite good-time oldies.

As they turned into town, Addy noticed her block was decorated and lined with people, all waving posters welcoming Addy back to Tampa. News crews were stationed on either side of her house and a huge black Suburban was parked in the driveway. The house had been painted. And landscaped. It looked great.

Addy stepped out of the truck to cheers from the crowd and hugs from classmates, church friends, and strangers, all of whom knew Addy and had been rooting for her over the last month. Addy was overwhelmed and tried to thank them all as she made her way to the newly repainted front door.

Mike stood on the front steps and called out, "Thank

you, folks, for this great welcome. I know Addy appreciates that you all came here. But she is exhausted and ready to just relax at home for a while, so please excuse us if we say good-bye here."

Mike opened the door and Addy gasped. The entire house had been redecorated. It was perfect. The walls were beige, the new couches were full and a deep brown. Red accent pillows lay on either end of both couches, and a plush brown leather recliner replaced Mike's tattered old one. Addy was amazed at how the room really fit both of them—not ornate, not too feminine, very functional.

"Who did this?" Addy asked.

Mike looked to make sure the front door was shut and the blinds were closed. Then Mike's bedroom door opened and Mrs. Jackson walked out.

"Guilty." She laughed, Jonathon trailing behind her. "But you haven't seen everything yet. Come see your room. I hope I got it right. Jonathon helped." She grinned as Addy opened her door.

Addy couldn't believe it.

Jonathon Jackson and the First Lady are in my *house. Mrs. Jackson—renowned interior designer—has redecorated my house.* Addy was speechless.

Her room was freshly painted light blue, with thick brown stripes three-quarters of the way up the wall. Her old metal bed had been replaced by a deep chocolate sleigh bed, covered in a cream comforter with a brown stripe and blue and brown pillows. She had a new desk in a matching shade in the corner, and her favorite books and photos were housed on shelves above the desk.

Mrs. Jackson had framed a picture of Addy and Jonathon at Augusta and placed it on the desk. A huge dresser was on the far wall. The whole room looked like a picture from a magazine.

"Do you like it?" Jonathon asked, standing beside her.

"I don't know what I like better. My house or the fact that you are in my house."

Jonathon smiled. "I couldn't wait until this summer to see you."

Addy looked into Jonathon's eyes and swallowed hard.

"Addy, check out my room." Uncle Mike popped his head in Addy's doorway.

"It's fantastic, Mrs. Jackson." Addy looked around. The entire room had been gutted and made to look like the inside of an old log cabin. "This is perfect for him. You are an amazing designer."

"I may not ever leave." Mike sat on a leather recliner and leaned back.

"Thank you so much," Addy said. "It's incredible."

"You're very welcome, Addy," the First Lady replied.

"But why?" Addy asked.

Mrs. Jackson linked her arm with Addy's and led her to the new couch in the living room.

"First, because your uncle was instrumental in saving my son's life." She placed a loving hand on Jonathon's knee. "A little video clip—though very well done," she acknowledged, seeing the mock offense on Jonathon's face, "was just not enough. This isn't even enough, but it was something personal, from me."

Mike walked into the living room. "All that happened

was that I was in the right place at the right time. God is the one who deserves the thanks for that, not me."

"I do thank God." Mrs. Jackson smiled. "Believe me. But if you hadn't gone straight to the Secret Service . . . if you had waited even one day." She wiped her eyes. "I don't even want to think about it. You are a hero, Mr. Scott. And I will never forget what you did."

"Thank you, ma'am." Mike bowed his head. "It was an honor."

Mrs. Jackson took a moment to compose herself, and Jonathon wrapped a protective arm around his mother's shoulders.

"I also did this because I watched you, Addy, and I like you." Mrs. Jackson patted Jonathon's knee. "You're the real thing. You're a good influence on my son and on everyone who meets you. And I just wanted to do something special for you to let you know how special you are."

Addy was moved to tears, feeling inadequate in the face of such a powerful woman.

"You are very kind," Addy said through her tears. "But when did you do all this? The show just ended a couple of days ago."

Mrs. Jackson stood. "Oh, I had my crew come down here a week and a half ago. They've been hard at work. I sent them with my plans, and they taped each day's work so I could review it at night before they started again the next day."

Addy was stunned. She turned to look at Jonathon. "So you knew about all this?"

"Who said I can't keep a secret?" He laughed.

"You too, Mike?"

Mrs. Jackson responded, "Him too. We wanted to keep it from both of you, but we had to get in the house somehow. Plus, we wanted to make sure the changes were made in a style you'd both like."

"They are," Addy said, looking around once again. "Thank you so much."

"You are more than welcome, Addy." Mrs. Jackson pulled Addy in for a hug. "I just wish we could stay and enjoy it with you."

"We can't?" Jonathon said.

"You have school tomorrow, young man," his mother said.

Jonathon groaned. "Could I have just a few minutes alone with Addy before we have to go?"

Mike motioned to the First Lady. "I've got a fancy-looking new coffeemaker in my kitchen. Care to join me for a cup?"

Mrs. Jackson smiled. "I'd love to. Bull, Jeff, you and the others can come in here too. I think these two will be safe in the living room for a few minutes."

Addy watched as the Secret Service agents filed out of the living room and bedrooms and into her small kitchen.

Jonathon scooted closer to Addy on the couch. "I've really enjoyed reading John."

"I know." Addy pulled her cell phone from her purse. "You've texted me through every chapter, remember?"

Jonathon laughed. "Has it been that much?"

"I don't mind, though." Addy smiled. "It's been fun seeing it through your eyes."

"Have I also told you that I really wish it were you I was taking to prom instead of Lila?"

Addy nodded. "But she's a much better dancer, so I really think you lucked out. I would have broken a toe or two."

Jonathon grabbed Addy's hand. "So have you decided what's next?"

"For what?"

"College, life . . . us." Jonathon gazed hopefully into Addy's eyes and her heart began to pound. *Will I ever get used to those eyes?*

"I'm not sure. For the first time in my life, I don't have a plan. I'm praying about all of it. God knows what I need to be doing. He just hasn't shown me yet."

"Fair enough." He squeezed her hand. "I'll be praying too. Do you think God has a plan for me?"

"I know he does."

"Does that plan include you coming to visit me this summer?" Jonathon raised his eyebrows.

"Do I get a guided tour through the White House?"

"Of course."

"Commemorative photo with the First Family?"

"Absolutely."

"Okay, then. I'll be there . . . There's only one stipulation."

"What's that?" Jonathon asked, weaving Addy's fingers through his.

"No camera crews allowed."

"It's a deal." Jonathon laughed.

Acknowledgments

*H*ave you ever been around a potty-training toddler? It is messy. Literally. Puddles on the floor, presents beside, but not quite in, the toilet. Yellow Elmos and soggy Spider-Men. And it's a group effort. Mom and Dad are involved, of course. But so are the older siblings, grandparents, aunts and uncles, the babysitters and nursery workers. It's a thankless, stinky, exhausting job. But it's so worth it.

I am kind of like that toddler. As a writer, I am like a little girl trying to put my words where they should go, and sometimes they just don't make it. But, thankfully, many people have come along to help me learn what to do with all these words. People who have held my hand through the process of writing this book. People who have run with me, cried with me, sat with me, and cleaned me up.

My husband believed in me enough to give me a whole summer to drag my laptop to our local library and type, just because I had an idea and I wanted to see if I could turn that idea into a book. My kids give me constant inspiration and encouragement, reminding me that no fictional characters can ever be as amazing and fun as the three characters I have living right under my roof.

My proofreaders, Alexis Scott, Jill Ferguson, Amy Busti, and Laura McKenzie, read as I wrote, encouraging me to keep trying, keep working. Their input was, and is, invaluable. Their friendship is priceless.

My students at Citrus Park Christian School allow me to daily peer into their hearts and minds, giving voices to my characters. I don't even think I would have thought about writing this if it weren't for my AP Lit class of 2010. Those four girls became more like little sisters than students. I still miss our "Starbucks Fridays."

My agent, Lauren Yoho, spent hours reading my book, offering suggestions, talking me through the process I knew so little about. She is fantastic. Amanda Bostic, Becky Monds, and the entire fiction team at Thomas Nelson have been incredible. I am honored to be working with such talented people. Julee Schwarzburg edited this manuscript. Then edited it again. And again. (I wasn't kidding when I said I was like a toddler.) But she always did it with happy faces and encouraging comments. Her suggestions and advice have made me a better writer, and I am so excited to get to work with her again.

But this book is really a result of one person: Jesus Christ. It is by him, for him, and because of him that I write and that I live. As I grow as a writer, I am growing to know his heart more. The creator, the author. The stories he tells are breathtaking. I never get tired of reading them and thinking about them and praising the God who shows himself behind the scenes and on center stage to a world he loves so very, very much. My prayer is that you know his heart better every day and that his story in you will take your breath away.

Reading Group Guide

1. Addy's story is loosely based on Esther. What parts of the biblical story did you see in *First Date*?
2. Addy did not want to be on *The Book of Love* reality TV show. How would you feel if you were asked to be on a show like that?
3. One of Addy's biggest fears is sharing her faith with others. Is that hard for you? Why or why not?
4. Kara loves being on the show, but she doesn't get caught up in all the "drama" like Lila and some of the other girls. Why do you think that is?
5. Lila will do anything to win. Have you ever known anyone like that? How did you respond?

6. By reading her mother's journals, Addy learns more about her parents' life in Colombia, South America. Have you ever known any missionaries? What did you think about their experiences living in another culture?

7. If you were on *The Book of Love*, which of the challenges would be your favorite? Which would be your least favorite? Why?

8. Uncle Mike tells Addy, "Nobody makes Jesus look so bad as those who say they're following him." What do you think about that statement?

9. In the book of Esther, God prepares Esther to stand up for the Jewish people. How does God prepare Addy to stand up for her faith?

10. Mike teaches Addy that we are happiest when we are obeying God. Have you experienced that in your life? Have you experienced the opposite?

11. Addy says she won't date Jonathon unless he is a Christian. Do you think it's important that guys you date share your faith? Why? Why not?

12. What do you think Addy learned most from her time on *The Book of Love*? How did she change from the time she began the show until it ended?

Message from **Kara McKormick**

Addy,

So I know you're still basking in the "Jonathon loves me so much he had his mom redecorate my house" glow. But I need you to take a break from thinking about you so you think about . . . me! I have HUGE news. And when I say huge, I mean, monstrous, colossal, enormous (that's right, I'm using my thesaurus) news. Earth-shattering, sky-is-falling, I-can't-believe-you-can't-hear-me-screaming-all-the-way-from-New York news. But you have to call me. No way can I tell you this over something as impersonal as a computer. Because—did I mention?—this is HUGE!!!!!!

Kara

Kara McKormick is back! And this time, she's the star . . .

About the Author

Author photo by Amanda Allotta

*K*rista McGee writes for teens, teaches teens, and, more often than not, acts like a teen. Along with her husband and three kids, Krista has lived and ministered in Texas, Costa Rica, and Spain. Her current hometown is Tampa, FL.

Visit KristaMcGeeBooks.com